Strangers No More

IT'S A VIBE: BOOK III

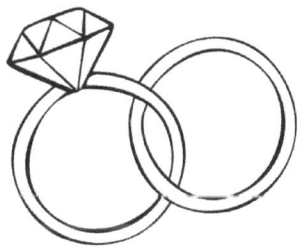

BY: J.D. SOUTHWELL

Also by
J.D. Southwell

40hrs With a Stranger
https://mybook.to/xEH6O

They're Not Strangers
https://mybook.to/A77E

You Belong to Me, Period
https://mybook.to/Rv82

Dating is Ghetto
https://www.amazon.com/dp/B0BTN31YB8

Copyright © 2025 by J.D. Southwell

All rights reserved.

No part of this publication may be reproduced, distributed, or transmitted in any form or by any means, including photocopying, recording, or other electronic or mechanical methods, without the prior written permission of the publisher, except as permitted by U.S. copyright law. For permission requests, contact jd.southwell@outlok.com.

The story, all names, characters, and incidents portrayed in this production are fictitious. No identification with actual persons (living or deceased), places, buildings, and products is intended or should be inferred.

1st edition 2025

Annunciation/Translation

- Yeobo – Darling

- Seojun – See.oh.jun

- Seo – See.oh

- Agi – baby

- Chul-Moo – Ch-ull-moo

Start Here!

Hey babes! Before you jump into this book, let's get a few things squared away. If you have not read 40hrs With a Stranger (book 1) or They're Not Strangers (book 2) go read them before you start book 3. I'll wait ☺

Did you read them? **Nah, for real did you read them?** These books intertwine heavily, and I don't want you confused.

1. This book is <u>NOT</u> like the first two. Strangers No More is stepping away from the fluffy romance, like book 1, and away from the romance suspense, like book 2. This final book is taking place into the dark romance world. So, please check the trigger warning page.

2. Now that you are all caught up with the first two books, let me set the scene for book 3. The first three chapters are during the 5 months that Ashlynn and Denice were getting their shops together and just before Nick proposes. T is currently still MIA, but the group is keeping their guard up.

Trigger Warning!

Before you jump into this story please check your triggers! Book three is not like the other two and has a darker theme. It contains content not limited to:

- Violence

- Explicit Sexual Content

- Blood

- Assault

- Attempted SA

- Body Dismemberment

- Torture

- Foul language

- Domestic Violence

If any of these are not what you like, then please do not read. Now that we've got that out of the way, enjoy the ride!

Chapter 1

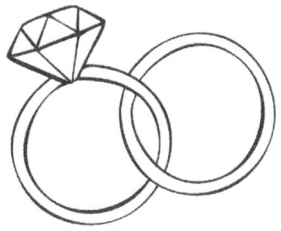

Seojun 5 Months Ago

I sat on the couch in my living room for a few moments after getting off the phone with my little cousin, Ayzo and booking my flight to Philly. Taking another sip of the vanilla Crown I was babysitting, I took in a deep breath. As much as I wanted to down the sweet beverage and enjoy the burn across my chest, I couldn't. After Ayzo told me everything that had happened since he left, I had to keep my head clear. Well, clear enough to be prepared for what I knew was coming my way. To be honest, I had my bags packed from the moment he called and had me freeze Denice's accounts. I had a gut feeling that some shit was about to pop off and I needed to be ready.

Stay ready so you don't have to get ready.

"Thanks for the advice, Dad," I huffed out a chuckle as I remembered my dad's constant reminder.

The motion detector pinged on my phone with an alert that a car had entered on my street. You heard that right, my street. I had the entire housing community fully equipped with cameras while the remaining houses were being built. So far, five of the houses were just about ready to go on the market, not including mine. Of course, when everything was ready to go, I'd take down the cameras, but while I was living here, alone, the cameras were staying up.

After I lost my chain of massage parlors and group homes, I decided to switch things up. Not the group homes that you are thinking of, but more like up-scale brothel houses. I still had some money saved and used that to become a buy-and-hold investor. I built homes from scratch or renovated properties before having my realtors sell them to families in need. Unlike most of the greedy realtor companies I've come across, I made my houses luxurious, yet affordable to low income families. If they could afford the mortgage without living paycheck to paycheck, they were handed the keys.

I knew what it was like growing up in a crowded apartment because my mother and father couldn't get into a house due to poor credit. I remember my dad arguing with the lender that they had the money to pay the mortgage months in advance, but were always denied. No bank would offer them a loan because of past mistakes they were continuing to pay for. So, when I started up my business, I made sure to not turn away those in need.

With that said, I wasn't a dummy about it. I knew how some muthafuckas would try and take advantage and lie their way through the system. Too bad for them, I knew all about it. I could smell bullshit a mile away and didn't hesitate to kick a fucker out of my office.

I took a long drag from the black and mild I was smoking before putting it out. I shook my head at the wood tip sitting in between my fingers. My dumb ass was going to have a nasty ass headache later, but I didn't want to light up a blunt – trying to quit that habit. Yeah, yeah, I know, black and mild's ain't no better. Shit, I needed something to prepare me for my journey to Philly and, from the four men hopping out the all-black Escalade across the street, this ass whooping I was about to hand out.

Standing up, I cracked my neck and rolled my shoulders before walking through the kitchen and down to the basement. I entered the four digit code on the door to reveal my stash of guns.

Tapping my index finger on top of my lips, I clicked my tongue. "Hmm, which one do I want to use tonight?"

I started to hum Archie Eversole's "We Ready" as I examined each of my guns. I wouldn't say I was a gun enthusiast, but I had my favorites. Personally, I liked to go old school and fuck somebody up with my hands, but since I had to be at the airport in a few hours, I didn't have time to waste. Picking up my Glock with the extendo, I walked over to the circuit breaker and switched off all the lights.

"What the fuck?" I heard someone yell out.

"Nigga, shut the fuck up!"

I shook my head and laughed. Of course, T sent some young boys to try and handle me. Either he didn't give a fuck that he was about to lose four bodies, or he was dumber than I thought. How could he figure out where me and Ayzo were hiding, but didn't know how dangerous I was? I mean, my family dominated the Midwest and parts of the east coast. Everyone knew who the Jaguars were, but then again, I guess he thought I was soft now. Yeah, everyone that was once a loyal Jaguar abandoned me and is now a Cobra, but that didn't change the fact that I knew how to handle my own.

I walked up the stairs and leaned against the door frame as I watched one of the boys rummage through my refrigerator. He wore all black and had his ski mask lifted up, exposing his sienna, brown face. I didn't have a good view, but from his profile, I could tell he was no older than nineteen. I cocked my head to the side and saw the Cobra tattoo on his neck and frowned. T definitely sent him. I contemplated on not killing these idiots in my house. I didn't like having to take someone's life, especially when they were this young.

"I'm about to tear this shit up!" the intruder murmured.

I tilted my head to the side and realized what the muthafucka was doing. First, he broke into my house, now he was in my shit. There were five things I didn't play about:

1. God

2. My family

3. My money

4. My trust

5. My food

I may have been a mere one hundred and eighty pounds, but I had big back energy. I could eat a three course meal with extra rolls and still stop by a shop and get me a triple scoop of double dark chocolate chip ice cream. Don't judge me!

"So, you just going to break into my house and make yourself a big ass sandwich?" I asked, crossing my arms across my bare chest.

The young dude popped his head up, a slice of peppered turkey hanging out of his mouth. His eyes bulged with the realization of who I was.

"Brody, what the fu–-"

His partner, an older white male in his early twenties, began to question as he came waltzing out of the pantry with a fresh loaf of bread, but stopped in his tracks when he saw me. My eyes zoomed in on his hand that was freely finger fucking the top four slices of the bread. To make matters worse, I could see the dirt caked under his nails. I didn't know this man from Adam but I for damn sure know I ain't hear no water running for him to wash his hands before he started touching on food.

I sent a bullet through his dome, instantly sending him to his permanent sleep. I smiled and was glad that I picked up the silencer before I left my basement. No one was around for miles and wouldn't hear the gun shots, but I had two more dumb asses upstairs and I didn't want to alarm them. Yet.

"Like I was saying, you just had to take the last few slices of the turkey? You couldn't have made you a damn ham sandwich? It's bad enough your dirty nail ass homie had to touch all over the bread, but you just straight up inconsiderate. Hell, you could've at least left me a few slices." I ranted, feeling anger boil through my veins.

Look, I didn't mind sharing my food, but you had to ask. This little fuck not only didn't ask, but he was going to take all of it with no hesitation. Ignoring me, he smirked and shoved the rest of the turkey into his mouth.

"Fuck you and this dry ass turkey."

He attempted to go for his gun in the back of his waistband, but he wasn't fast enough. I sent two bullets in between his eyes.

"Little rude ass," I scoffed, closing the refrigerator door.

T was definitely dumber than I thought. He failed to prep these men about how I operated. Hell, he could've just asked one of the ex-Jaguar members about my training. Yes, I was computer savvy and was always dressed in my business formal best, but I was a killer. I spent hours at a time training and fighting with some of the best assassins under my father's rule. Hell, me and Akeno trained together and had very similar fighting styles. Oh well, not my problem.

"Yo, his ass not here and probably heading to Philly. Let's go!" I heard a deep voice bark from upstairs. "Brody, Drew, y'all hungry asses better not be in that damn kitchen."

Arching an eyebrow, I stepped over the two bodies bleeding all over my floor and headed towards my living room. I listened as the two other men began stomping down the stairs, muttering that coming to my house was a waste of time. I had to agree with him because if they hadn't brought they ass up into my place, they'd be able to breathe another day.

The first to hit the bottom of the steps was a stocky Hispanic with a bald head and face tattoos. If I had to guess, I'd say he was in his mid-thirties. Trailing behind him was a thin Asian who looked very familiar, but I couldn't quite put my finger on where I've seen him before. He was probably my age with platinum blonde hair that was slicked down his head. I squinted my eyes and damn near giggled with glee. Now I knew where I recognized the guy. The little muthafucka still had the Jaguar tattoo on his neck. I could tell he was working on getting it covered up with a Cobra, but I guess he ran out of time. Dash aka John used to flirt his ass off with the girls in my massage parlor. He had just got into the crew, but his young ass was more interested in pussy than doing his damn job. I shook my head. Of course, his bitch ass jumped ship.

As soon as the Hispanic dude hit the bottom of the steps, I picked up the lamp from the living room side table and chunked it at his head. He flew backwards and hit the ground with a thud. Dash whipped his gun out, but I already had mine aimed at his face.

"I wouldn't do that if I were you." I tsked.

"I knew you were here somewhere," Dash snarled.

"Your friends didn't. Sad you lowkey killed them since you ain't tell them how I operated."

Dash shrugged his shoulders. "I wanted to be the one to bring you in. You see, even though majority of us crossed over to the Cobras, the bosses are cautious around us. We still have to prove our loyalty and bringing your ass in was going to secure my spot."

"Well, aren't you a go-getter?"

"That's the one and only thing I liked about your teachings. Take the initiative and get what you want or you'll never succeed in life."

I nodded my head and smiled as I started to lower my gun. "So, you remembered one of my daily affirmations? Too bad you missed the important line after that."

I watched as he pinched his eyebrows together, his hand slowly rising with his gun gripped tight.

"What was that?"

I tucked the gun into my waist band and placed my hands behind my back. Dash smirked as he pointed the gun at me. Dipping my chin, I huffed out a sigh.

"But never bite the hand that feeds you unless you're ready to die."

I yanked the knife out of my back pocket and threw it, connecting with the middle of Dash's throat. He dropped the gun and held onto his neck, panic dancing in his eyes. I maneuvered around my sectional couch and headed towards the stairs. The Hispanic guy was groaning in pain as he began to wake up from his little cat nap. I pulled my gun out and placed the barrel at his temple before gripping the trigger, sending him back to sleep. I continued up the stairs until I was standing in front of Dash. Thick blood oozed from his lips as he frantically moved his hand around the floor, looking for his gun. I picked it up for him and smiled.

"You know loyalty is on my list and the fact that you and fifty other men turned your backs on the Jaguars is crazy." I leaned down close to his ear. "But you know what? I am going to hunt down and kill each and every one of you before I burn down the Cobras."

Dash spit blood onto my chest as hatred filled his eyes. I shook my head and punched him. His head flew back, causing more blood to spill from his nose. His blazer slightly opened, displaying his phone. I snatched it from him and gripped the front of his hair, allowing the face id to unlock his phone. Going to the camera, I went into video mode and made sure the flashlight was on.

"Any last words? Oh, wait, you can't really talk right now. Don't worry, I'll speak for you. I, Dash Lin, thought that I could complete the impossible mission of killing Seojun. Little did I know, I was meeting my maker today. Seojun knows all fifty men who betrayed him, and he is coming after us. One by one – until the streets are drenched in our blood."

I took Dash's gun and held it to his forehead before pulling the trigger. His eyes rolled to the back of his head as his body went limp. Dark blood splattered onto the camera lens and across the wood floors before I ended the video. I went to his contacts and clicked on the only name available, Ms. K and attached the video. As soon as the message was delivered, my eyes landed on the time.

"Oh, shit. I'm going to miss my flight."

Throwing the phone at Dash's head, I jogged up the stairs and straight to my bathroom. I needed to take a quick shower and then grab my bags before my car arrived in the next hour. Before I forgot, I snatched up my phone and sent a quick message to the cleaning crew who would have the bodies gone, blood cleaned up, and new flooring installed by the time I reached Philly. I thought I needed to wait a little longer to take action on my plans, but the fact that the Cobras were coming after me sparked my motion into action. It took a while, but with Ayzo's help, I had the list of everyone who fucked me over. I didn't know who ran the Cobras, but I was done with hiding and ready to go seeking.

Chapter 2

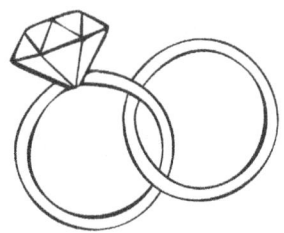

Luther 5 Months Ago

The familiar sting radiating off of my fists followed by the warm blood sliding across my knuckles almost warmed my heart. My hands hurt like a muthafucka, but I didn't care. Pain was that friend who gave you back handed compliments while providing you the attention you desperately yearned for. I welcomed pain with open arms, especially when I got to be the one passing along it's embracive love.

I watched in awe as T's head snapped to the side before falling down, his chin hitting his chest. A part of me wanted to slice this nigga's ears off and force feed it to him, but not tonight. Olivia had him already hooked up to an I.V. to help ease his pain. Once the medicine took effect and he got some sleep, then I'd continue knocking his ass the fuck out.

After Xavier found T hiding in New York, I decided to play cat and mouse with his ass. I couldn't count how many times I was in tears from laughter, watching him trying to stay low and out of sight. He was lowkey oblivious to his surroundings because I had eyes on him at all times. Hell, I allowed him to roam the streets for a month; just enough freedom and time to make him believe that he was safe. Once I saw him snooping around Denice's new business location, I had to admit that I was curious of what he was trying to do. I mean, was he trying to get into my good graces by finishing the job?

Well, the short answer to that was no. I had someone come back and tell me that his dumb ass was planning to start singing like a canary to save his own skin. He tried to get Nicholas's mom to set up a meeting with him and her son so that he could tell Denice of my involvement in their kidnapping. Luckily, Nichola's mom had gotten clean and didn't want involvement with T, but when I tell you I was livid, I was ready to fly out to New York and snatch his ass up myself. At that point, it was time to get rid of his ass. I sent a few of my goons to snatch his goofy ass up and I've been torturing him since. For the past four months, I picked a designated week to beat the muthafucka to the last inch of his life, before he was nursed back to health. I'd leave him alone for the other three weeks and then started over.

"Damn, baby. What did Uncle T do, anyway, to get put on the torture list?" Olivia asked, checking on T's vitals.

When she was satisfied with the results, she unlocked the wheelchair I had him bounded in and rolled him towards the piss stained cot in the corner. Wasn't nothing wrong with his legs, but she just found it easier to move him around, especially when he was barely conscious. Shit, she was better than me because I would have left his ass in the damn chair.

Observing Olivia some more, I couldn't help but feel a sense of pride. She has been in Vegas, holding it down for me at a few of my brothel houses and keeping these hoes in line when I couldn't. Over the past three years while I was traveling in between Philly and Chicago checking on my other properties, Olivia kept my Vegas property in check while she was in school to become a nurse. Not only did she retain just enough information to keep niggas alive for me to torture, but she was recruiting for me, too. She wandered through the campuses and sent men and women my way to work in one of my houses. Once people started asking questions, she'd drop out and start over at another school. Talk about loyalty! With her help, it was that much easier to snatch the Jaguars out of Seojun's hands.

"His slow ass didn't complete the job I gave him and then tried to snitch." I said, wiping my hands on the towel I had in my back pocket.

"Well, shit. Uncle T did raise you to take care of muthafuckas who couldn't get the work done." Olivia tsked, shaking her head at my uncle. "What job was it, anyway? You know I can get shit done for you, baby."

I smirked. As much as I loved Olivia's enthusiasm and willingness to please me, I wasn't going to hand her this assignment. Not that I didn't trust her, but I knew that she wasn't going to be successful. If that were to happen, then it'd be her ass being hooked up to an I.V. after getting knocked the fuck out. I cared about her just enough that I personally couldn't do that to her – I'd have to get Xavier to do it.

"He was supposed to ensure some bodies were dropped at the bottom of the river and to bring me what was mine. His stupid ass failed and now he has to die for it."

"What's yours?" Olivia asked, turning around to stare at me.

"Denice."

"Denice?"

I simply nodded my head, causing Olivia to glare at me through slanted eyes before she folded her arms across her chest.

"Since when have you cared about the likes of Denice? I mean, when we were younger, you wanted to fuck because she wasn't putting out, but you haven't uttered her name in years."

"Pipe that shit down, Olivia." I snapped.

Her lips tightened as she continued to glare at me. Olivia was my ride or die, but she didn't understand that was her only roll in my life. She would always be my bottom bitch – ready to take action and didn't mind getting her hands dirty. Not to mention, she knew how to suck the demons out of my soul through her mouth game, but that's it. She wasn't wifey material.

Denice, on the other hand, was. I wanted someone sweet and innocent on my arm that I wouldn't mind taking care of my future children. Olivia's ass was too selfish to worry about anybody but me and herself. If I were to get her pregnant, she'd hire a nanny and pretend like the child didn't exist. I wouldn't put it past her to even be jealous of the little muthafucka, because I planned on spoiling my seed. I shook my head. Nah, she not worth that hassle, but Denice was. Besides, if I didn't take Denice for myself, then I would be in trouble with my boss and silent partner.

"I thought this whole time you cared about me."

"Look Liv, you'll always be my main bitch. You've looked out for a nigga and got your hands dirty with no hesitation, but you and I both know I need to maintain my image. I need to be the family man in the eyes of the world and Denice is the perfect person to complete that image."

Her shoulders slumped. "Am I not good enough to be that for you, baby?"

I grabbed Olivia by her hand and pulled her towards me, wrapping my arms around her waist. "No, but you know this dick belongs to you, baby. I'm only going to fuck Denice on our wedding night and to get her pregnant. The rest of the time, I'm all yours."

Her eyebrows pinched together, and I knew she was upset because I told her the truth. Olivia would never be anything past my gutter bitch, and I had to remind her. The faster she understood her role, the better off she and I would be.

I gripped her chin and smashed my lips against hers, giving her no time to speak. If I wasn't on a strict strategic plan, things would be different. Olivia would be my wife, and we'd be overseas somewhere lying on a beach. Since I knew she wouldn't be still and had that same itch as me for the need to quench her thirst for blood, I'd have her as my personal sneak attack. She did it for me in that job in Philly with those two brothers, Nicholas and Garret. She played her role so well and I was proud of her.

However, that plan was out of the question. I was on strict orders to stick with my current plan, and I didn't want to disappoint my boss. Besides, I didn't want to leave this world behind without at least one of my spawns available to take over everything I'm working hard for, and unfortunately, Olivia just wasn't the nurturing type.

My phone vibrated in my back pocket, causing me to break our kiss. Checking the caller ID, I instructed Olivia to go get ready for some dick. Her frown turned into a seductive smile and she damn near sprinted out of the room. I may say some fucked up shit to her ass, but once I gave her this dick, she was over it. After I heard the door close, giving me the privacy I needed, I answered the phone.

"How are you doing this evening, Mr. Omba?" I asked, ensuring my professional tone was on full effect.

"I'd be better once you secure my request for a bride."

"Trust me. I understand but greatly appreciate your patience as I find what you are looking for. I can find you someone faster if she didn't have to be a virgin or of age."

"Absolutely not! I may buy men and women from your establishment for my clients but I don't fool with that tom foolery. I want her of age and intact."

"Of course, Mr. Omba. I'll make sure she gets weekly checkups with the doctor to prove it."

Mr. Omba hummed in delight. "I have to admit, when Ms. K originally sent me your way, I was skeptical. Not a lot of men are trustworthy, nor do they keep their word. I am delighted to know that y'all have yet to prove me wrong."

"We take our business very seriously, my friend." I chuckled, pulling out a blunt from my front pocket. "As soon as I have your merchandise, I'll have her there before you could say overnight shipping. Well, once the final payment is made."

"Yes, I know." Mr. Omba chuckled. "Remember, I would still like my future wife to be educated. I have enough airheads walking around here."

"That shouldn't be a problem. I'm sending a colleague of mine to a few of the college campuses tomorrow to check out potential candidates."

"You know, if for any reason my possession were touched, our deal would be off. I've worked with you and Ms. K. a long time, but if you fail to complete this task, I will be finding business elsewhere."

I swallowed and cleared my throat. "Yes, Mr. Omba. We definitely understand."

The line disconnected and I exhaled a shaky breath, lit my blunt, and took a hard pull. I was ready to get my hands on that half a million from Mr. Omba. I had been working for him for about a year now and have already made hundreds of thousands just by sending him men and women overseas to his country. Normally, he didn't care how they came as long as they were in a certain age range and not too doped up to the point that they weren't useable for his clients. This time when he hit me up, he was ready to spend big money, but not for his clients; he was looking for his own wife. He wanted someone smart, untouched, and wouldn't be missed when she got shipped off and I intended to find her.

I heard a chime come from my phone and saw a message from Ms. K aka Mama K, my right hand and silent partner.

Mama K: Remember I told you I was sending Dash to find the three idiots who let Ayzo, Nicholas, Denice, and Ashlynn get away?

Me: Yeah

When my goons failed to kill everyone but Denice and bring her to me a few months back, I was livid. Since Bobby was already dead and Kendra was locked away in solitary confinement, I made plans to torture Hector, Brody, and Drew. Unfortunately, T must have put them on game and kept them off the grid somehow. I had my best people searching, but they had no idea where those muthafuckas had disappeared to. If my uncle wasn't such a failure and snitch, I'd be impressed.

Mama K: Watch the video I'm sending to T and then get rid of him.

A few seconds later, T's phone began to vibrate against the table I had it sitting on. Following the instructions, I opened the message. I watched in disgust as Dash's bloodied face filled up the screen. Anger quickly took over as Seojun's voice came through the speaker. Dash's brains splattered across the floor and camera before the video ended. I snarled as I charged over to T who was knocked out on the cot.

I had been looking for Seojun's exact location for over two years and he had been right under my damn nose. I had knowledge that he was in Nevada somewhere, but he stayed under the radar and this grimy bitch knew his location the whole time. For how long, I didn't know, but I was pissed the fuck off. I didn't know if it was more because Seojun was right in my backyard at the moment or because T played in my face again. My uncle knew that taking over the Jaguars and ending Seojun's dynasty was my ultimate goal.

I reared my leg back and kicked him square in the face. He screamed out in pain, but I threw a punch to his gut, knocking the wind out of him.

"You backstabbing bitch. Not only were you going to snitch on me to Denice, but you knew where the fuck Seojun was this entire time!" I spat.

His head drooped to the side but he still managed to muster a laugh.

"You thought I was going to willingly give up the cobras? I been running shit since yo little ass was in diapers! The cobras are mine and as soon as I would've taken out Seojun, you would've been next!"

My nostrils flared as I yanked the I.V. from his arm and shoved the tube down his throat. He kicked and thrashed but I kept my hand over his mouth and nose as I squeezed the bag, emptying the fluid into his system and cutting off his air supply.

Chapter 3

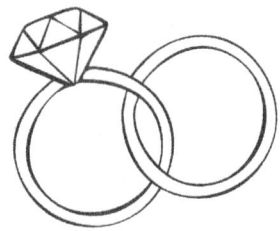

Addison 5 Months Ago

I stared at the overdue bills in my hands as tears fell down my eyes. I literally spent my all paying for the last few overdue bills and yet they continued to come. Clamping my eyes shut, I took a deep breath. I had no idea what to do. I was in my last semester of school, but I had depleted all of my income paying for my grandmother's personal caregiver.

My nana was recently diagnosed with advance dementia and needed around the clock care. I used to take care of her as much as I could, but her illness made it impossible for her to be home alone. The money she had for her retirement and the personal loans I pulled out weren't enough to cover all of the medical bills on top of her mortgage. I contemplated on putting her in an assisted living home, but I knew nana wouldn't like that.

I chewed on my bottom lip and anxiously bounced my leg as I pulled my phone out of my pocket and dialed the one other person's number who could help.

"Who the fuck is this?"

"Seriously, Ma? You can't save your own damn daughter's number?"

"Don't call my phone cussing and I just got this new number."

I briefly stared at the phone in disbelief. Was she serious right now? My mom has had the same number for two years now. The only thing she changed was the actual phone itself. She refused to not have the most up to date phone on the market.

I shook my head. Wanting to avoid an argument, I cleared my throat. "Mama, I called you about Nana Henrietta."

"What about her?"

"Well, her bills are piling up and I don't have any money to pay them."

"And you think I do?"

"Ma, I'm just saying she may lose her house."

"Ugh! Why don't you just use the rest of your financial aid? I know y'all be getting those refund checks. Hell, don't you have a job?"

I clenched my jaw as I bit down on my tongue. She was working my nerves and I was beginning to regret calling her.

"Mama, I don't have any money. What I did have, I used to pay the past due bills. I'm in work study at school, but that's pennies compared to everything nana needs."

"Damn, sounds like y'all shit out of luck."

"Are you fucking serious right now? Are you telling me that you won't help with anything for your own mother?"

"Bitch, please! I'm your mother and you don't help me with shit. I don't see you bending over backwards to help me pay for my own fucking bills, but you expect me to pay for Henrietta's?"

My mouth hung open. Was she serious?

"How can you be so heartless and selfish? That woman gave birth to you!"

"And I gave birth to you, so what that mean? Look, your Nana has lived a long life and that sickness is going to kill her. Let her old ass go in peace so we can cash out on her life insurance policy. Then we wouldn't have to worry about bills. I got to go. My boyfriend about to pick me up to take me shopping."

The line disconnected, causing me to scream out in frustration. How the hell that woman was my mother made no damn sense. She was a greedy, narcissistic wench and didn't care about anything or anybody.

"Whoa, is everything ok?"

I looked over my shoulder to see a thick Latina woman with brown curly hair and a tattoo sleeve going up her arm. She wore a red crop top and black jean shorts with a pair of red and black Nike slides. She had her backpack hanging off one of her shoulders and she held a medical terminology textbook.

I sighed and shook my head. "No, not really."

"Well, if you don't mind talking to a complete stranger, you could tell me what's wrong." She suggested, sitting next to me on the bench.

I glanced at her and took in her warm smile. She seemed genuine. I guess it won't hurt having someone to talk to. Besides, I probably wouldn't run into her again. I exhaled and explained my situation. From my grandmother falling sick to not being able to financially support her, I vented out all of my frustrations and worries. The girl stared at me and nodded as I spoke, taking in my words.

When I was done speaking, she pulled me closer to her and embraced me into a hug.

"Damn, boo. I'm sorry you're going through all of that."

We sat in silence for a moment as she nervously bounced her leg. Tucking a piece of hair behind her ear, she opened her mouth to say something but quickly shook her head.

"What's up?" I asked, observing her.

"Well, I had a suggestion that may help, but I don't want to overstep. Besides, I don't think you'd be up to it."

"At this point, I'll take any advice I can get."

A small grin spread across her face as she grabbed my hands. Okay, so I know this guy who actually helps other people by giving out loans."

"Is he like a loan shark or something?" I asked, squinting my eyes.

The woman threw her head back and laughed before playfully pushing my shoulder. "Girl no! Nothing like that. He just helps others who need help every now and then financially. You can pay him in installments or work in one of the houses he owns. Once he gets his money back, you're good to go. He doesn't double or triple the amount he gives you."

"When you say work in one of his houses, do you mean I'll be like his maid?"

"Yeah, something like that. How about this, I'll take you over to his office so he can explain it better? I was just heading over there to drop off one of my installment checks anyway."

I had a nagging suspicion in the pit of my stomach urging me not to trust her, but I couldn't figure out why. She was sweet and innocent and gave off the impression that she really wanted to help me. Besides, I was desperate. If this man could help me pay off grandmother's bills and prevent us from losing the house,

I could at least hear him out. Especially if all I had to do was clean up his house. Shit, I'll scrub the toilet with a toothbrush if he was able to get us out of debt.

"Ok, let's go!" I said, grabbing my backpack. "I'm Addison, by the way."

"I'm Olivia."

Chapter 4

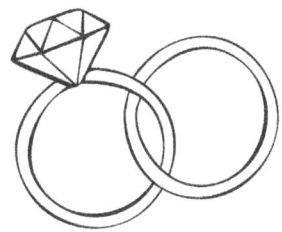

Addison 5 Months Ago

We pulled up to a massage parlor that had a black and green cobra sprayed on the side wall. The sign on the front door read L & K massages. Outside were two buff men, one Korean and the other Black, wearing a black shirt with L&K crew on it. They had identical bald heads and wore a pair of dark sunglasses with scowls across their faces.

"Dang, since when did a massage parlor need bouncers?"

Olivia laughed as she hopped out of the car. "Girl, you'd be surprised."

"They be wildin' like that?" I asked nervously.

"You'll be fine. Now c'mon."

Olivia walked towards the two men and gave them each a hug.

"You been staying out of trouble?" The Korean man asked.

"You know me," she said, winking. "Is Mr. L. in?"

He nodded his head and opened the door for us. We walked in and I expected to see a standard receptionist desk with potted plants, gentle lighting, and some sort of water fountain. To my surprise, as soon as we walked in, the room was lit up with a pink, fuchsia color. There was a sign that had one arrow pointing to the right that read play area and an arrow pointing to the left reading offices.

"This way," Olivia gently pulled my arm, taking us to the left.

The hall had two private offices on the left and right hand side with an executive office in the center. Olivia walked up to the center office and knocked three times.

"Come in." a loud voice boomed from behind the door.

I took a step back as my heart pounded in my chest. "I-I don't think I should be here."

"Girl, relax. Mr. L is cool people, trust me."

Olivia opened the door and stepped inside. I chewed on my bottom lip before following behind her. The office space was quite empty with the exception of a black leather couch on the far wall with a few affirmation posters hanging up. Focusing my attention to the center of the office, I saw Olivia sitting on the edge of the desk with a chocolate-skinned brutha eyeing me. He had small coils on top of his head and deep hazel eyes. His shoulders were broad, and I could see the tattoos going up his arms and across his chest through his undershirt. He was handsome, but there was something dark behind his eyes that made my stomach knot. I shifted uncomfortably as he licked his lips. His eyes traveled up and down my body before he looked over to Olivia.

"What you think?" Olivia asked, looking over at Mr. L.

"She's pretty. I can make some good money off of her."

My eyes scrunched up. "Hold up. What the hell are y'all talking about? Olivia, what the fuck have you brought me into?"

"Calm down, Little Bit. I'm not here to hurt you. I heard that you need some help, is that right?" Mr. L asked, leaning back in his chair.

I swallowed and nodded. "Look, I-I just need a little money to get my grandma's house up to date and to pay for a full time caregiver. I can't really pay you back in installments, but maybe I can clean one of your houses or clean around here."

Mr. L huffed out a hearty laugh. "Olivia, did you really tell this girl she'd be cleaning?"

"I had to say something. She looks so timid, and I couldn't flat out say what she'd really be doing."

My eyes widened as I stared between the two. "What the hell do you think I'd be doing? If you think I'm fucking for some money, then y'all got me messed up! I'm not having my first time be with some stranger."

The smile on Luther's face vanished as he abruptly stood up from his desk. "What did you say?"

"I-I-"

"She's a virgin, baby." Olivia cooed, licking her lips.

I slowly began to step backwards but Mr. L was already in my face with a maniacal smile. He grabbed my arm and pulled me towards his desk, pushing me down into the seat across from him.

"Look, I-"

"I can help you." Mr. L interrupted.

I sat with my mouth open before shaking my head. "Wait, you will?"

"Yes."

"So, I can pay you back in installments?"

He chuckled. "No. Let's make a deal. I give you the money to save your grandma's house and I will take full ownership of her medical bills if you accept my offer."

I scrunched up my nose. "What offer?"

"You agree to marry my client."

"What?" I shouted, hopping out of my chair. "You must be out of your fucking mind!"

"Girl, calm down. You were literally crying on a bench trying to come up with a way to get some money. The opportunity is right in your face." Olivia said, rolling her eyes.

"Yeah, but. I...I can't. I mean, marry some complete stranger? That's absurd."

"Welp, good luck getting the money. Maybe they'll allow your grandmother into a homeless shelter."

I swallowed the bile in my throat. Shit, what was I supposed to do? On one hand, I'd be giving myself away to someone I had never met. What if they were cruel or abusive? I'd be stuck with them until I had the funds to get away. Then again, that money would help out so much. I wouldn't have to worry about my nana losing her home or ending up in an assisted living facility. Shit! I stared down and briefly closed my eyes. I didn't have any other choice. My nana had done so much for me and helped me become the woman I am today. This was the least I could do for her.

"Fine. I'll do it."

Chapter 5

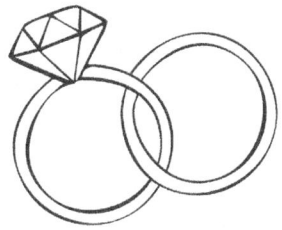

Seojun 3 Months Ago

I moved my head from side to side, giving my neck a much-needed crack. Rolling my shoulders, I closed my eyes and tilted my head back. The cool air caused a shiver to run down my spine, but this was still my favorite season. I didn't have much time to enjoy it since the summer heat was right around the corner. I gazed up at the night sky through the holes of the roof and smelled the rain that was due to arrive soon. I couldn't believe that it had almost been a year since Ayzo told me about Nicholas going on a road trip with a random woman to seek out his ex, Olivia. Maybe it was a coincidence, but since then, my own search for revenge has been nothing but rewarding.

A slow smile crept across my face as muffled cries echoed behind me. I slowly turned around and stuffed my hands into my pockets. Passing the toothpick around in my mouth, I eyed the five men currently tied up. The first man was Theron a.k.a. Ron. He was my third in command and in charge of recruiting the women for my massage parlors and group homes. I only hired women who wanted to make extra money. Nothing was by force, and I made sure no one abused my girls. Ron was the man who made all of that happen. You could imagine my disappointment when I learned he jumped ship to the Cobras.

The second man, Lewis, helped Ron with my group homes. He made sure anyone, man or woman, who came into one of my homes, was clean. No type of STD, fever, cough, not a single damn illness passed the threshold. Everyone had to be healthy as an ox. If one of the girls fell ill, she was quarantined. If she caught an STD, since they were free to come and go as they please as long as they got checked and stayed safe, then she was removed from my payroll. Trust and loyalty have always been big to me. If I was betrayed, then there was no coming back.

The last three men were a part of the security team. I cocked my head to the side and chuckled. Now that I thought about it, I never had a chance to learn their names. Ron had hired them on just before everyone turned their backs on the Jaguars. I shrugged. It didn't matter now.

"Can I be honest with you guys? Now, if I do, you promise not to tell anyone?"

Ron and Lewis glared at me while two of the nameless guards shook in their chairs with terror. My eye caught the last man frantically nodding his head in agreement. I chuckled as I pushed off the table I was sitting on while pointing at him.

"Ah, see guys! This man right here is a good man." I stood over him, baring the gold fangs in my mouth. "A man of his word, right?"

His eyes darted over to the other men. I snapped my fingers in his face and tsked.

"I wasn't talking to them, I'm talking to you, uh...dammit. What is your name?"

I snatched the duct tape off of his mouth, not attempting to be gentle. He yelled out in pain as tears welled in his eyes. Glancing at his face, I hurriedly examined the piece of tape and realized I took off a nice chunk of his mustache.

"Damn. My bad," I said, letting out a low whistle. "Here you go."

I ripped off the clunk of hair that was on the tape and stuck it back on his lip with a light pat. It limply fell on to his lap.

"Anyway," I said, holding back my laugh. "What's your name?"

He blinked a few times before he audibly swallowed. "J-Jonah."

"Ah, Jonah. So, are you a man of your word?"

He nodded.

I arched and eyebrow as I chewed on the toothpick in my mouth. "If you are, then why did you betray the Jaguars? Why did you renege on your word and loyalty to me?

"I swear, Mr. Seojun I–"

I yanked my gun out of my back pocket and sent a bullet through his mouth. Blood splattered the ground that I had littered with tarp. I shook my head in disgust. I knew for a fact that whatever was about to come out of his mouth was going to be a damn lie. When Ayzo and I went into hiding, we compiled a list of every muthafucka who turned their backs on me. I may not have remembered every single person's name who worked for me, but when I had someone tied up, you better believe they snitched like their lives depended on it. After almost a year, I finally had every single person who worked for me on my list. All I had to do was check off each name until I found the ringleader.

I placed my foot on the chair and pushed, causing the corpse to drop to the floor with a splat.

"Damn, you had to shoot the nigga in his mouth?"

Right on queue, Raheim came walking into the warehouse. Raheim was in his early thirties and ran a cleaning crew all across the Midwest. He was tall and stocky, which made it a breeze for him to haul away bodies with little effort. I remembered hiring him a few times when I ran the Jaguars and never had any issues. When those idiots ran into my house a few months back, he was the only one I could think of to accurately get the job done. Fortunately for him, when he heard that the Cobras needed a cleaning man, he declined. He said he wouldn't work for anyone that could do some shady, disloyal shit like that. It was a good thing he was loyal to me because I had originally planned to kill him, too, once he had my house put back together.

Right behind Raheim was my cousin Jay. He used to follow me and Ayzo around when we were kids before we were inducted into the Jaguars. He wanted so badly to be a part of the crew, but at the time, he was too young. Plus, his mom, my aunt Jenny, made me swear on her death bed that I wouldn't let him near the group until his 21st birthday. She had hopes that he would've changed his mind by then, but unfortunately, he didn't.

The pair began rolling up the body on the ground and I couldn't help the slight shake of my head. Watching my cousin work, I just knew that my aunt was probably rolling in her grave just as much as Jay was rolling up the body. I sighed. I did try to keep him away, but at the end of the day, he's a grown ass man. If he wanted to be a part of this life, at least he was going to do it under me. I was going to keep him safe.

As Raheim and Jay carried out the body, I spun on my heels to examine the other men. The two men that were already scared had pissed themselves. Hell, one of them had passed out. I snatched the toothpick out of my mouth and jammed it into his cheek.

"Ahh fuck!" he shouted through the tape over his mouth.

"I didn't give you permission to take a damn nap." His body shook with fright, but he kept his eyes on me. From the corner of my eye, I could see Lewis moving his head before he began mumbling.

I walked over to him and snatched off the tape from his mouth. Luckily for him, he didn't have any facial hair.

"What do you want from us, Seojun? You know that we all crossed over to the Cobras and that's grounds for execution. So, why torture us?"

I smiled before placing my hands behind my back. "That is an excellent question, Lewis. I have just one simple question and if you can answer truthfully, then we can wrap this up and call it a night. Does that sound fair?"

Lewis eyed me with suspicion. "Just one question?"

I held up my finger and nodded. "Just the one."

"And we are good to go for the night?"

"Indeed."

"Okay."

"Great! Who recruited y'all to leave the Jaguars and join the Cobras?"

Lewis shifted uneasily in his chair as he looked back over at Ron. I squinted my eyes as I stared at him. He knew something, but he obviously was afraid to say anything because of Ron. Even though I was the boss, Lewis reported to Ron for years and he hardly had to interact with me. I could respect that, but I wasn't Ron, and he didn't run shit - I did. I pulled my gun out and scratched the side of my head. My patience was thinning, and I was getting hungry. It was well after midnight and the taco spot; I liked was only going to be open for another hour and a half. I'd be damned if I missed out on some tacos because nobody wanted to talk.

"Either answer my damn question, or I leave y'all here while I go eat and get some sleep. It's going to be a cold one tonight – probably the low 40s with a bit of rain. Ehh, y'all not afraid of getting a little bit of pneumonia, right? Then tomorrow evening, I'll come back and chop y'all up one by one."

When Lewis chewed on his bottom lip instead of talking, I turned around and grabbed my keys off the table. I began walking towards the exit to talk to Raheim and Jay when Lewis called me to stop. I slowly halted in my steps before looking over my shoulder.

"A man named Z approached us at the group home off Langley Ave. We thought he was just another customer. I mean, he had all of his documentation and passed all the tests to get in. We assumed one of the girls invited him because it was like he already knew what the procedures were. After he spent time with Cinnamon, he came to us. He started telling us about how his job is similar to ours, but he just got paid more."

I rubbed the stubble on my chin. "Z, huh? He didn't have a last name?"

Lewis shook his head. "I'm sure he does, but I don't remember what it was."

I arched my eyebrow when I noticed Ron was glaring at Lewis. Probably because he was running his mouth and nobody liked a rat, but could you really blame the man? I mean, me personally, I wouldn't be snitching, but their hands were tied. Especially since he thought his only chance of living was to give up information.

"Any information you want to add, Ron?" I asked. "I bet you know more and the faster you tell me, the faster we can call it a night."

Ron's eyebrows scrunched up as the muffled cries of the two other men and Lewis's pleas filled the room. As I watched Ron's face go through a wave of emotions, I couldn't help but place my hand on my chest and wipe away an invisible tear. These men were begging for their boss to talk so they could be let go. To these men, it was a life or death situation, and he knew it. Ron finally sighed heavily before nodding his head towards me.

I walked towards him and removed the tape from his mouth.

He huffed out a breath before licking his lips. "He never gave his last name. The agreement was, he could see Cinnamon if he got us in with the Cobras. We were guaranteed a position at his house."

"And who does Z work for?"

Ron shook his head. "Nobody knew. Hell, not even Z knew. He reported to a man named Manny and that's all I know."

I nodded my head. "So, all fifty of you decided to jump ship because they were offering more money?"

Ron shifted uneasily in his seat. "I can't speak on everyone else, but that's not why I left." He exhaled and briefly looked down. "The day after I met Z, I received an anonymous text from somebody who threatened to hurt my family if I didn't betray you."

My back stiffened as I glared down at him. "Why didn't you just come to me?"

"They knew where my daughter laid her head every night! Hell, they even knew what school she was attending. If you thought I was going to stay loyal to you just for her to be killed, then you never knew me. You know how much I loved her. In the end, it was all for nothing."

I cocked my head to the side. "What do you mean?"

Ron let out a humorless chuckle. "My baby mother took our daughter and ran. The last time I spoke to her; she said she didn't want anything to do with me because she knew that I had betrayed you. She didn't want our daughter's life in danger when your wrath came knocking on our door. A month after she left, I found out they were dead – hit by a damn drunk driver."

"Damn, my condolences." I turned to look at Lewis. "What about you? I don't remember you having any children, so what was your excuse?"

Lewis stared down at his feet. "I- no offense, Seojun, but the women were beautiful, and we were allowed to have them. If you would have just let us pick a girl that we liked and paid us decently, a lot of us wouldn't have been so eager to leave."

"Money and pussy were all it took?" I glanced at the other two men who stared guilty at the ground.

"Damn, that's fucked up." Jay said, leaning against the door frame, putting on a new pair of gloves.

"Agreed!" Raheim said, his dark brown eyes raging with anger. "I would put a bullet in my own damn head if I fucked over the one person who put me on game and gave me a steady income, so I didn't have to work in corporate America. You fucked up a good thing and for what? Some damn pussy and the fact that you got greedy."

Shaking my head, I walked over to the two men and removed the tape from their mouths. I didn't want to hear all of their crying and begging for forgiveness, but I needed one more question answered.

"I got all of the information I needed so let's call it a night and y'all can go."

The look of relief spread across everyone's faces except for Ron. He slowly closed his eyes and dropped his head. Ron has worked with me long enough to realize what was happening, unlike these other three.

"So, my last question for you guys is where do you want me to leave your body? Of course, it won't be the full body because I need to send a few of your limbs to the others who betrayed me."

"B-but you said you were going to let us go." One of the nameless men stuttered.

I dropped my head back and laughed. "I said no such thing, but I can see where the confusion came. I said we can call it a night and y'all can go...to hell. This is your final night alive."

I watched anger fill the nameless man's eyes as he sneered at me. "You conniving son of a bitch! I'm glad I backstabbed you and I'd do it again."

He hocked a glob of spit onto my shoes before beaming with pride. I smiled back at him as I stood over him. Lifting my hand, I motioned for Jay to come towards me. He knew exactly what I was asking for as he picked up the metal bat that I had resting on the wall. This wasn't just an ordinary bat, but one I had specially designed. She had a smooth handle that was designed for my fingers to fit snuggly. The barrel had jagged nails welded into the base and was wrapped in barb wire.

"This is Tiffany. I got my inspiration to make her from my favorite villain, Negan."

"W-who?"

I scoffed. "Negan! From The Walking Dead TV show? I would tell you to watch it but, you know."

"Seojun, please!"

He began to beg but I ignored him as I admired my bat. "Tiffany baby," I cooed, wrapping my hands around the handle. "This no name fucker spit on your favorite pair of shoes. Do you believe that?"

"I'm sorr-"

His words were cut short as I introduced Tiffany to the top of his legs. His screams echoed throughout the warehouse as the nails dug into his skin. Yanking the bat back, pieces of his skin got caught on the barb wire and dangled freely. I smiled manically as I swung again, this time striking his stomach. The thing I loved most about Tiffany was that her nails never went in deep enough to kill but made the death slow and painful.

"Hold this for me," I instructed to him as I left Tiffany digging into his abdomen. "Now, where was I?"

"You were asking them which body part they didn't mind not sending to their families." Jay chimed in with glee. "Me personally, I say the fingers. They break off easily and fit in envelopes."

Raheim glanced over at Jay before shaking his head. "I haven't met anyone who enjoyed chopping up bodies as much as you."

"Blame my science teacher for putting a scalpel in my hand and letting me dissect frogs."

I huffed out a laugh. "Can you two handle these three? I'm starving like a muthafucka."

Raheim nodded. "I got you, boss man. We'll get this place cleaned up once we're done and have those special cargos delivered tonight."

"One finger for each person on the list," I instructed before glancing over at Ron from the corner of my eye. I turned and strolled towards him, pulling out my gun from my waist. "I don't agree with what you did, but I understand why. I just wish you would have come to me. You know how I feel about protecting family. So, I'll make your death quick."

A small smile crept across his face. "You're right, but I can't change the past. For what it's worth, I'm sorry, Seojun."

I nodded before putting the gun against his temple. He closed his eyes and exhaled a long breath. "At least I'll get to see my little girl again."

I gave him a half smile before pulling the trigger.

Chapter 6

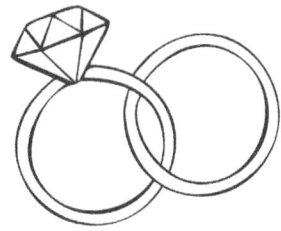

Luther 3 Months Ago

I gripped the bridge of my nose as I listened to Xavier, who I called X because he was my best friend, on the phone. It was barely seven in the morning and another one of my goons was found dead.

"Who did y'all find?"

"Lewis. You had just put him in charge of house Beta."

Over the course of three days, they've found pieces of three different bodies of my men. While the police scrambled to figure out what was happening, I already knew who was behind the mess. Seojun Yi a.k.a. the leader of the Jaguars.

"Yeah, I remember him." I sighed. "Crazy, Lewis's ass only wanted to leave the Jaguars because he wanted Sandy's ass all to himself and Seojun didn't allow fraternizing. Lewis was a stupid ass nigga for choosing loose pussy over loyalty."

"So, you didn't want him to join the team?"

"Every jaguar that switched up to be cobra is technically on my shit list until proven otherwise. They turned their backs on the boss with a snap of my fingers. Yes, it worked out perfectly for me, but I don't trust any of them. Those niggas aren't loyal to anything but money and pussy and I don't like that."

"That's why they get all the trash assignments?"

I snorted out a laugh. "Fucking right."

Xavier huffed out a chuckle before I heard him mutter a curse.

"What now?"

"I'm getting text messages from the other ex-jaguars. They all pretty much saying they got an envelope of either a finger or a toe placed on they doorsteps or car this morning."

I burst into laughter. I may not like Seojun, but I had to admit the man was ruthless. I made a mental note to do some shit like that to my enemies.

"Well, what do we do?" X asked.

"Nothing."

"Nothing?"

"Yup. Like I said, those ex-jaguars were disloyal and to be honest, they served their purpose with me."

"You and boss lady had them turn their backs on Seojun without a real need for them?"

I lit up a blunt and exhaled a puff of smoke. "All I'm going to say is, we got what we needed, and spare parts can be disposed of. Don't text them niggas back because they are good as dead. Go check on my houses, though, to make sure they straight."

With that, I hung up the phone. X may have been my best friend, but he didn't need to know everything that was in motion. The fact that I told him about Mama K was probably too much information, but I couldn't take it back. All he needed to know was that as long as he stayed loyal to me, then he was protected.

My phone chimed, causing me to roll my eyes. I wasn't in the mood for Xavier to get all sentimental or ask any more questions he didn't need the answer to.

Mama K: Seojun's out of hiding

Me: I heard. What do you want me to do?

Mama K: Nothing...yet. We have to see the plan through in order for this to work.

Me: Can't we just tell Mr. Omba she can finish school online and send her off? I'm ready to get my baby Denice and get rid of the rest of those muthafuckas.

Mama K: Patience, baby boy. With Seojun out getting rid of all those dumb ass Jaguars except for the ones we have in hiding, and his little family roaming around clueless of our plans for them, they'll never know what hit them when we strike.

Just before I put the phone down, I received another text notification, but this time from Mr. Omba.

Omba: I'd like an updated picture of my future bride. It seems the last one I retrieved suffered some water damage

I scrunched up my nose; ole nasty muthafucka.

Me: Sure thing

I started a new text thread and scrolled through my contacts until I found the name I was looking for.

Me: I need an updated picture of you.

Addy: Another one?

Me: Now!

Addy: I'm so sick of this shit, Mr. L

Me: Bet. I'll make sure that caregiver and mortgage company do not receive their payment for another two months. Then I'll send a few of my goons to your grandmother's home and she can make up for all of the money you owe. I know a few nasty niggas that like old pussy and would enjoy passing her around, especially since she can take her teeth out.

Addy: Please don't! I'm sending it.

Me: That's what I thought! And make sure you look sexy.

Addy: FYI if the mortgage bill isn't paid, the bank will add more fees and possibly foreclose on the house

I ignored her last text. I didn't give a flying fuck right now. I'll pay the shit when I get around to it. Within a few minutes, Addy had sent me over a pic that I knew Mr. Omba's ass was going to like. Hell, his ass liked all of the pictures she sent - that's why he kept messing them up. His old freaky ass was printing them off and jacking off on them.

I shook my head before forwarding them over. I was tired of dealing with his old ass, too, but that quarter million was on the tip of my fingers. All she had to do was finish school and the money was mine.

Chapter 7

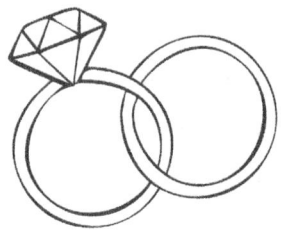

Addison 3 Months Ago

I stared at my phone in disgust as the notification updated from 'sending' to 'delivered', indicating the picture went through. I threw my phone down and placed my head into my hands. I hated this!

When Olivia approached me those few months back, I thought God sent her into my life as a blessing when she told me she could help and would introduce me to her boss, Mr.L. Honey, when I tell you my discernment was not powered on, because I would've known it was a test and not a blessing. Now I was stuck dealing with Mr. L and my soon to be husband.

If I wasn't in dire need, I wouldn't have accepted, but what other choice did I have? At first, Mr. L held up his side of the bargain by getting us caught up on all the bills and he even hired an around the clock caregiver for my nana. I thought I could rest easy knowing that while I was finishing school in Vegas, she was being taken care of back home in Philly. Of course, I was sadly mistaken!

Once Mr. L and I signed the contract making him the temporary guardian over my nana, he's done the bare minimum! Not only has he failed to pay the bills, but he's even forgotten to pay for nana's caregiver a few times. I should have known not to trust that asshole! Hell, I sacrificed my freedom so that my grandmother would be comfortable and safe, but it seems like it was all for nothing.

A knock came at my door, snapping me out of my thoughts. I took a deep breath and plastered on a fake smile. I may have been dealing with Mr. L's bullshit and lies and would eventually be given away to some old pervert, but I didn't let that get in the way of the little happiness I had. Opening the door, I found my friends Cindy and Sandy, who were cousins, and Akira standing there.

"What up, friend!" Sandy sang, pulling me into a hug.

"Hey, girls," I laughed, embracing her back.

I gave Cindy a quick hug and gave Akira, who I liked to call K sometimes, a kiss on each cheek. I may have been friends with everyone, but Akira was my best friend. I felt comfortable around her, and we told each other everything. We started at college together and damn near had the same major, so it was inevitable that we'd become close.

Don't get me wrong, Cindy and Sandy were cool, but I just met them a few months ago. They were freshmen on my floor and since I was the RA, I always talked to them. They eventually started to come around more and more until ultimately, we all became friends.

"What's the move tonight?" Cindy asked, sitting on top of my desk.

"I heard there was a new bar downtown, we should check it out." Sandy chimed in.

"I don't know about that. I have a few midterms tomorrow and I need to study." Akira protested, sitting crisscross on my bed.

"I'm with K. As much as I want to turn up, this is my last midterm, and I refuse to fuck up my GPA now."

"Ugh! I swear y'all are so boring sometimes. Live a little, why don't you!" Cindy pouted.

"Girl, you acting like you don't have two midterms tomorrow, too." Akira snapped.

"We do, but damn, we still like to go have fun."

"Yeah! Maybe if y'all come out and get the cobwebs dusted off y'all coochie, y'all wouldn't be so stressed about some tests." Sandy stated, snapping her fingers in the air.

"Bitch, fuck you!" Akira laughed, throwing a pillow at them.

"What? Just saying. When was the last time you made time for yourself and entertained the opposite sex? Or same sex, if you like eating more than sucking."

Akira rolled her eyes. "I'm talking to someone right now, for your information, but we both care about our future and are focusing on getting our priorities handled. Trust and believe, when the semester is over, not one speck of dust gonna be on either set of lips. You feel me?"

"I know that's right!" I cackled, giving her a high five.

"Aht, aht, not too much, miss ma'am. What about you?" Sandy tsked as she pointed her finger at me.

"She's talking to somebody," Akira interjected.

"Actually, that fell through."

"What?" Akira asked, her eyebrows pinching together.

"Y'all hoes and secrets - spill the tea." Cindy impatiently waved her hand.

I rolled my eyes before giving Akira a gentle smile. "Well, when I went back home over the winter break, I met this really fine guy at a bar called Jill's. I mean, nothing happened besides us having some really good conversation. I ended up giving him my number and on the last weekend I was in town, he hit me up to hang out. I spent over two hours doing my hair and makeup just for that asshole to cancel at the last minute."

"I know you fucking lying!" Akira gasped.

I shook my head as I sat down at my vanity. "That's what I got for letting a guy named Ayzo talk sweet bullshit in my ear," I huffed out loud.

Cindy and Sandy looked at each other, causing me to squint my eyes. Sandy cleared her throat and gave me a sympathetic smile. "Do you still talk to him? Maybe he's available now."

I shook my head. "Nope. After he stood me up, he sent me a text message the day I was boarding the plane back here, explaining that he still had feelings for some girl he used to talk to and it wasn't going to be fair to me to string me along. When I tried to reach out to him again, the number was disconnected."

"Or he blocked you." Sandy stated, matter-of-factly.

Akira rolled her eyes at her before looking back at me and expelling a small sigh. "At least he told you the truth. A lot of these niggas out here would have tried to fuck and then leave you on read without a second thought."

I nodded in agreement. "When you're right, you're right. Besides, when we met at the bar, I could tell that he didn't really want company, but he was fine as hell, and I would've been a fool not to talk to him. I should have listened when he slipped up and said some girl had him down bad and he was just looking for a friend to talk to, but this damn hussy in between my legs was ready to finally jump in the game."

"Girl, I can't!" Sandy chuckled.

Akira grinned before standing up and rubbing me on the back. "Don't worry, boo. When you find the right man, he'll want you and never leave you hanging."

I felt tears well at the corner of my eyes, but I quickly blinked them away as I hugged my best friend. I wanted so much to believe that would happen to me, but at the end of it all, my fate was sealed. I was already promised to be married to someone that I had never met. The dream of being able to find the love of my life was shattered the day I accepted help from Mr.L. Real love was never going to be in the cards for my life.

Akira's phone chimed, causing her to mutter under her breath. "Looks like I have to work early in the morning, so I definitely cannot go out."

I scrunched up my nose before looking at my watch. "Girl, it's almost seven in the evening. Why your boss just now saying something about somebody house needing to be cleaned this late at night?"

K shrugged one shoulder. "I've learned not to ask questions if I wanted to get paid."

"Big facts," I chuckled.

"Oh! Why don't y'all come with me? All of the heavy lifting will be done tonight, so in the morning, all we'd have to do is basic stuff like dusting."

"Hell to the no! I am not spending my weekend cleaning some nasty ass house," Sandy sneered, standing to her feet.

"Agreed! I'm trying to get my back blown out by dick not from scrubbing floors." Cindy chimed in.

I rolled my eyes as the pair waved goodbye and walked out the room. A part of me understood where the girls were coming from. At the same time, I've seen

Akira bring home at least a stack every time she was called to clean. Shit, I could use an extra grand right now, especially if all I had to do was tidy up.

"I don't mind going with you, Akira, as long as we're back before the afternoon."

Akira's nose crinkled as a questioning look danced in her eyes. We may have been best friends, but she still did not know everything I was going through. I had been able to keep my weekly doctor checkups and my arranged marriage hidden, but I could tell that she knew I was hiding secrets. It was written all over her face, but she didn't speak on it.

Akira cleared her throat and grinned. "Absolutely! If we get there by six, we'll be done by nine at the latest. They're offering three bands, so I'll give you half."

I jumped up and wrapped my arms around my best friend. "You are the bee's knees, boo!"

Akira laughed as she embraced me. "I'll shoot you the address tonight."

"Can I just spend the night with you? I mean, it'll be easier that way; we can just ride together."

Akira nodded her head. "I'm cool with that."

"I'm going to do a bit more studying and then I'll text you when I'm on the way."

"You know you can just study at my place, right?"

I shook my head. "The last time we had a study session, neither one of us actually studied because we were binge watching Martin. I almost put You Go Boy in my thesis paper."

"Girl, bye," Akira laughed out loud. "Okay, okay, I'll see you in a bit."

I waved goodbye and slumped against the door. As much as I loved my best friend, I really didn't want to spend the night at her house. I mean, she had a cozy one bedroom apartment next to the campus, but I wanted to sleep in my own bed, not toss and turn all night on a pull out couch. Unfortunately, this was my only option. I was on strict orders to be with Bruno, my personal driver, whenever I went outside of the campus — per Mr. L's orders. If I did anything on my own, my driver snitched, and all hell would break loose.

I sighed. There were times when I wanted to tell Akira everything that was going on. When I couldn't hang out or had to come up with an excuse for something so trivial like meeting at a location, I felt the tension in our friendship grow. I didn't think she'd stop being my friend, but maybe she'd start distancing herself to match my energy. I mean, would it be so bad if I told her what was happening in my life?

Chapter 8

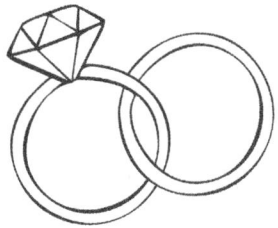

Seojun 3 Months Ago

The golden hue of the sun sprinkled sporadically through the room as the blinds on the patio windows swayed against the breeze. I caught glimpses of the large oak tree me and Ayzo use to play under. Jay was too little to play with us, but he followed us around anyway. I sat next to my father as he puffed on a cigar and watched a few reruns of his favorite TV show.

I had been out of hiding almost a year and this was my first time seeing my dad. Not because I didn't want to, but I was being cautious. I still did not know who set me up to lose the jaguars, but I was getting closer. There were only twenty names left on my list and coming to Chicago to visit my dad was the perfect reason to knock off a few more names.

"Adeul-a, eonje gyeolhonhal geoya?" (Son, when will you marry?)

"Abeoji (father), please." I huffed, taking a sip of water.

"You've been out of hiding for a while and have been chasing those cobras down. With all of the strategic planning you concocted, you didn't have an outline for when you would settle down to upend our deal?"

I rolled my eyes. "It is not time for me to marry."

Snatching the remote control from the side table, my father muted the TV. "Seojun, do you not understand how important it is for you to marry? I made a deal!"

I huffed out a breath of air, before folding my arms across my chest. I hated when my father brought up the fact that he bargained his only son for wealth. When we were financially struggling and barely surviving, my father met, Ernest, the leader of a group called The Reapers down in Texas. Ernest was an older man and did not have an heir to pass down his dynasty. Well, he had a daughter, but she was too concerned with spending his money instead of leading. So, he made a deal with my dad that as long as his first born son married a woman in the Reaper clan and continued the legacy, then he would help my dad out financially. The Reapers and Jaguars would merge as one and since my dad would become the new leader, the jaguars would be dominant. If for any reason the deal was broken, then the reapers in Texas, would murder us all.

Everything had been smooth for years. My dad would join The Reapers once a year to for their annual meeting. When my father stepped down and I I fully took over, I took over that responsibility. When I informed them about what happened to me and the Jaguars last year, they were understanding but put a deadline on our agreement. If I didn't marry by the time we were to meet again for our next annual meeting, they'd kill off the rest of the Jaguars. Us included.

"It is well past time for you to settle down. I understand that you want revenge for whoever did this to us, to the Jaguars, but you have to remember that we have a deadline. Do you want everything we've worked hard for to go to waste?"

I stared down at my hands.

"Exactly! My boy, you have to look at the whole picture. Your eyes cannot be fixed on one thing. If we want our legacy to continue and to keep the peace with the Reapers down south, then you must find a wife. Luckily for you, I found a woman you can marry that is a part of the reaper clan."

My eye brows shot up as I stared at my dad. "What are you talking about?"

"Her name is Bernice. She's been a part of the reapers for years and knows the ins and outs."

"Yeah, I know who Ms. Bernice. She's sixty-five! I don't mind an older woman, but how the hell do you expect me to have an heir if she's no longer able to have kids?"

"Well, you better find someone!"

I groaned. It wasn't like I didn't want to marry or understand how important it was, but my mind was not on that right now. Besides, there wasn't anyone who caught more than a day's worth of my attention. Not to mention, bringing someone into the middle of this war could be fatal to not only myself but to them. I already had to keep Ayzo, Denice, Ashlynn, and Nicholas in mind when it came to safety. I sighed.

"Father, I will not only get the Jaguars back, but I will marry a woman of the Reaper clan, of my choice, and produce an heir before our time is up."

He stared at me a long while before he nodded his head.

Chapter 9

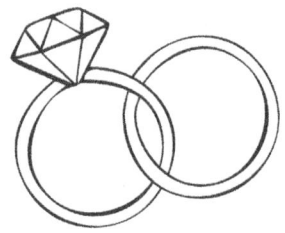

Addison Present

With each house that I assisted Akira with over the past few months, I could see why she did this as her side hustle. I already cleaned, so the fact that I was getting paid now was an added bonus. I didn't go to every job with my best friend, but when she had a huge house and minimal time, I came along. Besides, we were finally at the end of the school year, and I was graduating at the end of the week. Helping Akira these past few months was a wonderful distraction from my studies. The beautiful part of it all was that Bruno didn't suspect a thing. Therefore, he didn't have a reason to blab to Mr.L.

Not to mention, the money that I brought in was used to help out my nana in any way possible. We were still behind on the mortgage, but at least I was able to pay my nana's caregiver regularly. I even had enough money for the caregiver to take my grandma out to explore new hobbies. I knew that her dementia wouldn't allow her to fully participate, but at least she'd be able to get out of the house.

Akira slowed the car as we entered a housing development. When we finally stopped at the second house that was built on the block, my jaw dropped. To say the house was huge was an understatement. I swear Akira and I pulled up to a damn mansion. The home had a circular driveway that could easily fit five to six cars and a small fountain in the middle. It had a soft cream tint with a mahogany trim and a mixture of wide bay windows and sliding windows. The second floor had a balcony that wrapped around to the back of the house and the front entrance had double oak doors. I glanced around the area and realized this was the only home that was built so far. There were tools and supplies around the community, indicating other homes were being built, but this house was done.

"Mr. Adalyn does have some good taste!" Akira cooed, stepping out of the car.

"Mr. Adalyn?"

She nodded. "He's the owner of the entire neighborhood. He builds up homes for those in need and sells them at reasonable prices. According to my boss, he hasn't been here in months and just decided to sell this house which makes sense. He never stays in one home longer than a year. Well, except for this one. He was here for like almost three years, but he got into some drama and had to travel back home to handle it."

"How you know that man's business like that?"

Akira laughed as she waved me off. "Don't get no ideas. I have never met the man, but I've been working for him for almost two years. My boss, Raheim, has been by Mr. Adalyn's side for a long time."

I arched an eyebrow. "So...Raheim just voluntarily gives up his bosses info like that?"

Akira shifted uneasily before chewing on her bottom lip. She avoided my eyes as she fumbled with her purse, looking for the keys.

"K?"

My friend huffed out a sigh, her shoulders slightly dropping. "I don't need you judging me, Addy."

"Now you know I wouldn't do that. I don't know why you would even fix your mouth to say something like that. You know I'm not foul."

Akira rushed up to me and wrapped her arms around my waist, embracing me. "I know. I know. I'm sorry, love. You are my best friend, and you've always been ten toes down for me."

"You know you could talk to me about anything," I said, holding on to her hands. A swirl of guilt swam through my core, but I ignored it. Here I was getting offended that my bestie was holding on to secrets while I had one tucked away.

Akira nodded, quickly swiping away the few tears from her eyes. "It's Raheim. It has always been him. I don't know how it happened, but one day he stayed behind to help me clean one of the properties and the next thing I know, we're dating."

I gave her a playful smile. "If you're happy, then I am happy. I don't want anything but the best for you, boo. You deserve it!"

"How did I get so lucky to get a best friend like you?"

I smirked and shrugged. She pinched my cheeks before she turned to unlock the door with her spare key. My mouth dropped as I stared into the beautiful modern style home. Sleek black and deep gold color schemes decorated the living room to the left. To my right, was a wide staircase that opened up to a loft style upstairs before it branched off into the bedrooms.

"Girl, how many bedrooms are in here?"

"Eight bedrooms, six and a half bathrooms, two living areas, a basement, and a pool in the backyard. All this for one man, too."

I frowned. How could anyone live in this big house by themselves? As beautiful and impressive as this house was, I'd be too lonely to live here.

"Let's get to it! We need to get this house ready for a showing next week."

I nodded and followed Akira to the supply closet. We grabbed every cleaning supply that was in top tier condition and began our work. After an hour, we completed all of the downstairs area, except for the basement. Apparently, Mr. Adalyn had that specially cleaned already.

As Akira took out the trash, I began to make my way upstairs when my foot stepped on something hard. Looking down at my feet, I realized it was a phone.

"What the? Hey, K?"

"What's up?" Akira stood at the bottom of the stairs.

"Where do you put Mr. Adalyn's belongings that he's left behind?"

Akira's eyebrows scrunched up. "I don't know. He usually never leaves stuff behind – he must've been in a rush. I wonder how the first cleaning crew missed that."

I furrowed my eyebrows. "If he already had a cleaning crew here, why are we here?"

Akira shrugged as she typed away at her phone. "All I know is, Raheim usually doesn't need me to clean until Mr. Adalyn's ready to sell a house. Maybe the first crew thought he was coming back."

I pressed the power button on the side of the phone, but only the battery icon appeared on the screen, indicating the phone was dead. Akira exhaled an exasperated sigh as she stuffed her phone back into her pocket.

"Well, Raheem is no help. All he said was keep it and I know that's because his ass likes to call dibs on anything left behind in other people's houses. I done told him about that shit - gives us a bad look, you know?"

I nodded. "Well, when I get back to the dorm, I'll charge it. Maybe Mr. Adalyn has something in place to return his lost items. I mean, it's a long shot, but it doesn't hurt to try."

Akira nodded. "You are so sweet and go above and beyond to help other people. I, personally, wouldn't do all that, but you're the nice one."

We burst out into laughter. She wasn't wrong. While I was the nicer one and didn't mind giving people a chance, Akira had zero tolerance for people. Once she got a bad vibe or you did something fucked up, she cut you off. No ifs, ands, or buts about it.

"Well, since this is the newest iPhone, if this bad boy isn't claimed, oh best believe, I'm keeping it."

"Aye! Welcome to the bad side, Addy!"

"Girl, I am not about to play with you." I laughed out loud.

Akira and I finished cleaning up the house and headed back to school. Both of our final exams were due to start by noon and we had just enough time to shower and change. As promised, Akira sent me my half for helping her clean and I transferred it right to my checking account. I had the account set up for automatic payments and was sure damn near all of the money would be gone by the end of the day due to bills.

When Akira gave me half her money the first time, I tried to pay Mr. L so I could take back my guardianship of my grandmother and the house, but he refused. I thought about going the legal route, but thought against it. Not only could I not prove that I was financially stable to take care of my grandma, but there was no guarantee that I could even still help K with her houses. Hell, she probably wouldn't be cleaning after we graduated and her boss didn't know I was coming along to help. So, the rights remained with Mr.L. I had signed a contract giving him these things and wanted to kick myself but then again, I didn't have many other options.

After finishing up my last exam, I headed back to my dorm. Cindy and Sandy were not answering their phones and Akira was with her boyfriend. So, that left me by myself, but I didn't mind. Unlike a lot of people I ran into, I actually enjoyed spending time with myself. Nothing like soft music, candles, a box of pizza, and my kindle, reading some hot, messy urban fiction.

I set my belongings down onto the bed and sighed in relief when I finally took off my bra. My phone began to ring causing me to snatch it out of my back pocket.

"Ma?" I asked, answering the phone.

"Well, yes! Who the hell else would it be, girl?"

I scoffed. "Well, excuse me. I'm just surprised you actually saved my number this time."

My mother smacked her lips. "Anyways, did you get everything situated with your nana?"

I bit my bottom lip. Should I tell her what I did in order to not have the house foreclosed? A part of me wanted to, but then again, did she even really care? My mother didn't ask about me or her mother unless she wanted something. She for damn sure never called me out of the blue to check in on me.

I cleared my throat. "Yeah, sort of. I'm working and cleaning houses to keep up with the bills."

"A damn maid? Girl, you'd make more money stripping. Better yet, that's why I called you."

"You want me to strip?" I asked, looking at the phone.

My mother laughed out loud. "Girl no! You are your father's child and probably don't have any rhythm like me."

I rolled my eyes, but knew she was probably right. I could do a few dance moves from TikTok, but I was stiff as hell.

"I was going to say," my mother continued. "You can make thousands doing something a bit more...physical."

"Umm. Like what?"

"Damn, Addison do I have to fucking spell it out for you? Look, I know a few men who would pay a pretty penny to be with Ernest, the Reaper, granddaughter."

My nose scrunched up. "What are you talking about? Who is Ernest and what are the Reapers?"

My mother groaned as she huffed out an air of frustration. "Ernest was my dad, stupid and that's all you need to know. Anyway, since he died our family has been pushed to the bottom of the crew, but at least we're still a part of the Reaper family. So, I was thinking, if you at least get pregnant by one of them, they'll make sure to set you and me up for life."

"The fuck, ma! Why don't you do it since all you care about is how much money you could spend while being laid up?"

"Don't back talk me! Besides, don't you think I tried? My father made sure that I was off limits since I was kicked out. You, on the other hand, still has his blood. If only your senile ass grandma could stay focused for one minute to vouch for you."

"Don't talk about nana Henrietta like that!"

"Oh, grow up, Addison! She's old, senile, and needs to just kick the bucket already."

My mouth hung opened as I stared at the phone. "What the fuck is your problem? Nana hasn't done anything to you, but love you. She gave you her last and wanted nothing, but for you to spend time with us. Why the hell do you hate her?"

"Fuck her! Mama never stood up for me when I needed her the most. My dad kicked me out and disowned me all because I wanted to live my life. I minded my business and made sure not to go over my credit limit. The moment my dad gave me an ultimatum to either join him or marry within the group, I gave him my ass to kiss. He couldn't tell me how to live my damn life!"

"You have got to be kidding me. You are treating grandma like shit because you couldn't be a spoiled brat anymore?"

My mother scoffed. "Fuck you."

Three beeping noises echoed in my ear indicating that she had hung up. I paced the floor with my hands on my hips. After all these years, my mother chose to be a selfish evil bitch all because her dad wanted her to pull her weight. Sadly, I wasn't even surprised, but I couldn't help but wonder why these so called reapers never checked in on grandma. I mean, if she was my grandfather's wife, I would've thought they kept her living comfortably until someone else took over. I shrugged. I guess there wasn't any use thinking about that. None of them were around and I was already trapped into one engagement.

A loud chime echoed throughout the room, causing me to slightly jump. I looked down at my phone, but realized I didn't have any notifications. Scrunching my eyebrows for a brief second, I chuckled when I realized it was the phone

I found at Mr. Adalyn's house. I forgot I hooked it up to the charger when we got back earlier this morning.

I picked up the phone and to my surprise, the passcode was turned off. An uneasy feeling settled in the pit of my stomach. I mean, who walked around without a security code or face ID set up? I shook my head and tapped the screen to bring the phone to life.

My love: Where are you?

I frowned. Now I felt terrible. Mr. Adalyn didn't have his phone, and he was probably going to be in huge trouble for not talking to his girlfriend or wife. A wave of jealousy rushed through me; I didn't have anyone who worried about me like this. All I had was a creepy man who bought me. I would probably never experience love. I shook my head. There was no point in pouting over my own decisions. Besides, at the end of the day, as long as my nana was good, then I'd be fine. I exhaled and decided to text 'my love' back. Hopefully, they won't accuse me of being some mistress and just provide me instructions on how to get the phone back to Mr. Adalyn.

Opening the messages apps, I noticed one other text message that caught my eye. I didn't want to pry, but maybe it was someone who knew how to get ahold of Mr. Adalyn without getting him in trouble with his wife or girlfriend. Opening the message, I noticed there was only one item in the thread, and it was a video. My thumb hovered over the play icon before I closed my eyes. What was I doing? I couldn't be invading this man's privacy like that! Then again, the battle to do the right thing was losing against my curiosity.

As soon as I hit the play button, my eyes bulged in horror. Dash's face took over the screen. I hadn't seen or heard from Dash in over five months and just assumed he was assigned somewhere else. I mean, he was a big flirt and always told me how beautiful I was and that probably irritated Bruno. It's not like I ever paid him any mind because he literally gave the same line to all of the women he ran across, but even still, he was a sweetheart. On the outside, he tried his hardest to be this mean killer, but deep down, he was a softy.

The same gentle brown eyes that sparkled with excitement every time he saw me was now staring back at me and was full of terror. The kindness was replaced with fear and anger. I watched as he sat on stairs that looked like the one's at Mr. Adalyn's house while holding on to his neck. Tears formed in my eyes as I watched the blood seeping through his fingers.

"Any last words?" a deep male voice asked through the video.

I listened as the man holding the camera identified himself as Seojun. I scrunched up my eyebrows. Who was Seojun? I had never heard of him before, well, I haven't run across him before if he worked for Mr. L. I've had a few personal guards following me over the past year, like Dash, but I was good about remembering names. His was unfamiliar. Maybe he worked for Mr. Adalyn?

I screamed when I saw a bullet lodge into Dash's forehead, causing blood to splatter across the floor and onto the lens of the camera. Just before the video ended, I saw the profile of a deep honey-butter complected man end the video. Bile began to rise in my throat as I rushed into my private bathroom and heaved. Tears stung my eyes as the image replayed over and over again. Why did that man kill Dash? Better yet, who the hell was he? Was he one of Mr. Adalyn's cleaning crew members? I shook my head as I wiped my mouth with the back of my hand.

I couldn't wrap my head around what the hell was happening. Why would one of Mr. Adalyn's cleaning team kill Dash? This happened months ago, so what did they do with his body? Did Mr. L know about this? I wanted answers but I needed to tell Mr. L what I just saw just in case he wasn't aware. I may not have liked the man, but one of his followers was killed in cold blood.

My phone began to ring, causing me to slightly jump. Relief washed over me when I saw Mr. L's name highlighting my screen and I'm never excited to hear from him.

"Mr. L, I'm glad you called I found this –"

"Bitch, I don't give a fuck what you found! Why are you running out that damn apartment so early in the morning without telling Bruno?"

I briefly looked at my phone in disbelief as anger coursed through me. Yes, I was sneaking out with K to earn some money, but how the hell did he find out? I made sure to be discreet and the only people who knew I was leaving were my friends and they didn't know about Bruno.

"I am a grown ass woman. I don't even understand why I have to tell Bruno every damn thing. You know I'm not out here doing anything." I snapped, placing my hand on my hip.

"Don't back talk me! I've allowed you to stay on campus and hang out with your little hoe ass friends, but I think you getting a little too comfortable. How I know you not sneaking off to give away my pussy?"

I gritted my teeth as I gripped the phone tighter. I hated when he took claim over me. I wasn't a piece of property. Rolling my eyes, I dragged my tongue across my teeth. "I am not having sex. All I was doing was helping Akira at her job. Hell, I've been doing that for the past few months, and -"

"Is that right? So, Bruno needs to get fucked up, too, for not keeping a better eye on you? I swear it's hard to find competent muthafuckas to do their damn job."

Mr. L continued to rant on the phone. I wanted to yell at him to shut the fuck up so that I could tell him what I saw, but a nagging feeling was telling me to keep my mouth shut. I didn't know why, but I listened.

Mr. L exhaled a heavy sigh, causing me to listen. "Look, your ass graduates in a few more days and then we don't have to deal with each other anymore. Well, I mean once I get paid after shipping your stupid ass off to your new husband, but then that's it. No more contract and you can even take your old ass granny with you. But if you fuck this up, Addy, I swear that I will break your fucking neck. Do you hear me?"

My stomach rolled with more nausea as sweat began to coat the insides of my palms.

"Mr. L, please. I haven't been doing anything I'm not supposed to be."

"Yeah okay. If I find out you lying to me, bitch, I'll put you some place where you can freely whore yourself out."

"I said I wasn't fucking!"

"We'll see. Get your ass downstairs within the next hour so Bruno can take you to the clinic."

With that, he hung up. I screamed out in frustration as I threw my phone down onto the bed and began to pace the room. Why the hell did I get myself caught up with this nigga? I needed a way out, but how? Maybe I could take nana and run away? I shook my head – no I couldn't do that. She needs to be resting, and I don't want to put my burdens onto her and stress her out. It's not her fault that she has dementia. She only had one other living family member, her daughter a.k.a. my mother, but that money hungry wench wasn't about to take care of anybody. Hell, she didn't even bother to take care of me when I was growing up and left me with my nana so much that I just moved in with her. My mom didn't even bother to stop me or beg me to go back home with her.

I plopped down on the bed and placed my head into my hands. I was trapped. I tried to do the right thing by helping my nana and now I was in debt to a fucking monster who didn't give a damn about anybody but himself and money. I knew for a fact that the only reason he wouldn't let me buy myself out of this contract was that I opened my big mouth and told him I was untouched. I didn't think it was a big deal before, but the fact that an old muthafucka was ready to pay huge money so he could marry and deflower me made my insides churn.

No! I refuse to just give up and accept this fate. Yeah, I may have dug myself into this hole, but I was going to get myself out. One way or another. I walked over to my desk and opened my laptop. I shook my head at what I was about to do, but I was desperate. Then again, being desperate is what put me in my current situation. I closed my eyes and took a deep breath. I couldn't think about that right now. Besides, maybe this was going to actually help me instead of hurting me.

"Please Lord, let this work." I said out loud before typing in Mr. Adalyn's name in the search bar.

Chapter 10

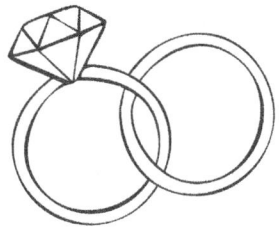

Seojun

I took a sip of my coffee and stared at my computer screen. All of the numbers were looking good for my business back in Vegas and so far, all had been quiet. After I handled the four men in my warehouse, I went on to find the other people on my list. So far, I was able to cross off everyone but the last five people. Manny, June, Arnez, Jackie, and Tiny. I was getting closer to who set me up and all the trails led me back to Philly.

"Morning, cuzo," Ayzo yawned, walking into the kitchen.

I chuckled. "I see Denice had your ass up all night…again."

"You already know! My baby can't get enough of Akeno." He started flexing his arms as he kissed each of his biceps.

"I don't know. I heard yo ass calling her name so loud, I had to leave the house."

Ayzo's jaw dropped as Denice came around the corner in a fit of laughter. "Now Seo, don't be putting our business out there like that."

I shrugged. "No disrespect – it's not like I was trying to hear that shit, but the muthafucka was loud as hell. You ain't turn that man loose for nothing."

"Okay, okay, chill out nigga!" Ayzo snapped, throwing an oven mitt at me.

"My bad, my bad." I laughed. "On that note, I think it's about time I got out of y'all hair and got my own spot."

"Oh, c'mon cuz, we'll be quieter."

I laughed. "Yeah, but at the same time, I'm sure you and baby girl want y'all space. Besides, you know I don't really like to sit in one spot for too long."

Ayzo nodded. "That's understandable. Welp, just know you have one of the best interior designers right here and we know of some quiet spots that you'd like to settle down in."

"I appreciate y'all."

"So, Seo, what's your plans for this weekend? Doesn't matter, you're going out with us!" Denice quipped, pouring herself a cup of coffee.

I shook my head. "Nope! I don't like big crowds; they make my balls itch."

"That might not be the crowd – it might be something you caught. Crabs, perhaps?" Ayzo arched an eyebrow before bursting out into laughter.

"Fuck you," I chuckled, throwing him the middle finger.

"Y'all a mess. I got to jump on a few meetings with clients, please behave." Denice instructed, heading out of the kitchen.

"Yes, ma'am." Ayzo sang, grabbing her arm and pulling her back towards him. He lifted her chin and gave her a few kisses before slapping her ass. She giggled and pushed him as she scurried away.

"That's what be having your ass singing in soprano every damn night." I snorted, downing my coffee.

"No shame in my game because…the neighbors know her name!" Ayzo busted out singing.

I laughed and shook my head. "You a fool, boy!"

"Don't get it twisted; the neighbors know my damn name, too. She was trying to get even because I been wearing that ass out and winning. She's very competitive, you see, and don't like to lose."

"Hold up! Are you telling me that y'all be in competition with one another on who gonna wear the other one out first?"

"Hell yeah! The shit be so fun because every time we step in the room, we are bringing our A game. Plus, whoever wins gets bragging rights for the week."

I laughed out loud as I sat back in my seat. "Well, that's one way to keep the bedroom entertaining. Y'all crazy, but it's nice to see you happy with the one you been chasing all these years."

Ayzo smiled as he glanced over his shoulder towards Denice's office. "I'd gladly do it all over for her, too. Enough about us, though, what's going on with you? I know that you are after blood for what happened back in Chicago, but is that it?"

I shrugged. "What else is there? I mean I got my new business going and once I get rid of all the muthafuckas that played in my face, then I'll be happy."

Ayzo hummed as he ran his thumb across his bottom lip. He stared into space for a few moments before he let out a sigh. "Look, I've seen my best friend literally go through that same song and dance. I know what happened to you and the Jaguars was the worst thing imaginable, but don't surround your life around just revenge."

I exaggerated a sigh as I stared up at the ceiling. "You sound like my father. He keeps reminding me to marry and produce an heir!"

"Uncle Chul-Moo is on to something. You're not a spring chicken, you know." Ayzo chuckled. "On a serious note, find at least a girlfriend within the Reapers. I know they have some nice looking women, not that I was looking."

I laughed.

"Anyway, that should make the people down south happy for at least a year. Maybe extend that contract a little, too."

I scoffed. "Akeno, I cannot walk around here and make believe that everything is peachy and try to find a wife when the person that fucked me over is still out there. Trust me, I understand the urgency, but I just can't make that my main focus. Besides, I've seen some of the reaper woman and none of them piqued my interest."

Ayzo nodded. "Alright. I'm going to leave you with this one reminder and leave it alone. Remember what Romans chapter twelve verses nineteen says. Leave it to the wrath of God, for it is written that vengeance is mine."

I rubbed my chin as I stared down at the floor. I didn't remember too many scriptures, but that one always stuck out to me. I chuckled under my breath. You would've thought I remembered more bible verses since I grew up with a black mom. She made sure to keep me in the church. Hell, Ayzo's dad was the same way, but over the years, I've kept my distance. Not because I've lost my faith or didn't believe, but it was just that I've done some terrible, unforgivable things throughout my life. I just felt that God was too disappointed in me to forgive me. Deep in my heart, I knew that wasn't true because God was merciful and forgiving, but there was always that tiny voice in my head telling me I was unforgivable.

Ayzo cleared his throat. "What else have you found out?"

I inhaled, shaking away my thoughts. "Honestly, nothing new. Every person on my list has pointed their fingers to June and Jackie. I still want to find the other three before I go after them. What about for y'all?"

Ayzo nodded his head. "All quiet over here." He swished his drink around in his cup before he stopped moving. "Well, except for this one thing, but I don't think it's nothing serious."

I arched my eyebrows, waiting for him to keep talking.

"Well, Nick told me that his mom confided in him that T was trying to contact her a while back. He followed up on it, but the trail was cold. No one has seen or heard from T since he kidnapped us. Hell, even the police stopped looking up until last week. I can't believe they found his body in a dumpster. I really thought he was behind all of this."

I nodded my head. "I thought it was him, too."

My laptop chimed, alerting me that I had a new email. I squinted my eyes at the email address because I had never seen it before. Then again, it wasn't uncommon for customers to message me directly about housing opportunities with my company.

Dear Mr. Adalyn,

I am in desperate need of your help and normally wouldn't stoop down to this level, but I am out of options. I have something of yours that could put you in a bad light if it fell into the wrong hands. If you are willing to listen to me, please text me.

I scratched my chin as the cover photo of the video sat at the bottom of the email. I didn't need to press play because I knew exactly what it was. It may have been months ago, but I recognized the cover. Staring at the phone number, I contemplated on hunting them down and killing them for knowing too much.

I leaned back in the chair. "Shit!"

"What's up?"

"You remember Dash?"

Ayzo thought for a second and then nodded.

"Well, he was one of the guys that came to my house a while back."

"Bruh! You didn't think to tell me that earlier? You know that bitch boy was the first one to jump ship when the Cobras came recruiting."

"I honestly forgot about his bitch ass. There was a whole lot of shit going down at the time and I didn't think twice about him once I sent that bullet to his dome."

"Cold blooded!" Ayzo yelled out, pretending to be Rick James from one of Dave Chapelle's skits.

"Boy if you don't hush! I'm on the phone." Denice yelled out from the other room.

I tucked my lips in while I pointed at Ayzo, taunting him and trying to hold back my laugh. This grown ass man just got in trouble, and I wanted nothing more than to keep teasing him, but I wasn't about to burst out into laughter because then I'd be in trouble, too.

Ayzo flicked me off and sipped on his protein shake. "Anyway," he continued, his voice lowered which caused me to snort out a laugh. "What about Dash?"

"Right, well, I sent a video to whoever his boss was showing proof that I meant business and was ready to go to war."

Catching on to where I was going, Ayzo put his cup down before rubbing his hands together. "That's perfect! You can go through the phone and track down the I.P. address you sent the text message to or whatever shit you do when it comes to tracking down numbers."

"I would, but I left the damn phone behind. I assumed I was going back after things quieted down here."

Ayzo scratched the side of his face as he thought for a moment. "Bet. So, call up your cleaning crew and get the information on where they dumped his shit."

I shook my head. "No need. Whoever has the phone just sent me an email and it's still in their possession."

"Oh fuck! What's the move?"

I shrugged as I ran my hand through my hair. "I'm not sure, but they want my help and if I don't want them foolishly going to the police, looks like I don't have another option."

I glared at this random sender's email address as my mouse hovered over the reply button. Stretching my fingers over the keyboard, I exhaled and began to type.

What do you want from me?

I need your help. Text me?

Chapter 11

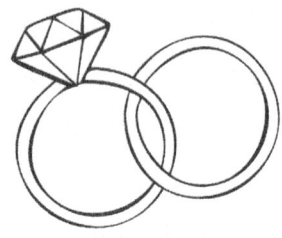

Seojun

How did you even find me?

Unknown: Is this Mr. Adalyn?

Yes

Unknown: It's a long story

And I got time. How do you expect me to help you if you don't even bother to answer my questions?

> Unknown: You're right. I'm sorry.

> Unknown: I was helping my friend clean your house and I found a phone on the stairs. I charged it and was hoping to find your contact info so that I could return it to you.

But instead, you went through the text messages?

> Unknown: …

> Unknown: No. I mean, I didn't right away. Your girlfriend had text, and I was going to let her know that you had accidentally left your phone. But then I saw that video of some man and Dash.

I sat up in my seat as I stared back at the screen, rubbing the small stubble on my chin.

I see. Well, how exactly can I help you, ma'am or sir?

> Unknown: It's ma'am – Addison and I would actually feel better if we discussed this in person.

Good idea.

> Addison?: I saw that you have an office just outside of Philly. Can we meet there?

It's a plan. Meet me there at 10am tomorrow?

> Addison?: Can we meet this weekend?

> Addison?: I'm sorry. It's just that I am graduating Friday, but I will be on a plane to Philly as soon as I get my degree.

I stared at her response and squinted my eyes. What was going on with this strange woman that she needed my help so urgently? I mean, it seemed strange that she was graduating from college and instead of celebrating with her friends, she was asking me for help. Abruptly standing from the table, I started to the back room I had been occupying.

"What happened?" Ayzo asked when I returned back to the kitchen.

"Well, so far this woman named Addison thinks the phone is mine and from the looks of it, wants to exchange a favor for a favor. She just asked to meet in person, and you know I need to run a thorough check before I agree to meet up with anyone."

Ayzo nodded his head in agreement as he came and sat at the table with me. He had never seen me at work so the intrigued look on his face made me feel proud. Even though we grew up together because of the Jaguars, my dad kept our training secret from one another. Well, besides learning how to fight and protect ourselves. I never understood why until when I went into hiding. We grew closer and he confided to me that it was to ensure we'd always stay in touch when one of us needed something. I made a mental note to thank him.

Focusing back on my other laptop, I searched the database with Addison's phone number and IP address from her email. After a few moments, I found everything I needed. Addison Billingsly: twenty-nine years old with one living parent in Texas and a grandmother residing here in Philly. Her grandfather,

Ernest Billingsley, passed away leaving her with a small trust fund. Unfortunately, it was emptied out on her sixteenth birthday.

My eyebrow slightly arched as a picture of Addison appeared on the screen. It was from a Vegas local news clipping, recognizing individuals who helped build tiny homes for the homeless. I slightly leaned back in my chair as I stared at the beautiful woman on my screen. She went to the University of Nevada, right in my backyard and I had never seen her before. Granted, Vegas is a pretty big place, and I didn't venture out too much, but still. Her beauty had me regretting not looking for her. Her deep mahogany skin glowed through the picture, causing my dick to slightly jump. Her hair was pulled up into a high curly bun, showing off the deep dimples in her cheeks as she grinned at the camera. Her curvy body had my mouth salivating and fists clenching.

One thing about me was that I loved me a voluptuous black woman. I couldn't explain it, but they were the most beautiful beings on this earth. The way they carried themselves, firm, independent, and strong. Yet, they were still soft and ready to submit to their man. Not just any man, but the one who would love, cherish, and respect them while allowing them to feel a sense of protection. I guess it was the way I watched my dad treat my mother as I grew up. I learned from him that it was the only way to treat the woman you loved. I just wished he fought harder for her.

Just like Ayzo, I was half black and half Asian, but a lot of people didn't know it. Don't get me wrong, I was never ashamed of it, I was just raised in a very private life. No one knew anything about my family except for the fact that we ran the Jaguars - business and pleasure never mixed. Hell, the main difference between me and my cousin was that my complexion matched everyone else in my family - deep beige and tawny.

I remembered being jealous of Ayzo's curly brown hair and hazel brown eyes when I was younger but learned how to embrace my appearance, especially as my dad, Chul-Moo's successor. I quickly realized how much I matched my dad's appearance when he was pissed off, which made it easier for the Jaguars to accept my authority. I had jet black hair and bronze colored eyes, but like my dad, when I was pissed off, my eyes turned just as black as my hair.

"Did you find her information?" Ayzo asked, breaking my train of thought.

I nodded as I took a sip of my coffee. "Yeah. Her name is Addison and apparently, she's from Texas but grew up here."

"Damn, really?"

I nodded again while turning the laptop around. Ayzo's eyes widened as he choked on his water.

"Damn bro, you, okay?"

"That's Bar Girl!"

"Bar Girl?" I asked, my eyebrow arched in confusion.

His head frantically nodded as he looked over his shoulder, checking to see if Denice heard him. He moved closer to me with a lowered voice.

"Yeah! Remember when I told you I was going to try and move on from Denice and was going to go out with a girl I met at the bar?"

"Oh, shit!"

"Exactly!"

"Well damn," I murmured.

Ayzo began shaking his head, his hands up in a defensive position. "We never hooked up." I opened my mouth to say something, but Ayzo wagged his finger at me. "I could tell by the way you were looking at her that you were interested."

"I don't have time for dating. Besides, she is only reaching out to me because she wants something."

Ayzo shrugged. "Whatever you say, cuzo." He grabbed the laptop and continued to read over Addison's information.

Addison: Are you still there?

I returned my attention back to my phone. I'd be lying if I said I didn't want to take Ms. Addison out for a date, but that's not why she reached out to me. She needed my help, that's it. Besides, she had evidence of me committing a crime. What type of woman would want a cold blooded killer in her bed? Granted, I don't think she actually knew it was me in the video, but still. Once she found out, I highly doubt she was the type to associate herself with killers.

"Yo, did you see this?" Ayzo asked, flipping the laptop back around. "Her grandfather was Ernest Billingsley."

I shrugged. "Yeah, so?"

Ayzo briefly closed his eyes and shook his head. "You can't be smart and dumb at the same time."

I glared at him. "Don't play with me cuzo."

"Fine, fine. Ernest Billingsly from Texas is also known as Big E. You know, the former leader of the Reapers and Addison's grandfather."

My eyebrows shot up as I took back the laptop. So, Addison had Reaper blood and now she was hitting me up. Could this all be a setup to see if I was going to hold up our end of the contract? I shook my head. No, that wouldn't make sense. I mean, the Reapers didn't give a damn who I killed and they for damn sure wouldn't be asking me for help. I needed to see what this Addison woman really wanted from me. Surely, she didn't really need my help. Snatching up my phone, I typed out a reply.

Okay, we can meet. Keep me posted when you land in Philly.

Chapter 12

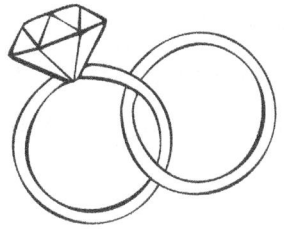

Addison

I exhaled a breath of relief as I shoved my phone into my back pocket. I couldn't believe that Mr. Adalyn had agreed to help me. Well, technically he agreed to meet me, but once I explained my situation, I'm sure he'd help me. He had to.

My phone pinged with a message from Bruno. I rolled my eyes and grabbed my purse as I headed out of my dorm. The fact that my grown ass had to have weekly checks from an OBGYN to confirm that my hymen was still intact was absolutely ridiculous. Mr. L knew my entire class schedule, the days and times that I volunteered at the hospital, and my overall daily routine. Hell, when impromptu events occurred, he was the first to know. It got to the point that he only contacted me when I needed to send half naked pictures.

I thought everything was cool and I could make some money by cleaning houses with Akira. To anyone else, it wasn't a big deal. Of course, that wasn't the case for me. Bruno's ass had to snitch and now Mr. L's ass was going to start checking my location constantly. I guess if I wasn't being sneaky about it, things wouldn't have been that bad.

I made my way downstairs and my eyes landed on Bruno. His black beady eyes glared back at me as his nostrils flared. He had a fresh line up and his hair was glistening with that hair in a can for men, but I could still see the small patches of hair that he was clinging on to. I shook my head. I don't know why he just didn't cut that shit off and move on. A lot of women liked a dark skin brutha with a bald head and thick beard. Plus, Bruno was about six feet tall and roughly 300 lbs. of muscle - another bonus.

I remember overhearing him brag about how he used to play football overseas and was about to go pro before he tore his ACL. I used to feel bad for him because his dream had been shattered, but when he opened his pompous mouth, all sympathy went out of the window. I didn't care how fine a man was, once he was disrespectful and said some off the wall shit, he was put on my shit list.

"Serves you right for trying to be sneaky. You and your hoe ass friend that was giving you rides could have cost me my damn job. Now, I don't micromanage you because I thought you knew better, but now ima be on you like words on a paper." His deep voice growled.

If I could roll my eyes any harder than I already was, they'd fall out. I looked up at him and squinted my eyes. "Bet if I slipped your Randall looking ass some money, you wouldn't have snitched to the male version of Ms. Finster."

"Don't fucking play with me, Addison." Bruno barked, his hand grasping my forearm. "I was tasked to make sure you keep your legs shut, but don't think for one minute that I won't knock you the hell out."

"Get bent, bitch." I spat, snatching my arm away before sliding in the backseat of the car.

I didn't care how big and intimidating his ass looked, I didn't take kindly to being threatened. Plus, Bruno was all talk. He knew if he laid a finger on me, the precious merchandise, Mr. L would fire his ass or put him six feet under. If the person buying saw that I wasn't in proper care, Mr. L would lose out on money.

I heard Bruno mumble under his breath as he slammed the door behind me. This was some bullshit! I hated that I got myself into this mess. Maybe I should have just told Mr. L that I was working. I shook my head. Fuck that! There was no way I was going to tell him that I was making extra money on the side. His ass would've either accused me of lying or made me give him everything I earned, and I wasn't having that.

If only I had found another way to help my grandmother. I mean, I knew my mom had the funds to help or at least she could've had one of her many boyfriends help. If I would have just begged and kissed her ass, she might've found sympathy and pitched in.

I pinched the bridge of my nose. Who was I kidding? That woman didn't give two damns about me or her mother. If she wasn't getting anything out of the deal, then she wasn't going to put in any effort to aid anybody else but herself. I sighed. Mr. L was my only option.

A thought ran across my mind, causing me to smirk as I relaxed in my seat. Mr. L was going to sell me as a mail order bride. That, I knew for a fact. If Mr. Adalyn wasn't going to help me, then I'd go along with Mr. L's stupid plan. I'd allow him to sell me and ship me off to wherever, but then I'd run. I wouldn't let some strange man touch me – fuck that! I'll make sure nana had everything she needed and as much as I didn't want to leave her alone, I was going to escape, and I wouldn't stop running.

As quickly as the thought crossed my mind, I instantly felt guilty. I couldn't just leave my nana all by herself. What if the person who bought me complained to Mr. L that I ran away? She could be all the collateral he'd need to get me out of hiding. I sighed and closed my eyes before muttering a quick prayer, hoping that Mr. Adalyn would help me.

We pulled into the parking lot of the OBGYN office, and I shuddered with anxiety. As I stepped out of the car, I tried my hardest to keep up my nonchalant appearance. Deep down, I was scared shitless. I didn't have a phobia of seeing doctors or getting shots like most people, instead, I was more anxious of what I knew was to come. I took in the one story deep beige office building that had beautiful flowers surrounding the front entrance and swallowed. It was ironic that the office looked appealing on the outside, but on the inside, it was a woman's worst nightmare.

"Go on!" Bruno snapped, breaking me out of my trance.

I looked over my shoulder with a scowl before heading inside. Walking to the receptionist desk, I checked in. Per usual, everyone here was nice and professional, offering me warm yet timid smiles. They knew what I was about to endure, but they turned a blind eye. Hell, when they could live carefree with a hefty salary, they'd be stupid to tell.

I wasn't always afraid to see the OBGYN. I mean, in the past, I had the best Black female doctor in the state, but once I gave myself to Mr. L, I had to use the doctors he recommended. I didn't think anything of it at first until I met him.

"Addison Billingsly?"

I looked up and made eye contact with the nurse.

"Dr. Johnston's ready to see you."

I swallowed the bile inching up my throat. Like I said, I didn't have a problem coming to the doctor's office, I had a problem with the doctor himself. You see, when I had my first appointment with Dr. Johnston, he instantly became infatuated with me. He begged and offered up money so that he could take my purity, but thankfully, Mr. L declined his request. However, because he was so intrigued with me and being the greedy evil bastard that he is, Mr. L made it to where he was my primary doctor.

After paying a substantial fee, the pair had an agreement that Dr. Johnston could be my doctor as long as he didn't penetrate any part of me. In other words, Dr. Johnston had free range to touch and grope any part of me without consequences and I couldn't say shit. In the beginning, I tried to go to the police, but that was when Bruno watched me like a hawk. If I was successful at getting past him, then one of Mr. L's other minions was tailing me. Hell, I never even made it to the police parking lot. Later, I found out that some of the cops were on Mr. L's payroll. I didn't know who I could trust, and it got to the point that I stopped trying.

I followed the nurse into an exam room where she did the usual – took my vitals, checked my weight, and blood pressure. After that, I was instructed to get undressed and to put on that thin ass paper napkin they called a patient gown and to wait for the doctor. At this point, my hands were shaking. I was ready to get this shit over with. Mr. L knew good and damn well that I wasn't being promiscuous and yet, he had me in this creep's office once a week.

A light tap came at the door followed by its opening. I rolled my eyes as Dr. Johnston walked in. He was a bit tall, maybe around 5'11, with salt and pepper hair that was styled in a small coiled afro. His skin reminded me of the pecans I used to pick up and eat when I visited my family back in Texas. On the outside, Dr. Johnston was a handsome man, bright straight teeth, hypnotizing brown eyes, and a matching salt and pepper beard. He was like that fine ass grandpa that had all the older women swooning, but all of that was diminished the moment he took action.

"Good morning, my beautiful flower."

I huffed out a sigh. "Can we get this over with?"

He expelled a low chuckle as the door locked behind him before he began walking towards me. "Why, Addison, baby, you just got here and you're ready to leave me so fast?"

"If I never had to see your ugly ass face again, it'd be a blessing."

"Now, you and I both know that I am far from ugly, sweetheart." Dr. Johnston laughed, running his hand up my leg.

I tried to snatch away from him, but he gripped his hand around my calf tighter. His nails began to dig into my leg, causing me to wince out in pain. His dark chocolate eyes bore into me as he yanked up my foot and placed it into the holder at the end of the table. Dr. Johnston grabbed my other leg and pulled, causing me to fall backward on to my back.

"Please, Dr. Johnston. No one's touched me, I swear."

Ignoring me, I watched as the doctor pulled up a chair and sat in between my legs. He hummed out a loan moan as I heard him unzip his pants.

"Now, let's take a look. Oh, I can see that you are still untouched."

His cold hands ran up my legs and pushed my legs apart. I used to fight him by trying to squeeze my legs closed, but that only made it worse for me. I suddenly felt his fingers spreading my lower lips, exposing my pearl.

"S-shit, baby. I wish I could suck on this fat clit." Dr. Johnston groaned. "I've never seen a pussy so beautiful. Nice, fat, juicy, and with a fucking piercing! Shit, baby! I bet you can get really nasty in the sheets once you were broken in."

I felt one of his arms moving rapidly as he continued to hold my sex open. The sounds of his low moans and curses filled the room, causing tears to brim my eyes. My stomach churned with the realization of what he was doing. He pleasured himself while staring at my pussy almost every visit and I shouldn't have been surprised. Still, I hated this! I was being violated and the only thing I felt was disgust for myself. Yet, I couldn't do shit about it.

Clamping my eyes closed, I thought about all of the ways I was going to torture and kill Dr. Johnston when I was able to escape Mr. L. If he felt comfortable doing this to me, I could only imagine how many other innocent women he's violated. When I make my escape, I vow to come back and cut him up piece by piece for every time he's touched me without my permission.

Dr. Johnston grunted and I could feel his body slightly jerking. His heavy breathing made nausea roll through me as he finally removed his hands from me. He took a deep inhale of my pussy before I heard him stand up and zip his pants. I refused to make eye contact with him as he rolled the chair back to the corner of the room.

"As always, Addison, it was a pleasure seeing you and I'll see you next week."

I laid still on the hospital cot until I heard his footsteps move towards the door and exit the room. I jumped up and snatched the gown off of me, quickly getting dressed. I didn't want to spend one more minute in here longer than I had to. I damn near sprinted out of the office and back to the car, not bothering for Bruno to open the door for me. As I sat in the backseat, tears rolled down my face, but I swiped them away before I booked my flight to Philly.

Chapter 13

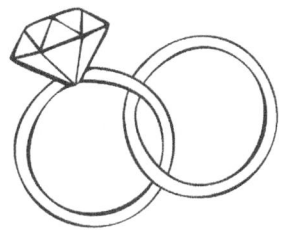

Seojun

Ayzo, Nicholas, and I tapped our glasses together before downing the shot of tequila. I laughed at the pair, who had their faces scrunched up as I enjoyed the burn in my chest. I was the only one who appreciated a smooth tequila while the others preferred brown liquor. It's not like I didn't mind some good ole Crown Royal, but Don Julio was my shit.

"Damn, Seo! I know this shit be getting you fucked up." Nicholas winced, squeezing lime juice into his mouth.

"It sure does - expeditiously." I laughed, refilling my glass with another shot.

We got another round of drinks and made our way back to the pool tables. It was a nice size crowd for a Tuesday night at Jill's, and I could see why. The drinks were cheap, not watered down, and Ms. Jill put her foot in her food. I damn near had almost everything off the menu, but my absolute favorite was the burgers. Her son, Junior, had his grill going and he made the best damn hamburger I've ever tasted. Between the burgers and the hot wings, Ms. Jill fed my big back at least three times a week.

I decided to order some mini sliders and fried pickles from Ms. Jill's app that I helped her create. Even though she insisted that I didn't pay since the app was doing amazing and had new customers in her establishment every day, I didn't mind giving up my money to her. Besides, after what I heard about Ms. Jill and everything her and her late husband, Benny, been through, she deserved to retire with her bank account full. Her son was a good man, too, and could keep the business running if she chose to stay home more.

I sat back in my chair before locking eyes with Ayzo who arched an eyebrow at me. I smirked and raised my glass to him. He knew me too well and knew that I was in my head. To be fair, I always am. At the moment, his words about giving up on my revenge had me in an internal battle. I mean, I could see myself being a silent partner with the realtor company and investing in Jill's while still running the jaguars. I could honor my father's wishes with the Reaper's contract by settling down and starting that family to bring in my heir.

I sighed and downed my drink because deep down, I couldn't do that. Maybe in another lifetime that type of living would be for me. If I were honest, the only way I'd marry was with someone for business purposes only. I couldn't marry for love because I was too far gone. I had done so many unspeakable and unforgivable things and I knew for a fact I didn't deserve happiness. I wasn't sad about it, though. Hell, I ultimately decided to stay in this type of lifestyle, even when my dad offered me an out when he allowed Ayzo to leave all those years ago. It was my decision to stay, mainly because I wanted to keep our family traditions and run the Jaguars just like my dad. I strived to make him proud of me, even if it meant sacrificing my own happiness. Plus, if I gave up, I would be destroying everything that he worked so hard for — getting us out of poverty and having generational wealth set up. I didn't want that burden or shame.

Ashlynn and Denice came towards my table laughing, breaking me out of my train of thoughts.

"What y'all two giggling about?" Nicholas asked, leaning over the pool table to line up his shot.

"None yah, nosey." Ashlynn chuckled, taking a sip out of her drink.

"Yeah, nosey!" Denice chimed in. "Besides, we came over to talk to Seojun, not you two knuckle heads."

"Oh! So now we knuckle heads? Was I a knuckle head when I had that big knuckle that's in between your legs in my mouth an hour ago?" Ayzo asked, leaning against his pool stick.

Ashlynn spit out her drink while Nicholas missed the cue ball when he made his shot before they burst out into laughter.

"Akeno!" Denice laughed before throwing him the middle finger. He pretended she was blowing him a kiss and caught it before putting it in his back pocket. He winked at her and waggled his eyebrows, causing her to blush as she shook her head.

"Y'all so damn nasty." Ashlynn laughed, wiping a tear from her eye.

"We nasty? Girl, the way Nicholas been putting you through the headboard since y'all met, I'm surprised you ain't pregnant."

Ashlynn and Nicholas briefly looked at each other, causing me to arch an eyebrow. They tried to play it off, but Denice had caught the interaction, too.

"Ash?"

"D?"

"Bitch!" Denice shouted.

"Yes ma'am!" Ashlynn cheered, sticking her tongue out. The pair started shouting with excitement and embracing one another.

"Uh, are they speaking in another language?" I asked, looking at Ayzo, He shrugged, and I could tell that he was just as confused as I was.

Nicholas laughed out loud at us before downing his drink. "Y'all are two of the smartest technical men I know, but couldn't pick up on their 'language'?"

Ayzo and I continued to stare at Nicholas, waiting for him to explain what was going on.

Nicholas laughed as he playfully threw his head back. "Seo, what My fiancé and her best friend were saying is we are going to be parents."

Ayzo dropped his pool stick and embraced his best friend. "Congratulations! First comes love, then comes marriage, now coming a baby in a baby carriage!"

I laughed and shook my head as I walked over to give Nicholas a congratulatory handshake. "I'm sorry about my cousin, he didn't come with a manual."

Nicholas laughed and clapped Ayzo on the back. "That's the reason he's my best friend."

I chuckled before waving the waitress over. "This calls for a celebration. I may not have known you and Ashlynn for a long time, but from the stories y'all have told me about how y'all met and got kidnapped, y'all deserve this happiness."

I ordered everyone another drink except for Ashlynn, who got another virgin margarita. As everyone excitedly talked amongst each other, I felt my phone buzz in my pocket. Glancing at the screen, I saw my associate Vincent, who was back in Vegas, calling.

Ayzo and I first met him when we touched down in Vegas two years ago. While we were still in hiding, I started up my business to keep money rolling in, but I needed someone to be the face for S&V Realty. After a thorough interview and background check, he was hired on as my lead real estate agent. He showed his loyalty to my company while working hard, and I admired that. Him and Ayzo became good friends, too. You could imagine Ayzo's surprise when he found out Vincent and Olivia, Nicolas's ex, were dating. I didn't know too much about Nicholas but heard about the foul shit that put him in the hospital and had his brother killed.

When Ayzo had called to tell me that Nicholas was on his way to get his revenge, I wanted to help and planned on keeping Olivia in a safe place so he wouldn't have to look too hard to find her. Hell, he deserved to get his lick back after the bullshit she pulled. Unfortunately, Olivia suddenly disappeared. My first instinct was that Vincent told her what was up, but I quickly squashed that. No one told him about Ayzo's connection with Olivia so there was no way of him knowing. Ayzo and I still decided to keep him at a distance until we could prove otherwise.

"What's up?" I said, answering the phone.

"Sorry, I know it's late over there but wanted to check in and run a few things by you."

I checked my watch and saw it was just a little after 8pm, but it was just past 5pm back in Vegas.

"You're good."

"Cool. So, since you are still out in Philly, do you want me to look into some investment opportunities in that area?"

"Nah, not yet. Instead, focus on Colorado. I'm thinking about opening up a few resorts."

"Finally! I'm telling you; tourist spots are where the money is."

"I never said I was going to stop making homes for families."

The line became silent. I knew Vincent was probably cursing me out on mute, but I didn't give a damn. If he wanted to open up his own establishment and setup overpriced tourist locations, then he was more than welcome to. I, on the other hand, wasn't changing. The only reason I wanted a resort in Colorado was because I wanted an affordable and family friendly vacation spot. I knew what it was like listening to the other kids in school bragging about spending summers on the beach or at some fun family resort. My goal was to have the option for every low income family to live comfortably and be able to enjoy a vacation every now and then.

"Anything else, Vincent?"

He huffed out a heavy sigh. "Mr. Adalyn, you are missing out on so much untapped money. If we can focus on raising the standards some and reaching the market with a higher tax bracket, we wouldn't have to keep working."

"I don't do this for the money! There are people out there who genuinely need help and don't need greedy people trying to overcharge them just to have somewhere to sleep comfortably."

"I understand, sir." Vincent bit out before disconnecting the line.

I shook my head with a laugh as I placed the phone back into my pocket and sat back down at the table. Vincent may be a disrespectful prick sometimes, but he knew how to do his job. As long as I kept him at a distance, then he was fine in my book.

"So, Seo," Denice said, resting her arms on the table. "What's your plans?"

"My plans?" I asked, arching my eyebrow.

"Yeah! So, I may have been eavesdropping a little and heard you had to start a family."

I laughed and shook my head. "Okay and?"

"Well," Ashlynn chimed in. "There's this client that comes in every two weeks asking about you. She's our height with honey brown skin and she keeps her nails and hair done. Oh, and she's single with three kids so you'll have plenty of practice raising a child. You just have to be careful with one of her baby daddies because he a little throwed off, but other than that -"

I shook my head. "Hold up, ladies. First off, I don't mind dating a woman with kids, but I don't do baby daddy drama."

Ashlynn nodded. "That's understandable. I told her that I'd at least mention her to you, and I didn't want to block. Plus, Belinda is cool people and beautiful, but she can be a little…"

"Easy!" Denice interrupted before taking a sip of her drink.

"No!" Ashlynn laughed, swiping her friend in the arm. "I meant, she just falls in love easily."

"Poor baby doesn't know how to distinguish between a genuine connection vs someone who's just trying to get in between her legs." Denice sighed.

"Exactly and I know that feeling all too well." Ashlynn huffed before giving us a tight lipped smile.

I'd heard bits and pieces of what Ashlynn had gone through with her ex-fiancé, Bobby. I wasn't the one to pry – if she wanted to talk to me about what happened then I'd listen. As for what they were trying to do, I was good. I didn't have time to worry about some woman that would be all in my space. My mind was on one thing right now and I didn't need to be distracted. Now, I didn't mind a woman temporarily warming my bed for a night or two, but that was it.

Ashlynn cleared her throat. "Anyways, I wanted to help her out. I've been giving her advice in hopes she'll learn from my past. I know that I am not perfect and went through a rough patch seeking validation from everybody else instead of practicing self-love. I can admit that I did stupid things and put up with a lot of bullshit, but thankfully I snapped out of it. Anyways, I'll keep praying over her with faith that God brings her the man for her. I'll do the same for you, Seo."

I huffed out a laugh which cause the pair to look up at me. "I don't deserve your prayers, Ashlynn. Besides, love isn't in the cards for me. I mean, marriage is but it'll only be out of convenience. It's what I deserve."

Her eyebrows scrunched together. "Everybody deserves true love, even if it's temporary. I don't know everything you are going through or have been through, but don't talk down on yourself like that. You are fighter and protector. So, what you've done some unspeakable things in the past? That does not get to determine your future."

I smiled at the pair as I excused myself from the table. I wasn't trying to be rude, but I did not want them attempting to play match maker. Even if I did want love, what good would that do me? Love causes pain and leave you in the middle of the night. Love can shatter your heart into a thousand pieces. There were so many nights I watched my father hold my mother's pillow or wait up for her as if she were coming back. But she never did. I'd rather marry because of convenience than go through that type of pain. While I waited to settle for whoever the contract bond me to, I'd keep my clip loaded and continue my hunt.

Chapter 14

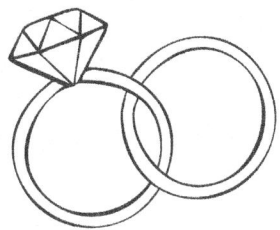

Addison

I stepped off the plane and stretched. I enjoyed flying but hated how tiny the seats were. I had way too much hips and ass to be trying to squeeze into those miniature seats. I wanted to upgrade to first class but of course Bruno would tell Mr. L since he had to fly with me. Normally, I wouldn't give a damn, but they didn't know I had money saved up. As soon as I would have upgraded my seat, I would have been asked a million and one questions about where I got the extra funds. I was going to keep my bank account secret as long as possible. If I couldn't convince Mr. Adalyn to help me, it was all I had left to escape.

After retrieving our bags, Bruno led us to a black on black Lincoln town car. A short young looking man, probably in his early twenties, was standing next to the trunk with a sign that read Bruno's name. I arched an eyebrow with realization that Mr. L must've sent for us. I inwardly groaned. I just wanted to go to my hotel and shower off the airlines, but I didn't have much of a choice.

I observed the driver and noticed he had on a formal black suit that was a size too big. The white shirt underneath his jacket was clearly a white beater and it had stains on it. His rich hickory skin was so ashy, I'm sure he could have started a fire by rubbing his hands together. The man's hair was in an afro that was matted on the side – probably from sleeping on it. I shook my head. Either all his uniforms were at the wash, or his ass wasn't paying attention in orientation about dress code.

Finally reaching the vehicle, I noticed the driver licking his lips as his eyes roamed down my body. I grimaced.

"My name is Jerome and I'll be your driver, miss. Nice to see you again, Mr. Bruno."

"Get in," Bruno snapped, ignoring the man. I shot my head towards him and back at the driver. Yeah, no way.

"Now!" Bruno demanded, pushing me towards the backseat.

"Damn, you not going to at least open the door?"

Bruno yanked the door open before pushing me inside.

"Fuck boy," I muttered under my breath as I settled in the backseat.

Rolling down the window, I took in the warm summer air and smiled. Since I lived in Dallas the majority of my life, I was use to the heat and the humidity. When I moved up north with my grandmother, it took a while for me to adjust to their type of summer.

"Roll the damn window up!" Bruno barked from the front seat.

I rolled my eyes and obliged. I couldn't wait to get away from this Berenstain Bear looking asshole. I continued to stare out of the window, enjoying the city.

Even with the window up, I could still hear the buzz of the streets. The honking horns as we steadily moved through traffic, the mixture of laughter and music as we passed a few restaurants. It was just after ten in the morning, the perfect time for brunch. I turned to my left as we passed Independence Hall, the ultimate tourist attraction.

I smiled as the memory of my grandma taking me there when we first moved in with her. I didn't want to go because I hadn't seen my mom for a few days. We had literally unpacked the last bag, and she was gone partying with her friends. I thought I was too boring for her because she would complain about how she needed more excitement in her life. So, when my grandma offered to take us to this historical site, I declined. I wanted us to go somewhere bold, fun, and entertaining so that my mom would stay around.

"I'm going to tell you something important and if you don't remember anything else I say, please remember this. Do not go through your life trying to please anybody, do you understand me? People in this world don't give a damn about nothing if it doesn't have anything to do with them. Go after God's heart, he's the only person that won't disappoint you as long as you keep your eyes on him."

I sighed. As much as I loved my grandma, I didn't understand how she could give me such advice when she was chasing after her daughter's heart. Over the years, I witnessed my mom being self-centered and greedy, yet my grandma begged her to come home. She pleaded with her to do something better with her life and that she would be there to support her through it all. Even when she knew my mom wasn't listening, she coughed up money or some type of presents whenever my mom asked or was mad at her.

I balled my hands on my lap as we began to slow in the car. A part of me wanted to be just like my mom - not giving a damn about anybody but myself. I could've shrugged my shoulders and let my grandma figure out what to do about her daughter and the house, but who was I kidding? I could never be that heartless.

The car finally stopped, and I noticed that we arrived at an office building on the edge of the city. Not too far from downtown, but far enough to have decent parking and minimal traffic. The building was two stories and a deep navy color. If the sun wasn't shimmering off the exterior, one would say the building was black. The parking lot was damn near full of cars and I couldn't help but wonder what Mr. L did for a living. I mean, I knew that he ran multiple brothel houses and sold men and women overseas, but that doesn't call for an entire office space.

"Head inside and the receptionist will tell you what to do next." The driver instructed Bruno.

"Can y'all help with my bags?" I asked, looking between the pair. I shouldn't even have to ask these grown ass men. I mean, they didn't even bother to help me load the bags in the trunk and I had to sit in the backseat with them. At least they can carry them to the door for me or to the next vehicle I was going to be in.

"Get out the damn car and leave your bags here. After we meet with Mr. L, the driver will take you to your hotel."

I opened my mouth to protest but thought against it. There really wasn't a point to argue since I knew it wasn't going to get me anywhere. Exhaling loudly, I yanked the door handle and scooted out of the car before slamming it in Bruno's face. I stomped towards the entrance, not bothering to wait for him. As soon as I reached the door, I felt his hand grasping my elbow and spinning me around. I tried to pull away when he grabbed my wrist and pulled me to the side of the building.

"So, help me, Addison, if you come in here showing your ass, I'll knock your teeth in."

"You can't touch me!"

"Oh, on the contrary, I can. As long as you stay pure, I can slap the shit out of you. And you know what the best part is? If you haven't noticed, Mr. L doesn't need to visibly see you every single day. Meaning, the bruises will be gone about the time you need to send your new owner a new picture of yourself."

My breath caught in my throat as his hand circled around my throat. I started to move away when he began to squeeze. My eyes bulged and I thrashed underneath his tight grip. A slow menacing smile crept across his face causing my heart to race. Was this really happening? As much shit that I talked to Bruno, he's never went this far. Yes, he's threatened me before, but I thought I was untouchable. How naïve of me.

"Now, am I going to have any more problems with you?"

My head shook as tears began to well in my eyes. He removed his hand, causing me to gasp loudly for air. My heart pounded through my ears as I bent over resting my hands on my knees, trying to regulate my breathing. The realization that I was truly trapped stabbed me deep into my core. I mean, I knew I had a plan to try and run away, but since Bruno was so comfortable putting his hands on me, I'm sure he'd tell the others to do the same. Like he said, I didn't physically see Mr. L and only had to send pictures when it was requested. Hell, even that, I had taken several pictures in advance so that I could just send them instead of dropping what I was doing to accommodate the perv's request.

Bruno sniffed as he fixed his blazer. He snapped his fingers in my face and pointed towards the front door. I didn't argue and did what I was instructed. I swallowed the lump attempting to form in my throat as I followed him up to the receptionist desk. Looking around, the space reminded me of any old office building. Off white walls with beige furniture were presented in the lobby area.

A few plants that were obviously fake and collecting dust sat in the far corners while magazines from three years prior sat unopened on the lobby tables.

"Good afternoon, sir. How may I assist you?"

I glanced over Bruno's shoulder to see a fairly young woman, probably in her early twenties, sitting behind the desk. She was gorgeous with her golden skin and long black hair that was pinned up into a bun. Her sharp green eyes looked Bruno over and there was no mistaking the lust.

"Hey Vickie, we have an appointment with the advisor to lease an office space."

Her smile slightly faltered as she looked at me and back to Bruno before she cleared her throat. "Of course, Manny will guide you at the elevators."

Bruno nodded before grabbing my wrist and pulling me in front of him towards the elevators. What the hell was going on? Why were we meeting somebody about renting out an office space. Where is Mr. L? My mind raced with a thousand questions, but my gut was telling me to keep my mouth shut.

Once we made it to the elevators, a tall Asian man, I'm presuming was Manny, stood with his arms crossed behind his back. He had on a black polo t-shirt that was tucked in to black jeans with a matching bomber jacket. His chestnut brown hair was pulled back into a low ponytail, and I couldn't help but notice the tattoo on the side of his neck - a snake baring his blood coated fangs.

If we hadn't spoken to the receptionist, I would have assumed he was just another man waiting to get on the elevator. From how he was dressed, compared to other elevator attendants, there was no way he worked here. Especially with his all black Air Force Ones on his feet. Hell, he looked like he was ready to beat somebody ass instead of ensuring other guests arrived at their proper locations.

Manny examined us as we approached him before placing a hand over his ear, showing the gun discreetly tucked into the front of his waistband. I realized that he had on an earpiece and the woman at the receptionist was providing him instructions to lead us to that advisor. Was he a part of security, too? It would make sense to have undercover security posing as a regular client. With a quick nod and affirmative to the walkie talkie on his wrist, he pressed the button to call for the elevator.

We stepped on the elevator, and I watched as Manny pulled out a badge from a pocket inside of his jacket and scan it over a kiosk that was located under the elevator buttons. After the scanner lit up green, he pressed the number for the top floor. I opened my mouth to ask where we were going but thought against it. Not only did I not want Bruno trying to choke me again, but I didn't want any problems with Manny. From the way his eyes were roaming over me, I couldn't tell if he wanted to pistol whip me or bend me over. Either way, I stared down at my shoes and avoided eye contact with him.

Chapter 15

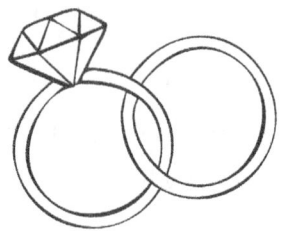

Addison

After passing all of the other floors, we finally made it to the top floor, which is usually the executive suite for the owner. Now that I thought about it, Bruno had to give the receptionist a secret phrase to get access to Mr. L and Manny was most definitely a part of the security team. I bit my inner cheek to surpass my laugh. Of course, Mr. L would have all of those obstacles just for someone to see him.

Once the elevator doors opened. I noticed an average size white man, probably no taller than 5'7, with sandy blonde hair sitting in the lobby. He had a scruffy beard which was braided and tied on the end with a rubber band. He looked up at us and smiled, showing off his white teeth that had diamonds incrusted on the bottom row.

"Yo, what's good, baby?"

Bruno pulled me off the elevator and inside of the room before walking up toward the man. Bruno grinned before grabbing the man's hand and pulling him in for a quick hug.

"X, my boy, just trying to get this money and keep these hoes in line."

"I feel that 100%."

Bruno tilted his head towards me. "This heifer been getting on my damn nerves for the past year and I'm so ready for Mr. L to get rid of her."

Oh, I know this muthafucka didn't!

"Man, I wish Mr. L would have let me watch over her," X said as he licked his lips and stared at my chest. "But then again, Mr. L knows best. I mean, we been best friend since high school and he knew my ass would've had my tongue deep in her booty as soon as I would've been put in charge."

I scrunched up my eyebrows as nausea rolled through me. I looked around the room to see if there was something I could throw. If they thought they could sit here and be disrespectful to me and I wasn't going to say anything, then they had me fucked up. I balled my hands into fists and glared at the ground. I took in a deep breath to calm down because at the end of the day, it was them two against me. Bruno already had no problem choking me and I didn't know what kind of man X was, but I'm sure if he worked for Mr. L, he was just as bad.

Bruno threw his head back and laughed. "Man! See Xavier, that's why you not in charge of the merchandise, especially not the pure ones."

Xavier shook his head as he chuckled. "No arguments there, but you know what? I'm not complaining since I get first dips with the used merchandise."

What the fuck? How long have these sick fucks been manipulating and selling off individuals? I clenched my jaws as I dug my nails into the palm of my hand.

"Anyways, y'all came to see boss man?" Xavier asked, pulling a blunt out of his jacket pocket.

Bruno nodded as he tucked his hands into his pockets. I watched Xavier light his blunt and take two long drags before passing it to Bruno, who mimicked the movement. Xavier walked over to a closed office door and knocked. I could hear a low grumble coming from the other side before a deep voiced snapped.

"Man, what you want now?"

"Yo, Bruno is here with Little Bit."

I couldn't help but roll my eyes. Ever since Mr. L called me that when I first met him, everyone else thought they could too. There was nothing about me that was considered little and they knew that but continually gave me that nickname. I mean, I had wide hips, triple D breasts, and wore a size eighteen. I was a grown ass voluptuous woman. If I really wanted to, I could probably beat Xavier's ass. Hell, I was just pushing 5'8' and towered over him a good an inch. I tucked in my lips and looked down at my feet to hold back a laugh.

The office door finally swung open, and my jaw dropped. The first thing my eyes immediately landed on was a topless woman who was on her knees in the middle of the floor. Her long black hair exposed her smooth olive complected back as she attempted to put her bra back on. I squinted my eyes to see if I could get a better look at her profile, but my vision was blocked when Mr. L stepped out. I swallowed as I took in his 6'2" and sturdy build. He looked the same as he did when we first met. Even though he was cruel, I had to admit the muthafucka was fine.

As he tugged on his shirt, I noticed that his Caesar taper fade, which was freshly cut, showed off a very descriptive tattoo going down the side of his neck. I slightly squinted my eyes and realized the image was the head of a cobra that wore a large crown. Blood dripped down its mouth as it buried its two fangs into two different dates. I wonder what the two dates represented.

"Miss Addison, I almost forgot how breathtaking you were." Mr. L's sultry voice filled the room. "Don't get me wrong, the pictures you send to your new owner are great, but baby girl, they do not do you justice."

"I'm saying! Little bit is bad. Let me just lick her toes one time," Xavier begged.

My upper lip curled with disgust as I glared at all three men. Fucking monsters! Between Mr. L not having a problem taking advantage of men and women who are vulnerable, Xavier using our downfall as a way to get some, and their loyal dog, Bruno, willing to get physical to complete his job – I was absolutely disgusted.

"What I tell you, X? You can't touch the pure ones."

"And I don't want to. The ones we have are barely legal and I don't want that. You got lucky with Little Bit. Not too many women as mature as she is that hasn't been touched."

I'd be lying if I said I was surprised by Xavier's revelation. Of course, Mr. L had more people like me under his thumb. However, to hear that they were barely eighteen broke my heart. I ran into money issues well after the fact that I graduated high school and was in college. I couldn't imagine what those other poor souls have been through for them to seek out Mr. L for help.

"Hands off, X. Anyway, Addison, you know seeing you in person again has me thinking about upping your price. I could probably adjust the contract with your husband and get more money. You are fine as hell. You remind me of my own woman that's out here in Philly."

"Oh, so your girlfriend is cool with you selling others to pervs who want their virginities?" I asked, placing my hands on my hips. "If she does approve, then she's a dumbass or just greedy as hell because I'm sure you're offering her up some hush money."

"Just like I offered yo ass hush money? Oh, my bad I didn't mean hush money but money to save your sick ass Grandma."

My jaws tightened as I glared at him. Bruno and Xavier snickered behind me, and it took everything in me not to just start swinging on them.

"Exactly!" Mr. L said, snapping his fingers. "Everyone has a price so you can shut that other dumb shit up."

I exhaled as I shifted my eyes towards the window behind him. He was right and I didn't have an argument against him. I stooped down and came to one of his brothel houses for help and agreed to give myself away. Who was I to pass judgement when I willfully placed myself in this position. Yes, it was to help someone I loved, but still, I chose this path.

"Now that you're back in town, what are your plans?" Mr. L asked, lighting up a blunt that he pulled from his pocket.

I swallowed the bile in my throat and returned my attention back on him. "I want to visit my grandma, and I need to meet with the realtors so that I can get her house on the market. Since I am to be sold soon, there's no point of keeping her house. At least I can use that money to pay up my grandmother's bills until, hopefully, I can meet back with her one day, or have her move closer to wherever it is I'm going. If that's okay with you."

Mr. L nodded his head as he tapped the ashes from his blunt into a trashcan outside of his office door.

"I see no problem with that. While you handle your business, I can accommodate your room and transportation. Consider it your graduation present."

I provided Mr. L a tight lipped smile. He exhaled a long chain of smoke before his eyes shot over to the other men in the room.

"Unless she's still giving you problems, Bruno."

I stiffened as I glanced at my driver from the corner of my eyes and inhaled. I didn't have to look over to recognize Bruno staring a hole in the side of my head. Should I tell on him about what just happened outside of his office? I shook my head. No that would be stupid. It was his word against mine and I was already on thin ice for sneaking out with K. I held my breath and waited for his response.

After what seemed like an eternity, Bruno shook his head. "Nah, we're good. She has a smart mouth, but nothing I can't handle."

I exhaled a shakily breath as Mr. L threw his head back and laughed.

"Mr. O is going to love Little Bit." Xavier chuckled.

"Agreed. Addison, the driver who picked you up from the airport, will take you to the realtor office and then to your hotel. I need Bruno for a few hours but then he'll be back. I'll ensure he takes you to visit your grandmother, too. Don't try anything stupid with this new guy."

I nodded my head. "Understood. Anything else?"

"At the end of August, the ink will be dry on the contract, and you no longer have to deal with us. Instead, you will be moving to your new home."

My eyes bulged. "W-what? At the end of August? That's barely a month away."

He shrugged. "I'm glad you know how to read a calendar but ask yourself, what the fuck does it have to do with Mr. L?"

"Well," I was floored. I literally was at a loss for words. I knew that Mr. L was selling me, but I didn't realize how much time I did not have. I took a quick breath and collected my words so that I could quit stammering. "That doesn't give me enough time to ensure the house is sold. That doesn't give me enough time to get all the affairs in order before I leave my grandmother behind."

Mr. L exhaled a fake yawn before staring at me nonchalantly. "Addison, I. Don't. Give a. Fuck. Like I said, you're gone at the end of August. You're dismissed."

I scoffed before spinning on my heels to head back toward the elevators.

"Addison?"

I stopped in my tracks as Mr. L's voiced called after me. I kept my back to him as I slightly looked over my shoulder.

"I forgot to mention, Dr. Johnston will be flying out this evening and will continue to do your weekly checkups, so don't get any fucking ideas."

The elevator dinged before the doors opened. I hurriedly walked in, not caring that Manny was glaring at me again. I had to get the fuck out of there.

Chapter 16

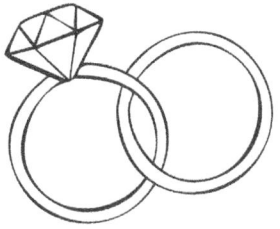

Luther

I watched Addison's ass unintentionally bounce as she damn near sprinted out of the room. If I wasn't so in love with Denise, I would've made her my own. Addison and Denice had so many similarities that it was impossible not to recognize – smart mouth, independent, and pure. All they needed was for someone like me to break them into submission. Blood rushed to my dick with the thought of both of them on all fours on my bed.

I briefly closed my eyes and exhaled, attempting to calm the monster in my pants. I had to stay focused and stick to the plan. Within a month from now, Addison would be shipped overseas, and Denice will be married to me. I win.

"Xavier, any news from the trio and my beautiful Denise?" I asked, leaning against the doorframe of my office.

"No, just the same old same old. Ashlynn has been working in her new salon while Nicholas has been at the tire shops with her dad. Well actually, I heard her dad was heading back home to Cali and leaving Nicholas to take care of the shops. In my opinion, I think he's doing really well. Way better than that dumbass, Bobby – may he rest in shit."

I stared at Xavier. "I don't give a damn how well the shop is doing. I'm not making any money off of it anymore."

"Damn, my bad bro! I was just saying."

"Yeah, anyway, what about bitch ass Ayzo?"

"He's usually at the shops with Nicholas, or at Denice's office, but that's really it. Either Ayzo is super boring and sits around their house or he's good at staying undetected. I mean, Nicholas and Ashlyn have been trying to stay hidden. They take different routes to work and make sure to observe their surroundings for the most part, but they aren't that good at it. Ayzo on the other hand, that motherfucker is good."

"Well, would you expect anything less from The Shadow? He must be the one showing Nicholas and Ashlynn how to observe their surroundings and not keeping the same routine."

Xavier nodded. "That makes sense. We've been doing a decent job with keeping up with the pair but eventually, they'll get better and then it'll be harder to keep eyes on them. I think we need to make a move now before we lose track."

I waved my hand, dismissing his suggestion. Sure, I could have ambushed Ashlynn and Nicholas, but it wasn't time yet. I had to wait on the word from Mama K. Besides, without knowing Ayzo's whereabouts at all times, our plan to finish what was started a year ago wouldn't work. Plus, Ayzo wasn't the only person I didn't have constant eyes on. I knew Seojun's ass was around here somewhere, but the fucker stayed hidden in plain sight.

While he was playing hide and seek, Seojun managed to kill damn near everybody who crossed over from the Jaguars to the Cobras. I mean, I knew he was unhinged, but he's single handedly slaughtered almost 50 men within the year. I used to pray for him to come out of hiding, but I didn't think he would come out swinging so hard.

Thankfully, I still had the last five ex-Jaguars, who were close to Seojun, by my side. They knew how to get all of his money, massage parlors, escort houses, and community on my side. On top of that, they knew where the majority of his safe houses were. When I took over all of his territories across the Midwest, Seojun had no choice but to flee. The first two years were blissful, and I was on top of the world. I had money and power in the middle of my palm, and nobody could touch me.

This was all thanks to Mama K. She told me the truth about my past and came up with the plan to take back everything that belonged to me. First, I needed to blend in with the community. So, I started up a financial advisor business. Of course, it was fake and I used the money I made from my brothel houses to transfer in and out of there. To complete my image of a businessman, I needed a wife. I already knew who I wanted. Hell, I wanted Denice all to myself again. Imagine my surprise when I found out that Ayzo's bitch ass was back in the picture. I wanted to be upset when I saw him at the bar with Denice a few months back, but it actually set everything in motion.

I took a pull from my blunt and exhaled. When Mama K gave me the plan, I was more than happy to oblige. When I learned the truth, I wanted Seojun to understand the why behind me ruining his life just like how that motherfucka ruined mine. She designed a strategy that was specifically for Seojun that she had in the development stages for years but when I saw Ayzo, it was finally ready to execute. I wanted to make all of their lives a living hell and taking the Jaguars from Seojun was just the beginning. Once I got rid of his little close-knit family and made sure no one else was by his side, then I'd go in for the kill. However, before we could get the plans in full motion, I needed to get Addison out of the way. Once I sold her to Mr. Omba, I would have enough money to take Denice and leave the country and we can live happily ever after while everyone else laid in their final resting place.

I motioned for Bruno and X to follow me as I headed back into the office. Sandy was still in position on her knees, where I left her. I'm glad that her back was facing Addison, or I would have to reveal who my closest informant was when it came to her behavior. When Cindy and Sandy told me that Addison was leaving with that other friend every morning to clean houses, I didn't really give a damn. Hell, as long as she was keeping her legs closed and not messing with another nigga, she was good in my book. The only reason I got pissed off about the situation was because Bruno wasn't paying attention to Addison. He literally had two task for his job – watch over her by keeping her a safe distance from niggas and driving her around. That's it! So, for him to not even notice that she was gone every morning made me want to pistol whip his big bitch ass.

My phone chimed and I noticed it was Mama K. It didn't matter what I was doing, I always stopped to answer her.

Mama K: Denice has been looking good and will be your perfect wife. You deserve her. Once your last assignment is gone, you can take her for yourself.

Me: Does that mean I can finally take out all of the trash?

Mama K. Yes. I'll be down in a few days and then we can kill them all.

A wide smile spread across my face as I sat my phone down. I had been waiting for so long to get the ball moving and it was finally time.

"Sandy, go sit on the sectional but take the rest of them clothes off. You're gonna be going to work in a second, I just need to handle something with Bruno."

She nodded as she did what she was told. I smirked when I noticed Bruno's ass watching her from the corner of his eyes.

"You see something you like, Bruno?"

He snapped his head back in my direction before he cleared his throat. "No, no sir."

I huffed out a chuckle as I sat on the edge of my desk. "It's okay, man. That's what she's there for. I'm not like your form boss, Seojun. You can participate in the merchandise as long as you pay. However, I won't charge you this time."

Bruno's eyebrows rose as he stared at me with suspicion.

"Look, I'm gonna give you an assignment real quick and then you can take her back to your place."

Bruno looked between me and Sandy before he stood up straight. "What do you need me to do?"

Xavier covered his mouth as he chuckled. He already knew what it was. Most men didn't turn down free pussy and Sandy was a nice looking woman.

"In two days, you'll go to pick up Olivia from the airport. As soon as she arrives, I need you to take her to a hair salon."

"A hair salon?"

"Yeah, and while she's there, I need you to go to a bar. It's a pretty popular bar downtown called Jill's."

"I'm a bit confused. These are just normal tasks you usually send me in a text message."

"True," I said, rubbing my chin.

I made eye contact with Sandy and nodded my head. Knowing what to do, she got on her knees while she propped herself up on the couch, pressing her breast together causing Bruno to swallow loudly.

"You see, Bruno, I'm going to be busy planning two weddings, mine and Addison's. So, unfortunately, you are going to be tasked with a few tedious chores."

Sandy reached for Bruno's belt and gently tugged him closer to her. Lust filled his eyes as he stared down at her. A bead of sweat began to form at his hairline as her small dainty hands roamed up his torso.

"W-what do you want me to do when I go there?"

"It'll be a cater order so all you have to do is pickup the supplies."

"That's it?" Bruno asked, looking at me from the corner of his eyes.

I stood up from my desk. "That's all! Do we have a deal?"

Sandy grabbed a handful of his balls and gently squeezed, causing a low growl to escape his mouth.

"Fuck. Yeah, yes, sir. I can do that."

"Perfect." I exclaimed, clapping my hands together. "Sandy, take him to the red room on the fifth floor and take a friend with you. Hell, take two. Bruno, I'll text you in the morning with more details."

Sandy grabbed Bruno's hand and pulled them out the door. Xavier shook his head and laughed.

"She's gonna have him eating out the palm of her hands."

"That's the plan. Despite his prior mishap with Addison and not reporting her whereabouts, Bruno has been loyal to me. Good deeds deserve a reward every now and then. Besides, he doesn't know that Seojun is out and about."

Xavier's eyebrows rose in surprise. "So, you're sending him to Jill's as bait?"

A wide smile spread across my face as I passed him the blunt. Seojun will get a nice surprise when he sees Bruno a.k.a. Jackie pop out of thin air because I knew he was somewhere watching. Phase two of our plan has begun.

Chapter 17

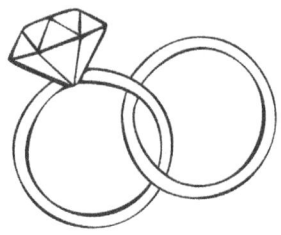

Addison

We pulled up to Mr. Adalyn's office and I exhaled. I couldn't get away fast enough from those men. Granted, I had to spend the next few hours with this new driver, Jerome, who was obviously checking me out, but beggars couldn't be choosers. As long as he stayed behind the wheel and didn't touch me, I could care less. The only thing that was really bothering me was the fact that he was getting on my nerves.

"Boss, after obtaining Denice again from your office, we arrived at-"

"You cannot be serious right now!" I heard Mr. L's voice boom through the phone. "At what point did I tell your dumbass to call me every single time Addison's ass did something? All I said was to let me know if she is doing some shady shit."

"But sir, we are at some real estate office."

"Did you really just forget that she already told me she was going to visit a damn realtor about selling her grandmother's house? Like nigga, it hasn't even been an hour, and you've already forgot what the fuck was going on?"

The driver did not respond, but I could see the bead of sweat rolling down his temple. I almost felt bad for the guy. I mean, he may have been a creep, but he was just doing his job. Not very well but still doing his job.

"I asked you a question," Mr. L's voice sliced through the silence.

"Y-yes sir. I mean, no I didn't forget I just –"

"How about this, do not call my line unless Addison's ass has run away or got some nigga in her face."

"Yes, sir."

"I swear hiring this young muthafucka was a mistake."

The line disconnected and I heard the driver let out a shaky breath. He quickly cleared his throat and exited the car. I wanted to give him some words of encouragement, but I didn't. Besides, he was literally there to tell on me. Not my fault his ass got in trouble.

A few seconds later, my door was opened and I hastily stepped out of the vehicle, avoiding eye contact with the driver. I tilted my head back to see S&V Realty in bold white letters on the front of the building. The green lawn was carefully manicured and held neatly trimmed bushes and a few tall trees around the permitter. The modern four story building had large windows across the front, allowing the natural glow of the sun to beam into each office. The sleek black glass façade gave the building an intimidating yet powerful appearance, which made my confidence for Mr. Adalyn to help me that much stronger.

Taking a deep breath, I headed towards the revolving doors and made my way inside the building. Stepping inside, the open layout was decorated with hues of black and gold. I stepped closer to a picture on the wall displaying happy families holding up keys to their new homes. I even saw a picture of a beautiful Black couple about to cut the ribbon in front of a bookstore. I couldn't help but smile at all of the contagious joy radiating off each of the memories. Across all of the pictures, I noticed that S&V really helped the local community. I read their reviews online and I was impressed by how much they were really for the people and not just after their money.

"Good morning, can I help you?"

I jerked my head to the side to see a petite woman with shoulder length curly red hair and hazel eyes smiling up at me.

"Oh, good morning. My name is Addison, and I have an appointment to see Mr. Adalyn."

Her eyebrows dipped as her red coated lips slightly frowned. "I'm sorry dear, but Mr. Adalyn is not in at the moment."

"What? He told me that I could meet him at the office today."

"Let me double check with his assistant. Sometimes he sneaks in and leaves without anyone knowing. Addison, correct?"

I nodded my head.

"What's your last name, hun?"

Oh, right. I never gave him my last name. I bet he had hundreds of clients named Addison and probably couldn't remember which one to add to his list for meetings.

I swallowed and cleared my throat. "Billingsley, but you can tell him we texted about a meeting the prior week."

She smiled with a nod. "Sure thing. Just give me a second, sweetheart." The woman said, gesturing towards the lobby area.

I smiled and took a seat, trying to control my racing mind. Did I get the day mixed up? No, I couldn't have. I've read and reread our text thread over and over again. Hell, it was the only hope I had and it gave me the strength to keep fighting for my freedom. Maybe this was a prank. I mean, maybe I emailed the wrong address or was texting the wrong number. Maybe it was Mr. Adalyn's girlfriend or wife this whole time. I shook my head. No, that was dumb. Why would his partner get mad about a business proposition?

I bounced my leg as sweat began to creep down my neck. I was nervous and becoming afraid. What if there wasn't any Mr. Adalyn? What if there was but he was a big creep like Dr. Johnston? I clamped my eyes shut and inhaled through my nose. Counting softly to five, I exhaled through my mouth. I was overthinking and assuming the worse for no reason. I needed to stay positive. I had a good feeling when I reached out to Mr. Adalyn, and I was going to see this meeting through.

"Ms. Billingsley?" the receptionist called.

I stood to my feet and headed back towards her desk.

"You may go up. Security will get you to the right place."

I looked over my shoulder to see a Black woman in a white button down blouse, black blazer and black slacks holding her arm out, pointing towards the elevator. Around her waist was a baton, gun holder, flashlight, and a can of mace. She had on gold framed glasses and her hair was styled into a pixie cut. She had a medium frame, but I could tell by her demeanor that she was probably toned. Hell, her tight jaw and pinched brows let me know that she could most definitely kick anybody's ass that get in the way of her boss.

I followed behind her as we stepped onto the elevator. She pressed the top floor and used her thumb print to bypass the security code when prompted. I couldn't help but notice the few similarities between this office and Mr. L's. The main difference was that I didn't get an uneasy feeling here. I looked up and saw the numbers creeping closer to the top floor. My heart raced and sweat began to form in my palms. My anxiety was through the roof because this needed to work. Mr. Adalyn was my final option.

The elevator dinged before opening. We stepped off the elevator and walked through double glass doors. The sitting area had a leather sectional couch and gold end tables. There was a closed office door with a black metal door frame to my right that had V. Reense stenciled on the front. To my left was a similar door, but the name had S. Adalyn. In the middle of the two doors was a desk that the security guard took a seat in.

I opened my mouth to ask her if I should sit and wait when the door to my left opened. My lips parted as a tall, deep olive-toned man stood in the doorway. His black hair was pulled back into a low ponytail. He had on a black button down shirt that was partially opened, causing his gold chain that had a cross on the end to rest against his broad chest. A tattoo of a red and black scorpion ran down the side of his neck and underneath his chin. Another tattoo was on his chest, but I couldn't make out what it was. I could tell by the ink on his knuckles that he was probably tatted all over his body. His full lips spread into a smile, showing off a gold bottom grill and two gold fangs.

I fought the urge to lick my lips, but I could tell right now that my panties were ruined. I've seen some handsome men throughout my lifetime, but the one before me had me ready to throw my panties at him. If he were to command me to get on my knees in front of him, you would have thought my legs gave out by how fast I would drop.

"Mrs. Billingsley, I presume?"

My mouth was dry, and I couldn't speak. What the hell? Talk dammit!

"Uh, Billingsley, yes. Me."

He arched an eyebrow and briefly looked over at the security woman. Oh shit, he had small gold hoop earrings on, too? Fuck! I briefly looked down and glared.

"Hussy, if you don't calm the hell down!" I inwardly shouted. Clearing my throat, I looked up and smiled. "I apologize. Yes, I'm Ms. Billingsley."

His eyes roamed down my body before he licked his lips. "Not married?"

Arching an eyebrow, my head slightly tilted to the side. "Why do you ask?"

"Because you wouldn't be here by yourself looking that good."

I swallowed. Was he flirting with me right now? Wait, this was not the reason I came here. I exhaled. "Uh, no but that doesn't mean I don't have a boyfriend."

I don't know why I said that because I was not entertaining anyone, but at the same time, I didn't want him to think I was easily available. I mean, I kind of was, but he didn't need to know that. I didn't want to cloud his judgement from helping me if he was thinking with the head in between his legs instead of the one on his shoulders.

He huffed out a small chuckle before taking a few steps closer to me. His cologne of sandalwood and mahogany infiltrated my nostrils, causing a shiver to creep up my spine. He stared at my lips before looking into my eyes.

"Yeobo, didn't anybody tell you that you're single until you're married?"

My eyes widened as he laughed out loud. He cocked his head to the side and motioned for me to follow him into his office. I exhaled and ran my hands down my skirt.

Lord, help me stay focused so we can get through this meeting.

Chapter 18

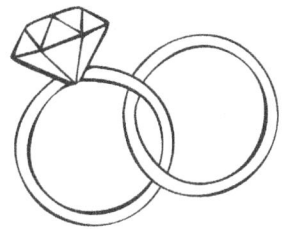

Seojun

I was two seconds away from telling Bishop, my personal security for my floor, to leave so that I could bend Addison over and dip my tongue in between her legs. The people who took her picture in that newspaper article that I originally saw did not do her justice.

Baby girl was breathtaking with her deep almond skin that seemed to shimmer from the sunlight coming through the window. Her curvy hips filled out her black pencil skirt, making my dick jump and the cream colored blouse made no attempt of hiding her full breasts. The way her full lips parted for me when I stepped out of my office made it damn near impossible not to imagine them wrapped around my dick. I needed to focus! Addison was here for a reason, and it wasn't for me to lust over her.

I stepped around my desk and motioned for her to sit down at the seat across from me. Her nervous deep brown eyes stared between me and the doors leading back to the elevator and I couldn't help but smirk. She wanted to run away. Whether it was because she was scared or turned on, I didn't know, but I hoped she stayed so that I could find out. I moved from my desk and stood next to her. I inhaled the mixture of her sweet yet subtle floral perfume and body wash.

"Addison, come, please sit."

She nibbled on the corner of her mouth as she stared up at me. She seemed so pure and innocent, but that couldn't be the case. I mean, Addison literally set up this appointment in an attempt to blackmail me into helping her. I wasn't about to let her innocent act affect me. Addison broke her eye contact with me and stepped inside my office. I nodded my head toward Bishop before closing the door.

"So, Ms. Billingsley, let's get right down to it. What do you need from me?"

She shifted uneasily in her seat before she tucked one of her braids behind her ear. "Please, call me Addison."

"Okay."

"Can I call you a different name besides Mr. Adalyn?"

"No."

"Well damn," she uttered, pinching her brows together.

"So, what can I help you with." I asked again, sitting in my chair.

"Just straight to it, huh?"

I arched an eyebrow at her. "If I recall, you emailed me and made sure to attach some interesting files. So, excuse me that I'm not interested in small talk."

She huffed out a sigh. "I suppose you're right. Shit, how do I even start?"

"Preferably from the beginning." I stated nonchalantly, leaning back in my seat.

"Well, my grandmother became really sick, and we had to use all of her money for her care. I ended up getting help from this man, Mr. L."

"Mr. L? You don't know his real name?"

She shook her head. "So anyway, I didn't know that Mr. L was very dangerous."

I rubbed my chin. "And I'm assuming this Mr. L gave you the money and now wants it back but doubled."

She shook her head. "N-not quite."

I tilted my head to the side, waiting for her to explain. Usually, when a loan shark offered up a lot of money, they wanted double, sometimes triple of what they gave out.

"He, uh," she closed her eyes and took a shaky breath. Looking back at me, I noticed her eyes were beginning to water, but she didn't allow them to fall. "He didn't want my money, but instead, he wanted my.... purity."

My eyebrows shot up as I sat up right in my seat. "Your purity?"

She nodded her head. "It's exactly what you are thinking, too. The agreement was that he would take on temporary guardianship to pay for my nana's caregiver and mortgage so that she had help and wouldn't end up homeless. In exchange of his support, I had to marry his client. Well, Mr. L lied and hasn't been taking care of our financial debt. The mortgage to my grandmother's house is behind again and I barely have enough money from cleaning to pay the other bills and her caregiver. I only have until the end of the month before the final transaction goes through and I'm shipped off."

"Damn," I muttered.

I honestly didn't know what else to say. I've heard of men and some women selling others for a profit, but I kept away from people like that. I may have run an all exclusive massage parlor and upscale escort homes, but it was always my workers choice to be there. I never made them do anything that they didn't want to, nor did I coerce them into it. I could tell from listening to Addison that she was desperate, but ultimately bamboozled into this type of trade.

"Mr. Adalyn, I need your help."

I sighed. "How am I supposed to help you, Addison?"

"I saw the video."

"And?" I asked, standing up from my desk and walking towards the window.

"Maybe you can hire that man for me. I mean, he was able to do that to Dash a few months back with no hesitation and I thought maybe he could take care of Mr. L for me. I know this is asking a lot, but I don't know what else to do!"

I spun around to face her. "You want me to hire the man that handled Dash?"

She nodded. "I promise I'm not some undercover cop or anything like that. I just need someone to help me escape my fate."

I faced the window again and placed my hands behind my back. She didn't recognize that was me in the video – interesting. Granted, I didn't show my face, but I thought she would notice the voices were similar. Maybe I could use this to my advantage, but I wasn't sure how just yet.

"How exactly do you plan on escaping your fate? I mean, say that we take care of your current problem, what about the man that you're already being sold to? I'm sure he's already invested some money in you. Do you think he's going to be fine if his investment was lost or damaged? You could be putting a lot of people in danger. And what about your grandmother? If this Mr. L is paying her bills, what would happen if that stops?"

I glanced over my shoulder to see her head bowed as she chewed on her lip. She didn't think this through all of the way, but who could blame her? She was at her last options and determined to try anything.

"Do you know who you were sold to?"

She kept her head down and shook her head. I rubbed the side of my chin and hummed. As much as I didn't want to get myself involved with someone else's issues, I had a gut feeling that I needed to help this woman. To see her so defeated, did something to me. I wasn't the most sentimental man, but listening to Addison's plea had my stomach in knots. Plus, the thought of her being married off to someone else pissed me off. I barely knew the woman and had no business being jealous, but still.

I let out a sigh as I folded my arms across my chest. "How do I know that I can trust you, Addison? You don't know me and I for damn sure don't know you. Yet, you are willing to risk your life, all from a video that you currently have in your possession? How do I know that you're not gonna go to the police once you get what you want?"

She shot her eyes up at me and began to frantically shake her head. "I would never do anything like that. I know you don't know me, but I'm not that type of person."

"Why not run?"

Her face scrunched up in irritation. "I can't because they'll find me or worse, hurt my grandmother. Look, I can pay you everything I have and if that's not enough, I could work off my debt. I can sweep floors or clean toilets in your office, hell, it doesn't matter what it is. I just need a way out of my situation. Mr. Adalyn, I just came to you because I figured whoever that guy was in the video didn't mind getting his hands dirty. From what I saw, Dash had made some bad dealings with him, which ultimately got him killed."

"You knew Dash?"

She nodded. "Yes, he worked for the same man that is selling me. Look, it isn't my business what Mr. Seojun has going on. The only thing that ran across my mind was the fact that he didn't allow anyone to fuck him over."

I flicked my tongue across my bottom lip as I quietly chuckled. She really had no idea that I was Seojun. Did she think because I owned a multi-million dollar business and looked like this uptight man that I didn't get my hands dirty? Then again, I had been in hiding for so long and only a few people knew what I looked like. Of course, there were a lot more people that could point me out, but I've already checked them off my list and had their remains scattered to send a message to the remaining five ex-Jaguars.

"So, you want revenge? I asked, turning around to look at her.

"Hell yes!" Addison eagerly replied as she stood to her feet. "You don't know what this asshole has put me through. Not only is he selling me, but he's allowed others to abuse me, and I want them all gone. Honestly, if I could, I would do it myself."

I arched an eyebrow. I had to admit that I thought Addison was going to be this sweet woman who just needed financial help, but I have been mistaken. Her thirst for revenge has me intrigued and the fact that she wanted to be involved turned me on.

"Please, Mr. Adalyn." Addison whispered. "I know this is probably not the norm for you, but I'm dolorous."

Rubbing my chin, I walked towards her with my hands behind my back. "How about this; you come with me tonight to handle some business. There, you'll be able to see how Seojun works. If you can handle it, then me and you can come up with some type of deal."

"I'll be there. Just tell me when." She eagerly stated.

"Hold on, dear Addison; you need to understand what I am saying. If you cannot handle tonight, the last thing you have to worry about is being shipped off to a new husband. If you fail tonight, then it just may be your last night here. Are you willing to risk your life for your freedom?"

She looked down at her hands and took a deep breath. Her honey brown eyes slowly stared into mine. "I'll do whatever it takes."

A small grin spread across my face as I extended my hand to her. She placed her dainty hand into mine before sealing our deal. I hope Addison was ready for tonight – I'd hate to have to kill her.

Chapter 19

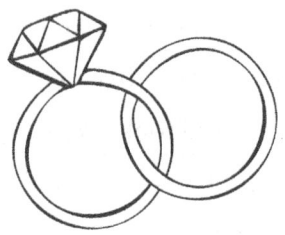

Addison

I exited the car without bothering to wait on Jerome. He was useless as a driver and I hated to admit it, but I would rather have Bruno here. I may not like the man, but at least he knew what the hell he was doing.

I mean, Jerome had gotten us lost after bragging that he grew up in Philly for the first twenty minutes after leaving Mr. Adalyn's office. Mind you, according to our GPS, the hotel from the office was only 20 minutes. We had been in the car for damn near an hour before we finally made it to my hotel. If I wasn't in my right mind, I would have called Mr. L to beg him to bring me Bruno back. Not that I wanted to deal with his shit, but like I said, at least I could get from point A to point B without being lost in the middle of nowhere.

"Do you need help taking your bags upstairs?" Jerome asked, unbuckling his seat belt before rubbing his hands together.

"Hell no!" I spat, slamming the car door closed.

I heard Jerome mumble a 'fuck you' but at this point, I didn't give a damn if he was mad. Instead of trying to make his way upstairs in my space, he needs to learn how to follow the damn GPS, which shouldn't be hard. The woman is literally telling him turn by turn instructions and yet he still got lost.

After getting checked into my hotel room, I jumped in the shower and finally washed away the day. Between dealing with Xavier, Bruno, Mr. L, Jerome and Mr. Adalyn, I was completely drained. My thoughts were running rampant, and my nerves were on ten thousand. I needed a drink.

My phone began vibrating on the side table next to the bed in the room. Checking my notifications, I saw I had a text message from Akira who was checking in to make sure I landed safely. I smiled as I sent her a quick message back explaining that I would call her in a few. As much as I wanted to tell my best friend everything that has happened to me since we graduated, I couldn't. Not yet anyway. If I passed this so called test tonight with Mr. Adalyn and Seojun, maybe I can tell her what I was going through. Of course, I wouldn't tell that I was pretty much hiring someone to unalive Mr. L, but at least she could know what I've been going through this past year.

After texting Akira, I sat on the bed and dialed my grandmother's number. I hoped today she was feeling up to talking. Usually with her dementia, there are days when she's not all the way with me. She thinks I'm either my mom or her sister who had passed when she was in her late thirties. Those days were hard for me.

My grandma was my first best friend, and I could talk to her about everything. When my mom was demonstrating her famous disappearing acts, my grandma stepped up to the plate. She taught me how to be a strong independent woman, but she didn't teach me how to handle my mom without her. She didn't prepare me on how to handle impossible situations like her getting sick and how to get away from people like Mr. L. The only thing I didn't mind during her episodes was that I could confess everything that was happening to me, and she wouldn't remember a thing.

I took a deep breath and called her phone. I briefly chuckled because my nana was one of those people who still had a landline in her home. After a few rings, I heard the line pick up.

"Henrietta Billingsley's residence."

A smile spread across my face as I heard the chipper voice through the line. "Hey Ms. Yolanda. How are you doing?"

Yolanda was my grandmother's caregiver. She was an older Jamaican woman with a no bullshit tolerance, but she loved hard. My grandma loved Yolanda and when she was in a better state, they would be sitting around gossiping and cooking like old friends. Yolanda was family and with her around, I never worried over my grandma. Even though I despised Mr. L, I was grateful that he allowed me to hire her with little input.

"Oh, Addison, baby! It is good to hear your voice. I am blessed, baby girl, but I owe you a congratulations on graduating with your bachelor's degree."

"Thank you! It was a lot of hard work, but I'm kind of sad that it's over. I mean, I guess I liked the distraction."

Yolanda hummed. "Well, that is understandable dear. I know that you and Henrietta are really close and watching her having to go through this sickness hasn't been easy. Just know that she is really proud of you – whether she's going through an episode or not. Hell, I'm proud of you too. Not too many folk able to take care of their family while trying to go to school full time."

Tears began to fall down my cheek. As much as I appreciated everything Yolanda was telling me, she didn't know everything I had to do to walk that stage. She didn't know how down bad I was and didn't have two pennies to give towards my grandmother's care until after I did what I had to with Mr. L. If she knew the truth, then she wouldn't be so proud of me.

I cleared my throat and swiped away the tears on my cheeks. "You are a treasure, Yolanda, and I am so grateful that you've been here with our family during this rough time. Before I forget, about your payment for next month-"

She playfully scoffed and I knew she was waving a dismissive hand in the air like she always did. "We'll talk about that later. So, do you want to speak to your grandma?"

"Yes, please."

"Okay, dear, but just know that she's having a bit of difficulty with memory today so be prepared-"

"I know, Ms. Yolanda." I interrupted. I didn't mean to be rude, but I already knew what to expect.

After a few moments, I heard Yolanda passing the phone to my grandmother.

"Hello?" her fragile voice filled my ears.

"Hey, love bug," I said, swallowing a fresh batch of tears.

"Ruthie? Why aren't you in school?"

I briefly closed my eyes and exhaled. Ruth was my great aunt. She was only a few years older than me when she passed away, but my nana still thought she was alive.

"Girl, I graduated yesterday!"

"What! Get out of here. Are you serious?"

"Yes ma'am. I am officially done with college."

"Shit, I'm sorry I didn't make it sis. It must've slipped my mind."

My heart ached as I finally allowed the tears to run down my face. "It-it's okay, love. I knew you were there with me in spirit. Besides, I recorded it for you so you can watch it."

My grandma huffed out a small chuckle. "I knew you would. I can't wait to see you Ruth. My daughter, Delilah has been acting up again, but my baby girl Addison has been my sunshine. She's so sweet and smart, just like you. I reckon she's about to graduate, too."

A soft sob escaped my lips, causing me to quickly cover my mouth.

"What's wrong, Ruth?" My grandma asked, her voice laced with concern.

"N-nothing, beautiful. I'm just so happy to hear that Addison's doing so well."

"Oh yeah! She's been working hard at school and doing everything she can to keep me comfortable at home. I just pray that her mom comes around and finally get to know her. I mean, she has an amazing daughter and she's missing out on so much. Anyway, what else you been up to sis? Any new beaux after your hand?"

I shook my head in laughter. "No, not quite. Well, there is this one man that wants me, but he just wants to use me because I'm still a virgin. I've tried to get away from him, but he has people following me and I don't know what to do."

"Ruth! I thought I told you to stay away from assholes like that."

"I know I know. It's just, he's helped me with a few financial situations, but now he feels like he owns me."

"That's usually how they work. I've run across men like that back in my day, but luckily, I had Ernest there to scare them off. You remember how he used to snatch up them jokers by the throat every time one of them eyed me longer than three seconds?"

"What? You've never told me that grandp- I mean, Ernest got down like that."

"Oh, yeah! Ernest lived by the rules of the streets. As the leader of the Reapers, he had to. He handled business and took out anybody that got in his way."

My mouth hung opened as my grandmother continued explaining how my grandpa used to leave niggas bloodied up to protect her. I don't remember much about him, but what I could recall was that Grandpa Ernest was always so sweet and gentle with me. He used to take me down to the convenient store and by me ice cream before taking us to the lake to go fishing. Never in all my twenty years of living did I suspect him to be a cold blooded killer. Hell, I didn't know he was the leader of a major group back home.

"See, that's who you need by your side, Ruth." my grandmother continued. "Get you somebody who doesn't mind sending a few bullets through his enemies to protect you. We wanted Delilah to marry within the crew, but she was to busy chasing after some knuckle head named Rico."

"Rico?"

"Mmhmm. Something about him rubbed me the wrong way. He was so controlling and needed to know Delilah's whereabouts at all times, but he was her first love. She was blind to all of the red flags, but me and her daddy wasn't and good thing we weren't. We found out years later that he murdered his wife and then himself."

"Shit," I muttered.

"Right, but Delilah's ass was still pissed at us for forbidding her to speak to him years prior. She became so disrespectful, Ruthie. It was so bad that Ernest cut her off from the Reapers." Grandma exhaled a heavy sigh. "I tried to stick up for her, but she got so out of hand. Stealing, sleeping with her father's clients, exessive spending - we had had enough."

"What did she do?"

"When we stopped paying for her destructive habits, she got pregnant by some wannabe rap producer. Unfortunately, he died from an overdoes. Delilah having Addison was the best thing that could have happened for her, but she didn't care about that baby. She only cared about the next man that would take care of her."

A knot formed in the pit of my stomach. "That explains why she doesn't want to come around."

"Unfortunately. I mean, Ernest reached out to her with an offer to come back into the Reapers, but she'd have to work her way back up in order to take over, but she refused. I've been meaning to talk to Addison about that."

My eyebrows shot up. "Talk to me, I mean, talk to Addison about what?"

"Hmm?"

"You said you need to talk to Addison about something."

"Did I?"

My shoulders slumped with realization that her memory was slipping again.

"Anyway, Ruth, it's time for Yolanda to take me to my crochet club and then we are having a dance party after supper at Paul's."

"Oop! Ma'am who is Paul? Let me find out you about to get your groove on."

"I don't want another husband, but I don't mind stepping my toes in the pool if you know what I mean."

I burst out laughing. "I didn't need to hear that. Okay, I'll let you go get your freak on. I love you."

"I love you, too."

I sat my phone back down and smiled. It felt nice talking to my grandma, even though she didn't recognize me. I couldn't help but wonder what she had to tell me. I shook it off with a shrug. I guess it didn't really matter. Besides, after speaking to her, I felt a surge of confidence to handle whatever it was that Mr. Adalyn and Seojun were going to throw my way tonight.

Chapter 20

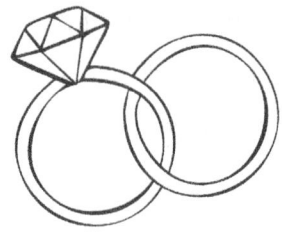

Seojun

"It was hard, but I found Arnez. He's been traveling back and forth between Cali and Vegas under the name Dr. Ralph Johnston. I spotted his ass last night going into a hotel. He had bags with him, so he must've just flown in." Ayzo said, sitting down in the recliner I had in my underground office.

I discovered this gem when I got to Philly and absolutely loved it. There were tunnels that led me throughout Philly and kept me undetected. Ashlynn, Nicholas, Ayzo and Denice were the only other people who knew about the tunnels. The agreement was that during the day, they kept up with their usual routine and only change it up just a bit. That way if T and his goons were watching, which we knew they were, they'd be under the impression that they knew our routines. Meanwhile, Ayzo and I would use the tunnels to keep an eye on everyone during the day. As soon as we got a whiff of suspicious activity, we'd be already on it. Of course, Ayzo was much better and faster, since staying hidden was planted in his core.

"That man was in my backyard the whole time," I scoffed, shaking my head.

Arnez or now known as Dr. Ralph Johnston, was not only a former jaguar, but my personal OBGYN for the group homes and massage parlors. He had a private practice and regularly did checkups for all of my workers. I had to fire him for trying to get with one of my girls. I didn't tolerate that bullshit. My girls were off limits.

"To be fair, we didn't know what we know now back then."

"True."

"So, what's the plan? I know that T is getting ready to strike because the hotel that Arnez checked into is barely two blocks away from Denice's shop. I doubt it was a coincidence."

"Definitely no coincidence, if we strike too soon, we'd be back at square one. As soon as Jackie, June, Manny, and Tiny hear that we got Arnez and are close to finding their locations, they'll disappear. Hell, they were trained to stay out of sight."

Ayzo nodded in agreement before he scratched the side of his face. "Don't be mad, but I don't remember a June or Tiny. I remembered Arnez, Jackie, and Manny, but them other two don't ring a bell. Did they start after I left the Jaguars?"

I nodded my head. "They were initiated into the Jaguars a few months before all hell broke loose which made me believe they are the ring leaders in this grand betrayal. I met them once, but I was too preoccupied to really pay attention to them because if I had, I would have caught the red flags."

Ayzo sat up in his seat. "What do you mean?"

"The day that June and Tiny came into my office, I remembered being annoyed because they were both young looking and had ugly attitudes. Now, I didn't mind helping young men get off the streets and better themselves with a job, but I don't tolerate the entitled disrespect. I was about to kick them out when they both showed me what they could do. They were able to pull up two of my highest paying customers' information within a blink of an eye. You know how I keep all of my things encrypted and locked away, so to see that they were able to pull that type of information had me intrigued."

"I don't blame you for adding them to the team. Hell, I would have done the same thing. That's a great skill."

"I thought the same thing, but if I were paying attention, I would have known better."

Ayzo tilted his head to the side, a puzzled look on his face.

"Those two customers had been in the shop within that same week. It could have been light work for those two to snatch up those elderly men and beat them up for information. I mean, they worked for the city and had never gotten into a physical altercation before."

"Oh, shit. I didn't even think about that."

"Exactly. I had so much on my plate and allowed those two to slip into my territory. The promises of free pussy and more money had all of them running out the door."

"Well, do you remember what they looked like? Better yet, don't you still have the files to the security system? We can roll back the tapes about two years ago and pinpoint them out. Then bingo, we got action."

I shook my head. "Great minds think a like, cuz, but I've already tried that. I pinpointed the so-called June and Tiny. They got hired to pose as the real June and Tiny."

"What!?" Ayzo shouted, standing up from his seat.

"Yup, those two guys were really called Philip and Bliz. Last I checked, Phillip was clean and working as a prison guard up in Jersey while Bliz was locked up in Rykers. They both said someone in all black approached them and offered them five grand a piece to pose as June and Tiny. The only thing they could remember that the person was a woman, but they couldn't see her face. So, not only did I get fucked over with everyone's betrayal, but now I have no idea who June and Tiny are for real."

Ayzo began pacing across the room while rubbing his chin as I sat back in my chair. As long as our enemy was out there breathing, we were all in danger. Nicholas, Ashlynn, and Denice were just as much my family as Ayzo was and I had to keep them protected. They put their lives on the line for my cousin and for that, they had my loyalty. Now was my time to step up and end all of this shit once and for all.

"What's the next move?"

I huffed out a sigh. "I was thinking about going through all of my old female workers to see if anyone was disgruntled against me to pretend to be June and Tiny. I mean, none of them were on the list of people who betrayed me and most of them are living comfortably, but you never know."

Ayzo quietly chuckled as he shook his head. I squinted my eyes at him and stared while he paced the floor. His laughter quieted as he made eye contact with me before stopping in his tracks.

"Oh, c'mon man! You treated all your workers with respect, especially the women who worked in the massage parlors and group homes. You actually listened to everyone on your payroll who were going through shit. Anybody that came to work and didn't give you no bullshit, loved your ass."

"And yet, they betrayed me."

"Only the disloyal ones that wanted to fuck and get their greedy hands on more money. Granted, that was damn near all of the men, but like you said, none of your female employees were on that list."

"I understand that, but right now, this is our best option."

Ayzo sighed and sat down in the recliner. "Or you could forgive and move on."

I blankly stared at him until he threw his hands up in defeat. I wasn't trying to hear none of that shit.

"So," I said, breaking the silence. "I had a total of 45 women on my roster between the massage parlors and houses. You take the first 20 and start vetting them and I'll take the other 25. One of them may have overheard or know something."

"Bet, I'll start tonight. Are you gonna start tonight, too, or do you have some paperwork to get through for that vacation resort you were planning?"

"Neither. I got something else for tonight planned."

Ayzo arched his eyebrow and waited for me to continue talking. Knowing my little cousin, I couldn't be vague right now, especially with everything that has been going on. I chuckled as his face began to scrunch up with annoyance. I didn't want to tell him, but at the end of the day, he was on the one I trusted to be there if anything went left tonight.

"You remember when I told you I had Ron, Lewis, and those other bodyguards in one of my warehouses a couple months back?"

Ayzo nodded.

"Do you remember that they all said that a man named Z persuaded them into joining the cobras?"

Ayzo nodded again while rotating his hand, motioning for me to get to the point.

"Well, it just so happens that I know who and where Z is."

"Hell yeah! We can get down to the bottom of who this damn ringleader is for the Cobras."

"Nah, Jay has already been with him the past ten hours and he don't know shit. He was reporting to either June or Manny."

"Dammit. If Aunt Jenny knew you had her baby boy Jay in the warehouse with you, she'd be having a conniption. That's my word of the day, by the way."

"I'm taking Addison with me," I blurted out.

The proud grin on Ayzo's face dissolved as his eyes widened.

I rubbed the back of my neck as I stood up from my chair. "She came to my office earlier today and wanted me to pretty much kill this person she calls Mr. L, who was going to sell her as a mail order bride."

"Whoa! What the fuck?"

"Exactly!" I exclaimed, pacing in front of my desk. "I have been blessed to have never run across a trafficker, but now that one is within my grasp, I most definitely want to fuck him up. However, I don't trust her. She still has the phone with the video of me handling Dash. Granted, she thinks that Seojun and Mr. Adalyn are two different people because I never showed my face in the video, and she didn't recognize my voice. Then again if she wanted to turn in the phone to the police, she would have done so already, right?"

I stopped and glanced at Ayzo who had his head slightly tilted and examining me. My heart raced in my chest and the room felt as if the air was thinning out. I then realized that I was rambling. Why the fuck did I start rambling as soon as I brought up Addison and, why the hell was my heart pounding? I swear not even two minutes ago, I was cool and chill, but the mere mention of her name has me prattling on like an anxious little bitch.

I exhaled a long breath as I calmed myself down. "Anyway, I was going to show her my plans for Z."

A puzzled look flashed across Ayzo's face before he opened his mouth to speak, but I rose my hand up.

"I want to take care of the person that's selling her because he's a fucking human trafficker and he needs to be buried under the dirt, but I also need to see if she can be trusted. If she tries to run or go to the police after she sees what I'm going to do to Z tonight, then I'm gonna put her in a shallow hole and she won't have to worry about being somebodies bride."

"And if she doesn't run?" Ayzo asked

"Then I'm keeping her in my protection until we get rid of her problem. Plus, I found out that her grandfather was the Ernest Billingsley. You know, the former head of the Reapers."

Ayzo squinted his eyes as a playful smirk spread across his face. "You sure that's the only reason you're keeping her around?"

"What does that mean?"

Ayzo grinned as he spread his arms across the back of the couch. "I know you very well, cousin, and I know that you will do anything to make Uncle Chul-Moo proud."

I scoffed. "Your point?"

"Well, I already saw you looking at Addison's picture in a way that was not business related. Not to mention, uncle wants you to bring a legitimate heir through marriage. So, the fact that you're attracted to this woman who just so happens to have Reaper blood is very telling."

"You got to be kidding me."

"What? You save her and she saves you. Win-win."

I blankly stared at him before heading out the door. I could hear him burst into laughter, but I ignored him. Was my cousin making sense? Yes. Was I going to entertain the idea? No. Well, maybe. I mean, if I were to marry Addison, that would void the deal she had with Mr. L since I would take over guardianship for her grandmother. I'd make sure to pay off all the past due bills, and sign the rights over to Addison. She'd be helping me by holding up my end of the contract with the Reapers since she was one. I mean, she didn't know it, but her grandfather was the former leader. I'm sure they would accept her with opened arms.

I shook my head, dismissing the crazy plan. I couldn't marry her. I mean, I doubt she would want to get out of one marriage deal just to jump into another one. No, I'd just have to find someone else. My interactions with Addison from here on out would be strictly business. I didn't understand why I became so anxious and giddy when speaking about her a moment ago, but I was just chalking it up to my exhaustion. Yeah, that's it. I just needed a nap.

Chapter 21

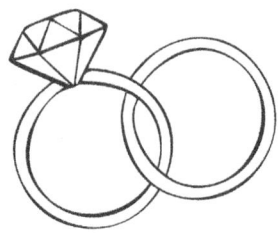

Addison

"Damn girl! You haven't even been gone for a day, and you already have a date tonight?" Akira asked, examining me through the phone.

I shook my head and chuckled as I finished putting on my eyeliner. I was sitting at the vanity in my hotel room and had my phone propped up on the mirror.

"Girl, it's not even like that."

"So, let me get this straight."

There was shuffling on the other end causing me to observe K. She had on a black moo-moo gown and her hair was pulled back into a low ponytail. After a few moments, she had maneuvered her phone so that I was staring at her and a whiteboard.

"Oh lawd." I muttered, picking up my lip gloss and applying a coat.

"So, you went into Mr. Adalyn's office to not only return his phone, but to get started on selling your grandmother's house."

I laughed as she drew on the whiteboard like she was breaking down a math problem. "K, if you don't stop trying to be like Brit and her Books off social media."

She waved a dismissive hand at me as she continued to draw. "I love Brit and would never post what I am doing. Plus, you know I'm a visual learner and I'm trying to see something."

I playfully rolled my eyes.

"Anyway, don't change the subject. So, after y'all meeting was done, he asked you to meet up with him tonight, correct?"

I huffed out a sigh. "Yes."

"So, if one plus one equals two, the muthafucking sky is blue, and you got to hide your snacks from that nigga Scooby Doo, then bitch how is this not a date?" She explained, drawing a big question mark and circling it three times.

I threw my head back and laughed. "Hold up, trick, when did you start dropping bars?"

K burst into laughter, too. "That shit was hot, right? My boo be letting me play around in his studio."

"Let me know when your first album is about to drop." I said, wiping away the tears.

"And will! But seriously, answer my question heffa."

"Ugh! I told yo big head ass it wasn't a date."

"Then what's up with the late night meeting?" Akira then gasped before she picked up the phone and stared at me. "Girl, is this a meeting to get your back blown out?"

"What the? No!" I yelled, falling into another round of laughter.

"Mmhmm."

I looked at my friend who was not laughing any more but instead had a look of concern on her face. I cleared my throat. If the roles were reversed, I'd be just as upset right now as K was. I haven't been telling her the truth for a while and for me to just be up and leaving at ten o'clock at night, during booty call hours, was very suspicious. I mean, I never did that when we were at school, except when I was going over to her place or we were going out to get snacks for our long study sessions.

"Akira, I love you and I promise I'm not meeting up with Mr. Adalyn like that. He's actually introducing me to his uh- assistant that's going to be working closely with me to get grandma's house taken care of."

"All right," she sighed. "Just make sure you keep your location on so I can keep an eye on you."

"Girl, you still in Vegas. How you going to get to me that fast if something did happen to me?"

"Don't worry about all that - just know I got your back. If you need my help in any way, say the word and I'll be there."

My stomach knotted with guilt, but I made sure to keep a playful look on my face. How could I look my best friend in the face and lie to her? K has been down for me since meeting in our first class together and she told me everything. Yet here I was, too afraid to tell her what I was about to do and what I was going through.

I quietly cleared my throat before smiling at her. "And that's why you're the best! Let me finish getting ready so I can head out of here."

"Okay girl. I love you."

"I love you, too"

We blew each other kisses before ending our FaceTime call. I sat back in my chair and exhaled. I allowed my thoughts to run before finally making up my mind. After all this was done, I would tell her everything. Hopefully, she wouldn't judge on my decision making skills.

My phone chimed with a text message.

Mr. Adalyn: Where can I pick you up at?

Me: That may be a problem. Mr. L has his driver watching my every move and unless I get dropped off by said driver, I won't be able to go out.

Mr. Adalyn: Fine. Meet me at this address. I'll be there in forty-five minutes.

I looked at the address and realized it was to a sports bar downtown called Big Shots. I couldn't help but smile because that was actually a good idea. Jerome wouldn't suspect a thing when he dropped me off and wouldn't have a reason to call Mr. L on me.

I stood up and gave myself a once over in the mirror. I had pulled my Boho braids into a high bun and wore a pair of small gold hoops with a matching necklace. My black tank top was tucked into my high waisted Levi's, showing off my thick curves. I completed the outfit with a black and red flannel and all black Steve Madden shoes. I was comfortable and cute. Not that I was trying to be cute for Mr. Adalyn, but if he were to flirt with me, I wouldn't turn down his efforts.

I sent Jerome a text message requesting a ride. He said he'd be there in less than five minutes. I wanted to respond that he didn't have to rush, but at the same time, I didn't want to be late. Besides, his ass should have already been outside since I had told him earlier that I was going back out tonight. After stuffing my key card into my crossbody bag and putting my phone into my pocket, I headed out the door.

I pressed the elevator button a few times before shaking out my hands. My nerves were getting to me and butterflies were swimming in my stomach. I know I had just met with Mr. Adalyn a few hours ago but knowing I was meeting Seojun, a cold blooded killer, was causing my heart to race. I had no clue what was in store for me when I met up with the pair.

The elevator doors opened, and I absentmindedly stepped in. Thoughts of my freedom was just within my reach, but I couldn't help but to think about those consequences. What if the man I was being sold to comes after me and my family? What if this was a trap and Mr. Adalyn is already working with Mr. L? I shook my head. I doubt that was the case. I mean if it were, Mr. L would have been outside waiting on me. Then again, what if this was a trap but it was Mr. Adalyn's way to getting rid of me. I was in his home when that phone was found, and I still had the evidence on me. He and Seojun could be working together to get rid of me since I am the only one who knew what they had done.

My palms began to sweat as the elevator got closer to the lobby floor. A part of me wanted to turn around and go right back to my room, but what good would that do me? At this point I had two options, deal with Mr. L and be sold or risk my life with trusting Mr. Adalyn. If I were to accept my fate with Mr. L than I was letting down future men and women. He would still be out on the streets manipulating them and I could never, in good conscience, allow another human to be put in the same type of situation that I was currently in. I closed my eyes and sighed. I may be taking a huge risk with Mr. Adalyn, but at least I would've tried to get rid of Mr. L.

The ding of the elevator had me opening my eyes. I stepped into the lobby just to see Bruno leaning over the receptionist desk flirting with the woman on duty. What the hell was he doing here and what happened to Jerome?

"Aren't you supposed to be on some special assignment and where's Jerome?" I asked, stepping up to him.

Bruno stood up straight and seductively smiled at the receptionist before turning his attention to me.

"First off, don't worry about my business and secondly, Jerome was only needed to get you to your little appointment earlier and to this hotel. With that said, where the hell are you trying to go this evening?"

"To the bar. Is that a problem? I just want a damn drink."

"Remember what I said earlier. Play any games and that's your ass."

I smacked my lips. I knew what he was cable of and he wouldn't hesitate to hurt me. He didn't have to remind me every thirty seconds. "Can we just go? I've heard that song already today."

He stretched out his hand, instructing me to walk in front of him. I rolled my eyes and stomped toward the front door. Stepping up to the car, I reached for the door handle and tried to open the door but heard the locks click into place.

"That's still my job."

"Congratulations! Want a damn cookie for memorizing your job description?"

I bit down on my bottom lip and instantly regretted opening my mouth. The hairs on the back of my neck stood up as I took a step back but Bruno had already broke the distance between us. He gripped my wrist and yanked me closer to him before his dark brown eyes stared down into mine.

"So, I guess my little chat with you today wasn't effective enough."

My eyebrows furrowed. I opened my mouth to speak, but he shook his head, his hand squeezing tighter around my wrist.

"I let your ass slide for a long time, but I'm tired of the shit. Watch who the fuck you're talking to, Addison."

"Let go of me!" I said through gritted teeth.

"You know, sometimes all you bitches need is for someone to go upside your head one good time for y'all to get some act right. I suggest you be nice to me or I'll do far worse than choke your dumb ass like earlier."

My jaws tightened as I glared up at him. Bruno lifted an eyebrow, challenging me to prove him wrong, but I wasn't a dummy. I broke our eye contact, causing him to chuckle a 'that's what I thought' before yanking the car door open. I made a mental note to add him to the list of people that needed to get fucked up.

Chapter 22

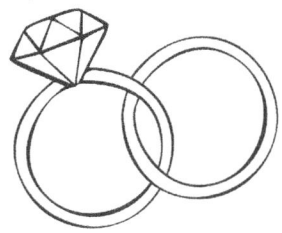

Seojun

I sat in the back corner booth of Big Shots bar and grill and took another sip of my tequila. It was Saturday night, and the place was crowded per usual. Big Shots had nothing on Jill's when it came to cheap drinks and good food, but it was a good back up bar. Jill's was mostly for the regulars while Big Shots was in the heart of downtown Philly and was swimming with tourists and college students. The music was a mixture of RnB and Rap and a few pop songs here and there. Since it was Saturday, karaoke was in full effect.

I watched as a tall petite woman with honey brown skin and wavey black hair sang Rihanna's "Sex with Me". Her eyes landed on mine and the sway in her hips became more seductive. I huffed out a chuckle before leaning back in my seat. She was beautiful, but I was in no mood to entertain tonight. My mind was focused on how I wanted to get rid of the scum I had tied up in the warehouse. The main thing that I didn't know would happen yet is if I was getting rid of one body or two.

A round of applause erupted around the room as the woman on stage finished the song. She ignored the other men trying to get her attention as she made her way towards my booth. I groaned.

"What are you sipping on, handsome?" she asked, sliding in next to me.

I stared at her for a long while before sighing. "Tequila."

"You must be the shy type."

"No, I'm just not in the talking mood."

"Mhm. So, what type of mood are you in?" she asked, rubbing her hands up my forearm.

The front door opened, and my attention shifted to the beauty walking through the door. Addison. Her brown eyes quickly did a search around the establishment before they landed on me. She took a small step towards me but hesitated. My eyebrows furrowed in confusion, but then I remembered the unwanted guest sitting next to me. Addison squared her shoulders and headed towards my booth.

"Good evening, Mr. Adalyn." Addison announced as she finally approached.

"Addison. I was beginning to think that you weren't going to show."

Her eyebrows pinched together before she looked down at her watch. "Uh, I'm on time."

"To be early is to be on time and to be on time is –"

"You are not about to quote Drumline to me, Dr. Lee." She interrupted.

I chuckled before finishing my drink and standing up from the booth. "C'mon, let's get started."

A scoff echoed behind me. "Really? You're just going to ignore me for that?"

I began to open my mouth when Addison beat me to it.

"Girl, please. There are plenty of other men in this bar for you to desperately throw yourself at until Mr. Adalyn returns."

"Desperate? Bitch, men chase after me daily. Plus, look at me. Does it look like I need to do anything to get a man's attention?"

"Yet, you're getting mad because the one you were just throwing yourself to is not giving you the time of day but has no problem giving it to me? Exactly! So unless you want to get your shit rocked for calling me out my name, I suggest you go pick a song to do karaoke to and calm the fuck down."

I smirked as the woman stood up and bumped past us. "She was pissed, wasn't she?"

"Bruh, I swear she had steam coming out of her ears like in those looney tune cartoons."

We looked at each other before bursting into laughter. "A woman who sticks up for herself – that's good."

"Mr. Adalyn, I promise I'm a nice person. She was just being rude."

I nodded before checking the time. "Well, we better get started. I don't want your driver getting suspicious."

I motioned for her to follow me before heading towards the back of the bar. Once we reached the back, I stopped next to Dylan, the owner's, office. I tapped twice on the doorframe, causing the older black man to look up at me. I briefly saluted him and he dipped his chin before hitting a switch under his desk that turned the camera off near the back alley.

Dylan and I had an agreement. I paid him a monthly convenience fee for him to 'lose' signal in his rear camera whenever I needed it. The entrance to one of my underground tunnels that led me to my warehouse was nearby and I didn't need anybody seeing what was happening. My dad taught me that with the right price, I needed to utilize all my resources. Mr. Dylan was an excellent resource. Besides, he knew the game and had plenty of clients he kept his mouth shut for.

I opened the exit door and lightly pulled Addison's arm, indicating for her to follow me. She was hesitant but didn't say a word. A small smile attempted to cross my lips, but I kept it suppressed. So far, she was doing good - following instructions without asking a million questions. Maybe she would be a good temporary wife?

We stepped into the alley where one flickering security light buzzed overhead, casting a singular uneven pool of yellow near the door of the bar. The rest of the alley was coated in black and tucked away from the rest of the world. I started towards the underground entrance catching whiffs of the smell of stale beer and grease from the nearby kitchen vent. As we moved deeper into the alley, the sounds of cars and chatter faded into the background. Soon, the only sounds that could be heard were our footsteps and her soft nervous breaths.

We made it to a small door that I kept hidden behind some boxes and I looked at Addison. Her chest rose and fell rapidly as she shifted uneasily on her feet. I could tell that she was nervous.

"Relax yeobo. We're about to go through my underground tunnel, but I need you to remain calm – the space is a bit tight."

"You have an entire secret passage in the middle of a dark alley and telling me to relax." She huffed out a humorless chuckle. "How do I know you not setting me up?"

I shrugged. "I guess you'll have to just trust me, won't you."

Chapter 23

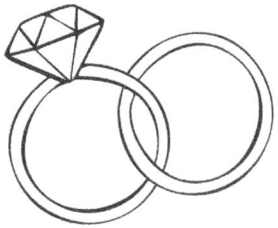

Addison

My heart was pounding in my chest as I watched Mr. Adalyn use his thumb print to unlock the door. I could just run. I mean, anyone with common sense would not be following a strange man into an alley that led to an underground passage.

I exhaled and followed him. At this point, he was the only hope I had left and there was no other choice but to trust him. Stepping into the door, the humming from lights going down the walls through the tunnel made my ears prick. Graffiti was painted down the tunnel, showing off one's artist skills and gang affiliation. I squinted my eyes and noticed one of the pictures was of a jaguar sinking its teeth into a cobra. Almost like the same one I've seen tatted on Mr. L and his minions.

The image even had one of the same dates in scripted inside the top of the letters. October tenth.

"Mr. L must've fucked with the wrong person on that particular day. I wonder what happened." I thought to myself.

The air around me felt cool, musty and thick with the scent of earth, mildew, and the faint tang of either rusted metal or old blood. My stomached knotted in fear. What the fuck have I gotten myself into? I pulled my flannel tighter around me as I continued to follow.

To distract myself from thoughts of getting murdered, I observed Mr. Adalyn. The man cleaned up nicely in his business attire but seeing him in casual clothes made my clit throb. He wore a black hoodie with a pair of matching sweatpants. His hair was pinned up into a bun, displaying his freshly faded haircut with two horizontal designs on each side. I flicked my tongue across my bottom lip before biting down on it. Just by the way he was walking, I could tell he was blessed in between his legs. Granted, I had no clue how I would be able to handle it if I were offered, but still.

"This way." Mr. Adalyn called out over his shoulder, breaking my lustful thoughts.

"So, what does yeobo mean? You called me that earlier and I have never heard of that before."

"It means darling, in Korean."

And just like that, my pussy was calling for him again.

The air suddenly shifted to a warmer temperature and was now laced with the faint scent of bleach and metal. The tunnel widened, and ahead of us stood a heavy metal door. I noticed a keypad blinked faintly beside it. Before I could get a better look, Mr. Adalyn blocked my view with his back facing me as he punched in a code. The lock clicked, causing the door to groan open. The night sky from an opening in the roof caught my attention as I looked up. The moon was bright, and I could see a few stars through the clouds. I briefly looked around the warehouse and for the most part, it was empty. There were a few crates lined along the far left wall and there was a staircase that led to a lone office door on the far right. A bay garage door with a white unmarked van was parked and I swear I felt my stomach drop out of my ass. Shit. Was that van meant for me when he kidnapped me?

Mr. Adalyn continued to walk deeper into the warehouse, and I hesitantly followed. My gut was pulling me in the opposite direction, but I honestly felt that I would only get lost in the tunnels. We walked behind a large plastic curtain that brought us into another room that was pitch black except for one light that shun in the middle of the room. My eyes bulged as a figure sat in a chair, their head down and hands bound. A metal table with different tools that were obviously there to cause torture sat next to the chair. I halted in my steps with realization of who was with us.

"Z," he called, shaking the man awake. "I brought an audience for your death tonight."

"What the fuck?" I shouted, taking a step backward.

"Addison this is Z and –"

"Yes, I know Zachary! A promoter for Club Jump. Why the hell does Seojun have him tied up?"

I watched as Mr. Adalyn's face scrunched up in confusion. "Addison, what are you talking about?"

"I ran into Z a few times at a few campus parties. He just promotes for a few clubs in the area. He hasn't done anything to anybody. Tell Seojun to let him go. Seojun, please come out!"

I called for Seojun as Mr. Adalyn just stared at me. This had to be a huge mistake. Zachary was the sweetest guy that I've met and wouldn't hurt a fly. All he did was hand out flyers to everyone on campus and then leave. There was no reason that Seojun and Mr. Adalyn had him tied up. Maybe they got him mistaken for someone else.

"Please, Mr. Adalyn, call Seojun in here so that Zachary can explain his innocence." I pled.

Mr. Adalyn walked up to me while he removed his cuff links. "Addison, yeobo, I am Seojun."

My eyes widened and bile began to rise in my throat. "Y-you? But you don't look like a...a..."

"Killer?" Seojun asked. A smile crept across his face that sent a shiver down my spine. "Why not? I am a very dangerous man, and I've sent a lot of men to their permanent sleep. Just like what I'm about to do to Z."

"B-but why? Zachary didn't hurt anybody. Like I said all he did was –"

"Zachary here used to put drugs in women and men's drinks and take them back to brothel houses. Some of them were able to move on without the memory of what happened to them. However, the ones that paying customers really 'enjoyed' were requested to return. Do you know how the news that they were drugged and taken advantaged of was given to them? By having videos or pictures sent to them as blackmail and the only way they could recover the evidence was that they had to work in one of those brothel houses for an extended period of time."

My eyes darted over to Zachary. Before I knew it, I was stepping toward him. "Is that true?"

Guilt and shame glinted in his eyes as he stared up at me. He opened his mouth, but didn't say a word. He shook his head as he cast his eyes down to the ground.

"Answer me!" I shouted, gripping his chin.

"A-Addy, please, it's not what you think."

"You know, when someone says that, 9 out of 10 times, it is exactly what you think." Seojun stated nonchalantly.

Tears slipped down Z's bruised face. "I was addicted to pills and I needed money to get my fix. I wasn't thinking about their wellbeing. I know it was wrong, but I was too fucked up to care."

"That's not a good enough excuse, you sick fucking monster!" Seojun shouted.

My hands shook with fury as I let go of his chin and stared down at him. I waited for my empathy to kick in, but it didn't. Hell, I didn't give a fuck about his crocodile tears because I felt that he only cared because he got caught. If he had an ounce of remorse, he would've turned himself in a long time ago. Or, he would have stopped a long time ago, but he was still 'promoting'. Not to mention, I saw him a few weeks before graduating on campus, urging people to come to some party.

"So, Z, are you ready to cooperate? It's the least you can do." Seojun asked. I looked over my shoulder to see him leaning on the metal table.

"Look man, I told you I don't know anything."

"You are telling me that one day you just decided to not only drug people but find a random brothel house to take advantage of them or sell them all on your own?" Seojun asked, crossing his foot over his ankle.

Z's jaw tighten. "No, that's not what happened, dipshit."

"Well, explain it to us because right now, that's what we're getting. How the hell did you even get yourself into this type of situation?" I asked, standing over him with my arms crossed over my chest.

Z tried to turn his head away, but I gripped his chin again. Leaning down, I stared into his eyes. There was guilt and anger behind them, and I was starting to feel sorry for him.

"Look at me. You have always been so nice to me, and we used to laugh and joke every time we crossed one another's paths. I never would have suspected you to be this awful person. So, maybe this is all just a misunderstanding, right? I mean, you would never hurt anybody on purpose, right?"

Z looked up at me before sighing. I stood up and watched as he dropped his head before shaking. My heart began to crumble in my chest. I thought Zachary was one of the good ones. I mean, it wasn't like I was attracted to him or anything, but the knowledge that he was an actual kind guy gave me a little hope that there were good people in this world. Now it was shattered. Was everyone just mean, corrupt, self-centered assholes?

I could feel my eyes beginning to burn with tears. Z peaked up at me before he tilted his head to the side. His shoulders began to lightly bounce as a low chuckle filled the space between us. I rapidly blinked away the tears to make sure my eyes weren't deceiving me and sure enough his ass was laughing.

"Addison, you're so naive!"

"W-what?"

"Look at you over there crying because you thought I was so sweet," he spat in a mocking tone. "I don't see how you can do it, but I'm bored with being nice. Oh, and for the record, I did everything he said on my own accord. You see, a man named Manny approached me outside of a club one night while I was working my dead end job as a promoter. He offered me more money than I had ever seen and all the sex that I wanted. Who the hell would turn that kind of offer down, huh?

"All I had to do was go after women like you, Addison. Weak, sweet, and innocent. You were the first to come to my mind, but your ass barely wanted to party. I was still waiting for the moment I caught you slipping because I would have made some stacks on you." Zachary licked his lips as his eyes roamed over me. A seductive smile spread across his face. "Oh, they would have loved you, too. I bet you are super sweet."

Z eyed me up and down before bursting into laughter. Fury rushed through me causing my body to burn with anger. Balling my hands into fists, I cocked them back and threw them into his jaw. Z's head snapped to the side, his mouth filling with blood.

"Shit!" I hissed, shaking my hand. My knuckles were radiating with pain. I had never punched anyone before, and I had no idea it hurt so much.

"Whoa there, tiger! I don't want you hurting your delicate hands on this shit stain." Seojun stated, gently pulling me towards him. "That's why I have these."

He gestured towards the metal table he was leaning on.

"As you can see, everything you need is right here– no need to hurt those tiny fingers."

I examined the table and noticed there were hammers, nails, bob wire, ropes, a nail gun, duct tape, and a metal bat all perfectly lined up. I ran my fingers across the tools before feeling Seojun step next to me. His scent was a mixture of cedarwood, rosemary, and jasmine – strong and sweet at the same time.

"These are just some of my favorite gadgets," Seojun murmured before brushing his thumb over my reddening knuckles.

He was standing so close now, that I could feel his cool breath tickle my ear. A small shiver ran up my spine and I fought the urge to moan. What the hell was wrong with me? This man barely touched my hand, and I was about to climax. I glanced over my shoulder to see Seojun's hooded brown eyes staring down at me. He was about 3 inches taller to my 5'8 height and that only turned me on more. My eyes drifted down to his full lips that had a soft pink and brown under tone. He tucked his bottom lip before a slow smirk began to form. The fact that this man was easily getting me hot and bothered was frustrating as hell.

"Does seeing all of my gadgets do something to you, yeobo?"

"W-what do you mean?" I asked, feeling my body warm.

"I mean, if I were to slip my fingers into your panties, would they be drenched with your essence?"

I briefly closed my eyes and bit down onto my bottom lip. Something was seriously wrong with me because he was right. Punching Z and seeing all of the items that I could hurt him with spread across the table, had me soaked. Was I the type of girl who would enjoy some type of discipline fetish? I mean, I enjoyed watching a bit of porn with that involvement, but I never thought I'd actually get to do it.

I cleared my throat and scooted away from him. I couldn't be thinking about that right now. Desperate to change the subject, I pointed at the table. "Uh, these are just basic items you can get from any hardwood store."

Seojun lightly chuckled and shook his head before he rubbed his thumb across his bottom lip.

"Exactly. I don't have to spend so much money just to have my fun. Besides, I have something special that I like to utilize for my own enjoyment – Tiffany."

I stared at him with an arched brow. "Tiffany?"

He nodded and I wanted to kick myself. Here I was lusting over this man, and he had a whole girlfriend. I should have known better. And fuck him for flirting with me like that knowing damn well he had a girlfriend. I had it in my right mind to tell her what type of man she was dating.

"So, you and your little girlfriend like to tag team bad guys? That's pretty cool. Was she 'my love' in your phone that you left back in Vegas?"

An amused smirk crossed his face as his head slightly tilt to the side. "Addison, yeobo, do I hear a hint of jealousy in your voice?"

"Yes," I shouted in my mind.

"What? No!" I laughed, attempting to cover up my annoyance. "I was…I was just asking, that's all. Besides, I don't think she would appreciate you being here with me, especially if this is y'all's thing."

Seojun threw his head back and laughed. I guess watching me flustered was hilarious to him. I rolled my eyes and continued to look over the items on the table. If he kept on, I was going to chunk one of the hammers at him. I watched as Seojun continued to chuckle as he walked toward an opening on the far left side of the warehouse that was covered up with a hanging plastic liner. He reached behind the curtain and pulled out a long metal bat.

"This, is Tiffany."

"Oh."

"And that phone you found in my house, that you still have, was not mine but Dash's."

"I see."

I could feel my cheeks warm with embarrassment, but at the same time, a small ounce of relief escaped me. I was really getting jealous of a damn bat. I didn't know this damn man but was about to get pissed off if he had a girlfriend. I had the same feeling when I saw that woman rubbing on his arms inside the bar. I don't know what the fuck was going on with me, but I needed to shake this shit off. Seojun was not mine nor was he interested in me. This was strictly business and nothing more.

As Seojun walked back towards me, I examined the bat closely and understood why it was his favorite. I briefly looked over at Z. "Are you going to use Tiffany on him?"

Seojun shrugged one shoulder. "Do you want me to use it or would you like the first swing?"

"Don't you need more information out of him before we start fucking him up?"

Seojun's eyes slightly widened before he burst into laughter. "Let me find out that this sweet innocent act of yours is all a persona and deep down you have a lust for blood."

I chewed on my bottom lip. I had never intentionally hurt anyone, but at the same time, I despised people who knowingly did evil to another person. My sympathy and empathy for why they harmed others was null and void. Hell, Z proved that shit to me. Besides, I literally had a list of people that I wanted to see hurt and I reached out to Seojun to make sure it happened.

"I am nice," I started, taking Tiffany out of his hands. "I just don't like people who take advantage of others to fulfill their sick pleasures."

"Interesting." Seojun stated, his eyes slightly squinting as I held onto his bat. "Tiffany is quite powerful, and I don't want you to get hurt."

I smirked before walking past him and over to Z who was rolling his eyes. He opened his mouth to say something, but I didn't give him a chance. I allowed all of my frustrations and anger take over me as I swung the bat down in between his legs. Adrenaline raced through my body as I watched Z howl out in pain.

I have never been a violent person, but I was tired. Tired of letting people push me around and tired of people thinking they can just man handle or manipulate me without consequences. Dr. Johnston, Bruno, Olivia, and Mr. L — all of them had pushed me to the edge. Yes, I talked big shit and that usually got people out of my face, but lately, it wasn't working anymore. Especially when I was dealing with these ruthless killers. If I was going to survive this trial, then I would need to become ruthless.

Chapter 24

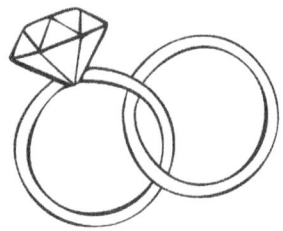

Seojun

Watching Addison slam Tiffany into Z and the way her eyes lit up with all of the tools I had laid out turned me on. I tried with all of my willpower to keep my dick under control while I was so close to her, but the muthafucka had a mind of his own. I've never met a woman like Addison Billingsley. Smart, funny, and had no problem taking matters into her own hands — especially when it came to injustice. It was like she was made specifically for me, but that was the problem. She was going to be a distraction if I got too caught up with her.

I slowly exhaled, blowing out a cloud of smoke. I knew I said I was going to stop smoking weed, but shit, the way Addison had me feeling, I needed it. Her voice echoed through the warehouse as she laughed with Jay. The fact that she wasn't fazed that he was rolling up Z's body in tarp made it that much harder to not like her.

"So let me get this straight, you thought Seojun and Mr. Adalyn were two different people?" Jay laughed out loud.

She playfully rolled her eyes before placing her hands on her wide hips. "Yes, but to be fair, I didn't see his face in that video. Plus, look at him! No one would think that he was capable of slaughtering a man without blinking an eye?"

I huffed out a chuckle. "Funny, I was thinking the same thing about you before you slammed Tiffany into Z's face."

She bit down on her bottom lip before she shrugged. "He was a bad guy."

I nodded, "I don't hurt anybody but bad people, too."

A slow smile spread across her face as she continued to lock eyes with me. Damn it! I just got my damn dick to calm down but now this fool was up and active again.

"Y'all two need some alone time?" Jay asked, staring in between us.

Addison quickly broke our contact before she cleared her throat. "Anyway, I need to head back. I don't want my driver getting suspicious. I've already been gone over an hour."

I nodded in agreement and looked over to my cousin.

"Don't worry big cuz, I'm already on it." Jay said, examining the scalpel he kept in his back pocket.

"Thanks. You be careful, love you kid."

"I'm not a kid anymore, jeez." Jay rolled his eyes before trading the scalpel for a saw out of his bag of tools. I wasn't the only one with favorites. I turned to walk towards the exit, when Jay called after me. "Aye, I love you too. Nice meeting you, Addison. I'm sure I'll be seeing you more."

He waggled his eyebrows before heading towards the back of the warehouse where I kept an industrial meat locker. Addison lightly chuckled before she walked past me towards the exit.

"Your cousin is funny."

"Yeah, a damn comedian."

She giggled some more, and I couldn't help but to smile too. We fell into a comfortable silence as we traveled back through the tunnels. I found myself glancing over at her from the corner of my eyes with every other step. She had me intrigued and I wanted to get to know her more, but that would be a terrible mistake. Did I find her attractive? Hell to the fucking yes, but this was all business. My father told me time and time again that I should never mix business with pleasure. Then again, my deadline to find a wife was approaching fast and the fact that she had Reaper blood in her veins made me want to throw out my father's logic. I shook my head. No, she wouldn't want me. Not in that way.

"So, Seojun, how is it that you own an entire realty company, but put bullets in people's faces like you did Dash and Z?" Addison asked, pulling me out of my thoughts.

"I could ask you the same thing, Ms. Bachelor's Degree Graduate."

She threw her head back and laughed, causing an echo throughout the tunnel.

"You were stalking me, Seojun?"

I huffed out a chuckle, shoving my hands into the front of my hoodie. "Let's just say, I make sure that I do a thorough background on everybody."

"Mmm." she hummed with a quick nod of her head. "Well, with my studies in psychology, I've always been fascinated with the human mind and reasoning behind why people acted the way they did."

"When and how did you become transfixed with that?"

She shrugged one shoulder. "I blame it on my mother. She is selfish and conniving. As I grew up, I couldn't for the life of me figure out why. I mean, my nana and grandpa were the most generous, loving people I knew. Hell, my nana would give you the shirt off her back and cook you a home cooked meal, but her daughter, on the other hand, would never!" She smacked her lips before shaking her head. "She wasn't always like that."

"Oh yeah?"

"Yeah. She used to be really nice up until my ninth birthday when grandpa died. I didn't understand when I was younger, but I found out my grandpa was a very powerful man. I know my mom was the only child and a daddy's girl, so his death must've hit her hard. At the same time, the person who gave her everything she wanted was now gone. So, she chased after wealthy men in hopes of replacing her dad."

"Damn. I'm sorry to hear that, yeobo."

She shrugged. "I'm over it. I'm more concerned with my grandma. She has always been there for me and I owe her everything."

I nodded my head because I understood exactly where she was coming from. Granted, my mom was actually sweet and loving like Addison's grandmother and I would've given her the world if she asked. Unfortunately, she left me and my dad in the middle of the night. She chose drugs over her family but instead of getting clean, she left. It was the most selfish thing she had ever done.

"Anyway, that's how I got into psychology. I wanted to understand my mother. Not in a sense that I wanted her love and affection, but more of what made her make the decisions that she did. Also, I wanted to understand why my sympathy meter was broken."

I gave her a puzzled look. "Your sympathy meter?"

She nodded. "Yup. Sometimes it works, but most of the time, it doesn't. For example, it works when I see people genuinely needing help or who have been hurt. Like, I have no problem with apathy when it comes to my best friend and nana. However, if someone is intentionally evil, like Z, then it's broken. I don't feel any remorse if I or someone else hurts them. Even when he was crying, I didn't feel anything. I say all that to say, I didn't have a problem mashing Tiffany into Z so many times. My broken sympathy meter wouldn't allow me to feel penitent. He deserved it for what he did to all of those men and women."

I smirked as we reached the door the led back into the alley. "I guess my sympathy meter is broken, too."

I opened the door and held out my hand, gently pulling her through. Her foot slipped on an empty beer bottle, causing her to trip. Stepping forward, I caught her in my arms. She stared at my lips and then up into my eyes before she smiled.

"Thanks."

"Any time." I muttered.

I wanted to kiss her. I wanted to feel her full plump lips against mine, either set would do. I've been attracted to a lot of different women in my life, but none of them had anything on Addison. Her delectable vanilla and lavender scent had me ready to explore every curve of her body to see if she tasted as sweet as she smelled.

She cleared her throat and stepped away from me. "I uh, I have to go."

"I knew that was your hoe ass in there!"

I snapped my head to the side and saw a tall yet lanky man storming towards us.

"The fuck. Jerome?!" Addison muttered before pushing off of me and heading towards the man.

I scratched the side of my face as I looked him over. I assumed he was the driver Addison was telling me about earlier, but I thought he'd be more intimidating. He probably didn't weigh no more than a buck fifty and I knew I would tower over him a good foot and a half.

"You should be receiving something in a minute, boss." Jerome said in his phone before tucking it into his back pocket. "You must be out of your damn mind! You have two of the most powerful men who own you and your dumbass out here with this muthafucka. Bruno is going to fuck you up!"

"Jerome, please, it's not what you think –"

Before she could get the words out, Jerome gripped her by the bun on top of her head and yanked, sending Addison to the ground. It took me less than half a step to get in front of him and slip my hand around his throat.

"You must have a death wish," I snarled.

"Fuck. Off. Me." He gasped, clawing at my hands.

I threw him against the wall before kneeling to help Addison up. "Are you okay, yeobo?"

"Y-yeah." She began, but then her eyes began to bulge as she scrambled backward.

I looked over my shoulder to see Jerome heaving with blood trickling down his nose as he pointed his gun at us.

"Get away from her!"

I smirked before I slowly stood up. "Or what?"

"I'll blow your fuckin' head off."

I laughed out loud before I reached out my hand towards Addison. "Come yeobo, let me help you up."

I kept my eyes on the driver as Addison grabbed my hand. While she stood up, I watched as Jerome glared at me, his hand shaking with either nerves or anger. I truly didn't care which because I knew he wasn't going to shoot. Hell, he would've done so by now.

Addison's phone began to chime over and over. "The fuck," she mumbled.

"I think you'd better answer that, Little Bit." Jerome smugly sang.

Addison smacked her lips as I heard her unzip her bag. The side of Jerome's mouth twitched up causing me to squint my eyes. What the fuck was so amusing? A loud gasp expelled from Addison's lips, triggering me to glance over my shoulder. A look of horror was written all over her face as she quickly swiped at her phone.

"What is it?" I asked.

She slowly looked up at me and swallowed before showing me her phone. Her hands slightly shaking as I took it from her. Staring down at a new group chat between Bruno, Jerome, and Boss, I saw a picture of Addison in my arms as the first message.

Chapter 25

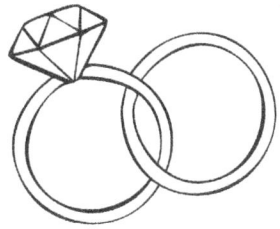

Seojun

The hug between Addison and I was completely innocent, but to any passerby and the way the camera was angled, we were in a passionate embrace.

"You're dead. The both of you!" Jerome chuckled. "I knew you was up to something when you asked for a ride. The fact that you didn't seem the type to go out drinking alone, I figured I needed to double check my suspicion. So, I followed you when Bruno said he was going to pick you up. Imagine my surprise when I saw you walking into the back of the bar with this muthafucka. Best believe I made sure to get everything recorded, too. Well until that old ass man tried to stop me. If he would've just minded his business, he wouldn't be dead."

My eyes squinted as I glared at him. "You only fight old men and women? How fucking pathetic! You didn't have to kill Dylan."

Jerome shrugged. "He knew where y'all went but didn't want to cooperate and let me through. So I pretended to leave and snuck around back. Thankfully, you had him turn those cameras off because he didn't see me sneak up behind him on his cigarette break. Don't worry, I made it quick. Anyway, as soon as I saw your fast ass all hugged up, I took a picture and sent it to my boss. He's going to be thrilled!"

"You dumbass! Mr. L is probably going to kill you for leaving me unattended and not informing Bruno!!" Addison spat.

Jerome threw his head back and laughed. "That broke muthafucka is not my real boss. Mr. Omba is."

"Who the fuck is Mr. Omba?" I asked, my patience growing thin.

"That's Addison's future husband. He's worked with Mr. L for a while, but did not trust him to keep his beautiful untouched wife safe. So, here I am!"

"You yanked me by my hair and threw me to the ground! How the fuck is that keeping me safe?" Addison snarled.

"I'm done with this conversation." Jerome snapped. "Addison, say goodbye to this nigga and I'll escort you back to Bru–"

Before he could finish his sentence, I picked up the bottle that Addison had tripped on with the top of my foot. Kicking it high, I spun and kicked the bottle into Jerome's face. His head dropped back before he fell to the ground unconscious. Not wasting a moment, I grabbed my phone out of my back pocket.

"Jay, I need you to take care of one more item."

"Sure thing. Send the address and I'll handle it."

"No need. I'm outside the door. I'll be there in 2 minutes."

I disconnected the line before walking over to Jerome and throwing him over my shoulder. Addison stared at me with her mouth open.

"Yeobo, listen to me carefully. Take my car and head back to your hotel. Do not stop and chat with anyone, but grab all of your belongings. We don't know how much time we have before any of Mr. L's people try to come after you. I am going to help you, but I need you to do this for me.

I said, pulling my keys out of my back pocket. I pressed the start button to show her my car was just across the street. She exhaled and nodded as she took my keys and headed towards the car.

Chapter 26

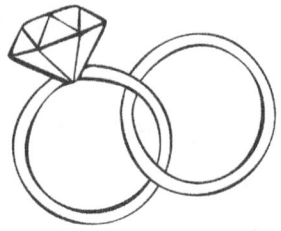

Bruno (a.k.a.) Jackie

I stared down at my phone as I leaned against my car, huffing out a chuckle. I knew Addison was up to something. After spending months with her, there was never a time that she voluntarily went to a bar by herself. She knew better to text Jerome for a ride because he was the new guy and I would've caught on to some bullshit early on. So, I left him there to keep an eye on her while I headed to the airport. I wasn't the least surprised by the pictures he sent. My phone began to ring causing me to quickly answer.

"Jackie, what is going on?" My boss, Mr. Omba, asked.

When I originally abandoned the Jaguars to be with Luther and the Cobras, I thought I was getting a great deal. Luther promised more money and all the pussy I wanted unlike Seojun's strict no fraternizing rules. Imagine my disappointment when all of the women that worked for Seojun disappeared. None of them crossed over which not only pissed me off but damn near everyman that became a Cobra. Luther did provide us women and men to use at our leisure, but we had to pay. If they were the Jaguar women, I wouldn't have minded, but the ones that Luther brought us were bottom of the barrel. I'm talking junkies and old hoes that been ran through more than a public soccer field that doubled as a little league football field.

When Mr. Omba first came around, I couldn't help but admire his work ethics. He was a man of his word and from chatting with a few of his employees during our drops, I liked his work ethics. It took awhile, but he finally gave me a chance to be apart of his crew. Since he didn't know Mr. L very well, he had me making sure all of his purchases and shipments went smoothly. From the outside, they did, but I was there to tell him all of the mishaps that we ran into during the process. Finding Mr. Omba's bride was Luther's last chance to stay in business with us before all ties were cut.

"Sir, things don't seem to be looking good. Mr. L doesn't have a hold on shit out here especially not your future property."

"That picture looked suspicious, but can easily be taken out of context."

I snorted out a laugh. "I agree, but I've been around Addison long enough to know that she doesn't want this deal to go through. So, if that means being a whore to get away from Mr. L, then I wouldn't put anything pass her."

Mr. Omba sighed heavily. "I was hoping things would work out for me. I really liked her."

I rolled my eyes. How the hell this nigga liked her, but only seen her via pictures was beyond me. Addison was a good girl, but she had a nasty mouth on her. Mr.

Omba wanted an obedient wife and she wasn't it. I tried to warn that to him before, but once he saw her picture, he wasn't listening.

"Look," I said, pinching the bridge of my nose. "I won't hold my breath with keeping Addison. If she's already hugged up with some man, it'd only be a matter of time before she's opening her legs for him. Then again, she may surprise us and go with the plan. Either way, I'll keep an eye on her."

I heard Mr. Omba exhale a breath of agreement. I opened my mouth to say something else when I saw Olivia walking out of the airport with her luggage.

"Mr. Omba, I have to go, but I will keep you updated with anything new."

"Good."

The call ended as Olivia stepped up to me.

"What's up Jackie? I mean, Bruno."

I laughed and wrapped my arm around her waist, pulling her closer to me. I leaned down to kiss her when she quickly turned her head and pushed away from me.

"What's your problem?" I asked.

"In what world are we on kissing terms?" she spat, taking a step back.

"The moment you wrapped them thick thighs around my head and let me suck on that fat clit."

She rolled her eyes. "I let you eat me out one drunken night and now you think we go together? Please!"

I chuckled as I flicked my tongue across my bottom lip. "It was more than once, baby."

"One time because you were thanking me for cleaning up your mess and another time because I was drunk. That still doesn't solidify us as being anything more than work associates."

My nostrils flared. I hated when she started talking like this. She had saved my ass when I wasn't able to secure Theron to join the Cobras. Theron was the most loyal to Seojun and wasn't listening to any of us who wanted him to leave the Jaguars. With him trying to stay loyal to Seojun, it was only going to be a matter of time before he told on us. Olivia stepped in by sending him threats against him wife and daughter. It caused so much fear into him that he agreed to join us. To show my gratitude, I sucked on her clit while Luther was on a date with Denice. The second time she let me in between her legs was just a few months back when she found out that Luther wanted Denice as his wife.

"Olivia I know you really love that man, but you need to wake up and smell the fucking bullshit he's been giving you. Luther would never want your ass. He will never love you."

Olivia's eyes furrowed before she reared her hand back and slapped me. She stomped toward the backseat of the car before she slid in, slamming the door behind her. I rubbed my face, still feeling the sting and clenched my jaw. I wanted nothing more than to snatch her ass out of the car, but we were in public and a nigga wasn't trying to catch a case. If she wanted to run after a man that didn't want shit to do with her, then she could have at it.

Chapter 27

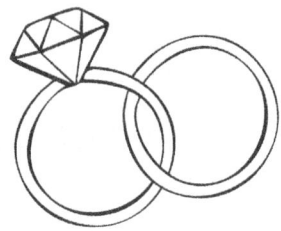

Addison

I was only about fifteen minutes away from my hotel, but it felt like I was being followed. I hadn't received any calls or text messages from Mr. L or Bruno, but that didn't mean they weren't after me. Fucking Jerome! If that nosy bitch boy had minded his business and not tried to be a kiss ass to his boss, then none of this shit would have happened. I slammed my hand down onto the steering wheel in frustration.

"Addison, get it together girl. Seojun is going to help you escape this shit." I said to myself as I pulled into the parking lot of the hotel.

Doing as I was told, I headed straight up to my room, not stopping to speak to anyone. My hands became sleek with sweat as I hopped on the elevator. Seojun said he was sending someone to get me. I wondered who. How would they know how to find me? I pulled out my phone and sent the address and room number to Seojun as I hopped out of the elevator.

Pulling my room key out of my bag, I quickly swiped the card and waited for the green light to pop up indicating the door was unlocked. I was in such a hurry to get into my room that I didn't notice the man coming out of his room that was across the hall from mine. As soon as my door unlocked, I was pushed inside.

"What the fuck?" I shouted, trying to get up, but a foot landed on my back, pressing me back down.

"Addison, baby, where have you been? I've been waiting a few hours for you."

My eyes widened as Dr. Johnston lifted his foot from my bag. I rolled onto my back to see him hovering over me. "W-what are you doing here?"

"Well, you had an appointment for a checkup this evening, but when I came by earlier you weren't here. So I waited until I received an interesting picture from Bruno."

I swallowed as I scooted backwards. "I don't know what you're talking about."

"Spare me, Little Bit. I saw the picture of you and an old colleague of mine looking quite cozy. Bruno tried to find you at the bar but saw that you had already left so he called me. You see, he knew that I had called ahead to ensure your room was close to mine and asked for me to be on the lookout for you. I am going to examine you and if all is still pure, then we won't tell Mr. L. However, if you are not pure," Dr. Johnston licked his lips as he grabbed the front of his pants. "Then I get to finally dip my tongue in between your legs."

"Fuck you!" I spat, scrambling to my feet.

"Oh, I plan on it. Now, let's get those pants off."

Dr. Johnston lunged for me, but I moved to the side, causing him to stumble into the side table. I cocked my hand back and threw a punch into his face and then his groin. He doubled over in pain as he gritted his teeth.

"Fucking bitch!"

As he held onto his dick, groaning in pain, I made a run for it. I reached the door and slightly opened it but was caught by my hair and pulled backward. My head hit the ground, causing my vision to briefly fade. I could feel Dr. Johnston's body fall on top of me as his hands clamped around my throat. Kicking and thrashing underneath him, I tried to break free from his grasp, but was failing.

"I am going to enjoy every minute of this." His raspy voice said as he squeezed harder.

I could feel my head become lightweight compared to how heavy my eyes were. He was going to kill me. A part of me wanted to just accept death with open arms, but I couldn't. I worked too hard and held on to sometimes nothing but a mustard seed of faith and I wasn't about to give up now. I lifted my hands off of his and plunged my thumbs into his sockets as hard as I could.

"Arrgh."

His grip loosened as he attempted to pry my hands from his face. Before I knew it, a large blue vase was floating in the air before it came crashing down onto Dr. Johnston's head. I turned onto my side and coughed, trying to get air into my lunges when a familiar voice called me.

"Addison, girl, I am going to kick your ass."

I looked over my shoulder to see Akira leaning over me, rubbing my back.

I opened my mouth to speak when she quickly shook her head.

"Don't talk. Let's get you some water. Raheem, baby, can you grab me a water bottle."

A small chuckle escaped my lips, causing me to instantly regret it. My throat was raw and on fire. I forgot that my best friend said she was dating one of Seojun's cleaning crew members. Lifting up, I chugged the water as Akira sat next to me, rubbing my back. Looking over her shoulder, I saw a tall buff man with rich coffee skin and a fresh lineup showing off his black coils.

"So, that's Raheem," I asked. "And you were the person supposed to pick me up?"

"Yes that is Raheem, and no, it was only supposed to be him picking you up, but we were on date night. I was going to call and let you know I landed, but me and Heem promised to give each other the full day. Unfortunately, our lonely ass boss doesn't care about that and sent us to pick up his special merchandise." Akira smiled at as she waggled her eyebrows.

"Girl, shut up. Seojun didn't say that."

"Oh, Seojun? Y'all on first name bases, too?"

I playfully rolled my eyes.

"Ladies, we really must be going. I don't know how long this guy is going to be knocked out and Seojun is waiting for us."

I nodded as Akira helped me up. I rushed to the closet and grabbed my suitcase, glad I didn't have time to unpack earlier. I snatched up my toothbrush and scooped all of my makeup back into the bag before heading out the door. Akira and I looked at each other as we hopped onto the elevator while Raheem took the stairs. We had a lot to talk about.

Chapter 28

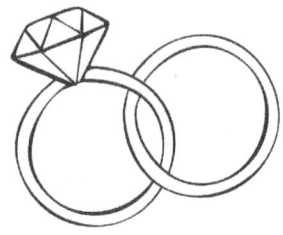

Seojun

Addison paced back-and-forth in the front office I had in the warehouse. I had escorted her here so that we could talk privately while Jerome and Arnez sat tied up with their heads hanging down. I sent Raheem to retrieve Addison for me, only to find out that he took his girlfriend with him. Originally, I was pissed but found out that Akira was Addison's best friend. She not only helped knock out Arnez, but she was actually helping her stay calm until she returned to me.

"What do we do now?" Addison asked, chewing on her thumb nail. "Since that picture was given to the person Mr. L was going to marry me off to, then I'm sure he's going to send his people after us to kill us."

"He's not going to kill us, yeobo."

"What do you mean he's not going to kill us? Look Seojun, I know that you are very powerful and dangerous but so is he. This could be a full out war with a lot casualties."

Walking over to where Addison was pacing, I grabbed her shoulders and made her face me. "Addison, breathe. In through your nose and out through your mouth."

Addison did as she was instructed and I could see her shoulders finally relax.

"Is that better, yeobo?" She briefly nodded her. "Okay, this is what we're going to do. You may have realized, but I don't trust a lot of people and only a handful of people know about this warehouse. Even a smaller number of people know and could've handled what goes on down here. So the fact that you not only know what happens but were a willing participant who actuality enjoyed themselves says a lot to me. So, I'm going to help you, but it's gonna be in a way that might seem unconventional."

Addison's eyebrows pinched together. "What do you mean, unconventional?"

I rubbed my hands together as I took in a breath. "How about you marry me?"

Her mouth hung open as she stared. "What? How does this solve anything?"

"Hear me out, yeobo. We are both in a predicament where we're being forced to marry. You need someone to sustain income for your grandmother while I need to marry someone to appease my father and uphold a deal that was made along time ago. You are the perfect person for me to complete that task."

"How is this different from what I have to do with Mr. L? And what do you mean I am perfect?"

"We both have something to lose. If I don't marry, the rest of my group and family are dead. If you don't secure a substantial amount of cash, you'll find yourself in a deeper hole of debt. From what you were telling me before when it comes to your grandma, you are her only source of income to handle her finances."

She stared down at her hands as she shifted on her feet. "What group? Seojun, who are you really? I mean, you know I'm just a girl in a fucked up situation, but you are a mystery. You come off as being just a businessman, but in reality, you are a killer. How can I go along with this plan when I don't know you? Hell, I might as well go with Mr. L's arrangement."

I tucked my hands into my pocket and sighed. "I used to run a powerful group called the Jaguars until about two years ago. Someone came into my territory and recruited all of my men. They abandoned me and I've been spending the past year hunting them down. When Z was tied up, it was because he helped make that happen. The same with that ass hat over there," I said, pointing at Arnez a.k.a. Dr. Johnston. "My goal has been to get my revenge on everyone who betrayed me and rebuild the Jaguars."

I opened my mouth to tell her about the deal my father made but thought against it. She knew enough for now. I watched as she chewed on her bottom lip, her mind racing with a million thoughts. Addison walked over to the window and looked around, probably hoping to see her best friend, but her and Raheem were still gone handling Jerome. I wanted Addison to help me with Arnez, but we had to get this deal in motion.

"So," she said, crossing her arms across her chest. "How do we do this?"

"Well, we'd only be married temporarily, yeobo. We'll get the marriage certificate and send it to Jerome's boss, which will end the contract between him and Mr. L. Also, because he will cancel the contract, that cancels the payment arrangement you made. Once we're married, you will have the proper income to prove that you can take care of your grandmother. I will add you to my bank accounts and show you as a silent partner in my realtor company. I have plenty of homes on the market, so you can move your grandmother to somewhere safe until we get Mr. L out of the picture."

Addison shook her head. "My nana loves her house. Can't she just stay there and have people watch over her?"

"It'll be safer to move her, but like I said, this will all be temporary. Besides, if she stays there, I can guarantee it would be the first place that Mr. L would go to either find you or hurt her."

"Shit, you're right. Okay, okay, you promise that if we get married, you'll allow me full guardianship of my grandmother? Plus, I can pay off all her debt using your money without retaliation?"

I nodded. "I am a man of my word."

Addison shook her head and sighed. "Well, shit. I guess I don't really have a choice. I mean, I know I have a choice, but this sounds like the best option. The good thing is at least I don't feel weirded out by you and you're not too bad on the eyes."

I threw my head back and laughed. "So you think I'm beautiful, yeobo?"

She laughed and shifted uneasily on her feet, refusing to make eye contact with me. Was my little darling shy?

"Anyway, when do we start? What do we do in the meantime?"

I arched in eyebrow at her before chuckling. "Yeobo, there's no 'in the meantime'. As soon as I handle Arnez, we are heading to my private jet and going to Vegas to a twenty-four hour wedding chapel."

Addison's mouth dropped open. "We're doing this today? T-that's not enough time! I mean, we don't have a marriage license and I don't have a dress." Addison rambled, pacing in my office again.

"Yeobo, yeobo, calm down. Listen, in Vegas you can get your marriage license and go to a chapel within the same day. They also offer 30 days to annul the marriage."

"Do you think we can get this all done within 30 days?" she asked.

I nodded. "Indeed. I only have three people left on my list and then I'll be able to get down to the bottom of who betrayed me those two years ago. Plus, the sooner we get your grandmother in a different and safe location, the better. After you are settled, I'll need to take you down to Texas for a meeting, but that would barely take a day. You win. I win. Easy as pie."

"Pie from scratch isn't that easy to make," Addison scoffed.

"Not if you don't know what you're doing and yeobo, I'm a master chef."

She chuckled before slightly shaking her head. "Well, Seojun, we have a deal."

She extended her hand towards me and a happily accepted it. The softness of her hands had my imagination running wildly in my head. I envisioned her hands moving down my back as I dug deep into her walls. I bet she was a screamer. That thought had my dick jumping.

Not wanting to risk her seeing how turned on I was, I let go of her hand and walked towards the door. "Ready to take care of our mutual friend?"

A wicked smile spread across her face before she practically skipped out of the room. I smirked as I followed behind her. Pulling up a chair, I sat down and watched Addison head over to the metal table in the middle of the room. She didn't tell me everything that Arnez did to her, but when Raheem told me what he walked into when he went to pick Addison up, I assumed the worse. I wanted her to get her revenge first, before I took my turn.

"Dr. Johnston?" Addison called, looking over her shoulder.

He slowly looked up and smiled when his eyes landed on her. "Little Bit. I was starting to think you were going to hide in that room all night."

She laughed before turning to face him. "Now why would I do that? Didn't we have an appointment this evening?"

His smile faltered as he cocked his head to the side. Addison walked over to him until she was standing over him. I arched an eyebrow as I continued to watch her. What was she up to? Placing her hands on both of his shoulders, she stared down at Arnez. My blood began to boil as lust filled his eyes. I began to stand up when Addison hiked up her knee and sent her foot crashing down in between Arnez's legs. She stomped over and over as if she were trying to kill a bug that intrude her space.

"You fucking bitch!" Arnez wailed out in pain.

"Shut the hell up!" Addison screamed, rearing her arm back and elbowing him in the face. Blood gushed out of his nose as his eyes rolled into the back of his head.

I watched on in awe as Addison pulled a knife from her back pocket and walked behind Arnez.

"W-what are doing? Look, I am sorry! I was never going to hurt you."

She scoffed as she grabbed one of his hands and began slicing off his fingers. "Everytime you inappropriately touched me, you were hurting me. If you wasn't tied up right now, you'd probably be doing it again when you forced yourself into my room."

My jaw clenched. "Yeobo, how many times did he hurt you?"

Addison yanked off his pinky finger before tossing it to the ground. Ignoring Arnez cries, I walked up to her and hooked my finger under her chin. Her red tear filled eyes locked with mine. "Once a week for the past five months."

I ran my thumb across her cheek before leaning over and kissing her forehead. Her breath shook as she exhaled a soft sob. Wrapping my arms around her, I held onto her tightly as she cried.

"I'm sorry." I whispered in her hair, running my hand across her back. No one deserved to be hurt that way.

Addison sniffled. "It wasn't your fault."

"It wasn't yours either. "

She looked up at me and smiled. "Thank you."

Wiping away her tears, I nodded. "Now, do you want to finish his fingers or do you want to move onto another body part?"

She smirked before tapping her index finger on her chin. "Hmm. I'll move on. I know Jay likes to chop up things and he can have at it. Then again, I am ready to head to Vegas. Let's end this."

She winked at me before walking back in front of Arnez and jamming the knife into his gut. Blood oozed out of him and onto her hands as she yanked the knife out and stabbed him again.

"Rot in hell you piece of shit."

"Yeobo, accept my early wedding present?"

I pulled out the gun from my waistband and handed it to her. She giggled with glee as she accepted it. Addison kissed me on the cheek before aiming the gun at Arnez's face. She smirked at the tears falling from his eyes before emptying the clip.

Chapter 29

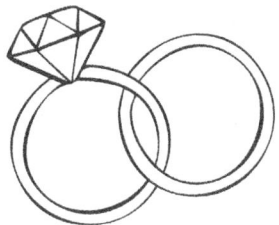

Addison

"I should kick your big headed ass!" Akira snapped, sitting across from me on the jet. "You had not one, but now two marriage arrangements and ain't tell me a damn thing!"

I reached over and grabbed her hands. "I am so sorry, love! I didn't know how to tell you about the shit that I had gotten myself into. My grandmother's bills were stacking up and the offer presented before me seemed like the only option I had. I should have confided in you, though. Hell, you would've slapped some sense into me."

Akira laughed as she ran her thumb across the back of my hand. "Yes, I would have. You know when someone gives me bad vibes, I shut the shit down immediately. Look, I owe you an apology too. I should have told you more about

Raheem and his boss. Granted, I didn't know much about Seojun, but I knew that Mr. Adalyn had no problem helping those in need."

I shook my head. "Girl, please. Nothing was your fault, it was mine. I kept my mouth shut instead of asking for help and got myself in this mess. I'm just grateful that you are by my side now and I can get your advice."

"Yes! Speaking of, you going to let Seojun open them legs tonight?"

I sat back in my seat and chewed on my bottom lip. "Uh, I don't know. If I was being honest, I'm scared. Don't get me wrong, he's fine as fuck and if it wasn't my first time, I would've been let him in."

K nodded. "It's completely understandable that you are scared, but think of it like this. Seojun will be your husband, even if it is only temporarily, but you should tell him what's up. I think he'll be very understanding."

"You think so?"

"Girl, yes! If you don't want to have sex, I'm sure he'd be cool with it. Hell, the man let you use Tiffany and from what I heard, no one is allowed to touch her. He must like you."

I smiled before taking a sip of my wine.

"I-I think I do want to have sex with him." I admitted.

"Like I said, talk to him and if that's what you want, go for it. Plus, he looks like he'll take his time, before he puts you through the headboard."

"Akira!" I shouted in laughter.

"What? It be them quiet ones that be the big freaks."

"Anyway," I said, hurriedly changing the subject. "How long have you been helping Raheem with the real clean up?"

Akira lifted her eyebrows before she nodded with understanding. "Yesterday was only my fourth time. He said he doesn't like me around the violence, but be having my head about to go through the headboard when he see's me fucking somebody up with my butterfly knife."

I burst into laughter. "Okay, see I thought I was tripping, but Seojun was staring at me like he wanted to snatch off my drawls when I was beating up Z."

"He probably did girl! These men are definitely different and when we show that we aren't afraid to be apart of their world, that gets them harder than trigonometry math."

We slapped hands in laughter and continued to talk and sip on wine until we dosed off. It had only been two days and I had been into so much drama that my body finally crashed. After a few hours, the plane landed in Vegas and we were placing our bags in the trunk of a car. I could feel my heart racing. This was it. In just a few hours, I would be married to essentially a stranger, but if I had to choose, I'm glad it was Seojun.

While I slept during the flight, he did everything that he promised. My grandmother and her caregiver were moved into one of his vacant homes and he added me to all of his bank accounts. The mortgage was paid in full and he deposited fifty thousand dollars into Yolanda's account so that she could take care of my nana without worrying about a missed paycheck.

"I'm starving. Let's grab some food," Seojun said, rubbing his stomach.

"Already on it, bossman. There's a barbacoa and shrimp burrito in the limo. Plus, a few street tacos for you, Addison. Akira and I will meet y'all at the chapel."

Seojun nodded and escorted me into the limo. "Good looking out."

"No problem. Oh, Seojun, don't be mean if Addison asks for some of one of those burritos."

Addison looked over her shoulder. "Why you say that?"

Raheem laughed. "Because Seojun's hungry ass don't like to share food."

Seojun threw him the middle finger before we got into the limo. My eyes widened when I saw all of the food sitting inside the car causing my mouth to water. I was grateful that it was mexican food, because I could never say no to some tacos. Seojun grabbed one of the burritos that was the size of a small chihuahua and rubbed his hands together.

"Damn, you going to eat all of that?"

"Hell yeah!"

As soon as Seojun got settled, he snatched the drawls off the burritos and was going in. I had never seen someone so lean and fit be able to eat so much food. Not that I had a problem with that because your girl knew how to throw down on some food, too.

"Here," Seojun said, scooting next to me. "Take a bite."

"You're willing to share your food with me? I assumed you weren't the sharing type after what Raheem said."

"I'm not. I maybe small, but I love food and I hate sharing. Well, except if it's with you. You, I don't mind sharing with."

A smile spread across my face as I leaned over and took a bite. Different flavors and seasonings burst into my mouth, across my taste buds. I closed my eyes and moaned with delight.

"This is the best thing I've ever tasted."

Seojun groaned causing me to open my eyes. He was gripping the burrito so hard, all of the filling damn near fell out. His eyes roamed over my body before staying on my lips causing my body to warm. His stare was so intense and full of desire that it caused my pussy to pulse with need. Seojun reached towards my face and glided his thump across ms the corner of my mouth. My breath quicken as he slipped the same thumb into his mouth, licking off the left over sauce from my face. I swallowed and squeezed my thighs together.

"Enjoy your tacos, yeobo."

Seojun and I got our marriage certificate completed at the county office and were now in the wedding chapel. Standing at the mirror in the bridal's suite, I looked over the dress that Akira had picked out for me. It was a beautiful white strapless wedding gown with lace intertwined down the sleeves. The back had buttons going down the middle of my back to the top of my ass. It was asymmetric and flowed just past my feet, but it wasn't long enough to make me trip. The way this dress hugged my curves while showing off my full breast made me smile.

"Girl, you look fine as fuck!"

I laughed out loud. "Thanks boo."

"Did you put that special gift I gave you on, too?" Akira asked, fixing my hair in the veil.

I huffed out a chuckle before rolling my eyes. "You mean those two thin ass pieces of fabric they call undergarments."

"That lingerie is sexy. When Seojun sees you in it, he won't be able to keep his hands off of you."

I swallowed. "You think so?"

K nodded. "Girl, that man been staring at you since I got here. I don't think he'd care if you had on a tablecloth and flip flops, he still going to want you."

A knock came at the door before the officiant poked her head inside, advising us that everything was ready to go. I hugged my best friend, grateful that she was here with me, and followed them to the chapel. My palms began to sweat as Fortunate by Maxwell began to play. Akira stepped out first as my flower girl and maid of honor. I took a deep breath and stepped around the curtain.

My eyes immediately found Seojun's and my breath got caught in my throat. He looked so handsome in his black on black tailored suit. His long black hair flowed down the middle of his back with his right side tucked behind his ear, showing off those damn gold hoop earrings. I could feel my clit throbbing for him and by the way his eyes roamed up and down my body before a mischievous grin spread across his face. I knew he wanted me too. I briefly closed my eyes and said a quick prayer, hoping that Seojun would be good to me during this temporary agreement.

I exhaled and moved down the aisle towards him. Once I made it to the officiant, Seojun reached out and grabbed my hands as we stood in front of each other. His thumb moved idly across my palms as the officiant began the ceremony.

"I see that the pair wanted to use the traditional vows, is that correct?"

Seojun nodded but then turned to the officiant. "I wanted to say something first."

She nodded as I stared at him in confusion. What was he doing?

"Yeobo, I know how we met was not conventional, but I promise to cherish you while you are by my side. You are my once in a lifetime chance and I refuse to let you slip by. No matter what happens, I pray that you lean on me for comfort, support, and safety."

Tears formed in my eyes as I smiled at him. "I promise to hold you down on your good and worst days. It doesn't matter what may come for us in the future, but I vow to be by your side through thick and thin."

A slow smile crept across Seojun's face as he leaned closer to me.

"Aht, aht, first the rings." The officiant demanded.

We laughed as we placed the rings on one another's fingers. "I now pronounce you Mr. and Mrs. Yi, you may now kiss the bride."

Seojun wrapped his hand around the back of my neck and pulled me closer. His nose brushed mine as he inhaled my scent.

"I am going to devour you, Mrs. Yi." He whispered onto my lips before smashing them to mine.

Chapter 30

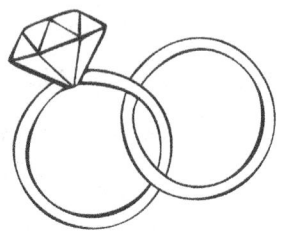

Seojun

Raheem and Akira wanted to celebrate by walking the strip and finding something to eat, but I didn't want to hear any of that bullshit. My meal was standing in front of me with a white dress that I planned on ripping off.

"Well, see y'all later." I said, grabbing Addison's hand and pulling her towards the limo.

"Oop," Akira laughed out loud. "I'll call you in the morning, girl, and we can meet up for brunch. That is, if you can walk."

Addison looked over her shoulder and chuckled before throwing her friend the middle finger. To be fair, K was right. I had been thinking about Addison's body ever since I met her and I hoped she let me have her.

It took less than ten minutes for us to leave the chapel and make it back at the condo I had rented. I jumped out of the car before the driver could and helped my wife out. Addison's eyes lit with excitement as she stood before our temporary two-story modern home. It was a mix of stone and glass giving the exterior a polished look while the subtle lighting along the entrance and balcony created a soft, inviting glow.

"Seojun, this place is amazing." She gushed.

She turned to look at me, but I wasn't paying attention to anything she said. Instead, I scooped her up into my arms and carried her bridal style to our suite. Addison's sweet laugh filled my ears before she pressed her lips to the side of my face. Her soft lips grazed from my jaw to my ear causing me to damn near sprint into the house.

I finally put her down once we made it inside. Wrapping my arms around her waist, I stood behind her and kissed the side of her neck. Addison moaned and rested her head against me.

"Seojun, wait, I have to tell you something."

I stared down at her with concern. Was she okay? Maybe I was moving too fast. I mean, I knew I wanted her, but she probably didn't feel the same way about me.

"I can sleep on the couch if you are not comfortable with me," I stammered, stepping back from her.

Addison lightly chuckled as she turned to face me. "It's not that." She chewed on her bottom lip and exhaled. "It's just that, remember I told you I was...pure."

My eyes widened with realization. How could I have forgotten about that? Hell, it was the main leverage Mr. L used to sell her off in the first place.

"I'm sorry, yeobo. If you are not ready, then we can wait."

She shook her head. "I-I do want you, Seojun." She slowly walked towards me, pulling at my belt. "Just be gentle."

I smiled and smashed my lips against hers. Our tongues moved melodically, and it felt as if I found the person who was meant for me. As our kiss deepened, her hands frantically pulled off my belt before she began unbuttoning my shirt. Pushing my shirt down off my shoulders, Addison stilled. Her hands ran up my chest, her fingers outlining every one of my tattoos.

"Your tattoos are hiding your scars?"

I closed my eyes and exhaled before nodding my head. "I had to train to become a leader and a fighter. Sometimes that involved scare and bruises."

I watched as a frown spread across her face. She continued to examine each of my marks before her hand stopped on my shoulder. Stepping around me, she traced the details of my tattoo.

"This date. I've seen it before."

I stiffened. What did she mean she's seen it before? Looking over my shoulder, I opened my mouth to ask her where she'd seen that date when she spoke.

"October tenth. What does that date mean?"

I briefly exhaled. "It was the day my life fell apart."

Her eyebrows dipped. I could tell she wanted to know more but I didn't want to ruin the mood. That day was traumatic for me and the last thing I wanted to do was talk about it on our wedding night.

Wrapping my hand around her neck, I pulled Addison towards me. I placed my lips against hers and moaned by how soft she was. Her hands roamed down my back before she grabbed a handful of my ass.

"Yeobo, you can't tell me you want me to be gentle when you are being naughty."

She chuckled as her teeth sunk into my jaw, causing me to growl. I spun her around and pulled the fabric of her dress, causing the buttons to fly off.

"Seojun! This dress is a rental," Addison pouted, looking over her shoulder.

"You have ten seconds to get the rest of these clothes off, before I tear it off of you."

"You wouldn't!"

"Ten, nine, eight," I began to count, causing her to run towards the bedroom. Her giggles filled the condo as I reached one and sprinted after her. Reaching our bedroom, I saw her sliding the dress down to her ankles, exposing the white lingerie set she had on.

My mouth salivated as my eyes roamed down her voluptuous body. Her full double D breasts were barely covered up and I could see her hard, pierced, nipples staring back at me. My dick fought in my pants, begging for me to release him. Walking over to Addison, I hooked a finger inside her panties and pulled them off. Her sweet vanilla aroma filled my nostrils, causing me to lick my lips.

"No one has kissed you here, yeobo?" I asked, running my finger up and down her slit.

Her body shuddered as she shook her head. I hummed in delight as I pulled her to me, sliding my tongue into her mouth. She hungrily accepted my tongue as I used one hand to grab a hand full of her ass and the other unhooked her bra. Her bare breast pressed into my chest as I walked us toward the bed. She broke our connection and sat down on top of the comforter.

"Lay back for me." I instructed.

She obeyed. I stared down at her before yanking out of my shirt and climbing on top of her. I kissed her lips and moved down to her neck and then her chest. I set up and pushed her breast together allowing both of her nipple piercings to stare up at me. I dragged my tongue from one nipple to the other before sucking them both into my mouth.

"Oh, my fuck!" Addison moaned, her hand running through my hair.

I smiled before moving my tongue down the rest of her body. My lips grazed her inner thigh before I bit down. Addison moaned out as I wrapped an arm around both of her thighs and spread her open. My eyes bulged as the shinny ball glinting in my face.

"Why yeobo, you have your nipples and a triangle piercing?" I asked, making a circular motion around her piercing with my thumb.

"Y-yes." She squirmed.

"Does pain turn you on?"

She nodded her head. "I just haven't had the chance to try out things I've seen in videos."

"Oh yeah? How about this, tonight, tell me what you want to try first."

"I want you to kiss her." Addison whimpered as I tugged at the ring in between her legs.

I smiled. "Anything for my wife."

Leaning closer, I flicked at her ring with my tongue before sucking her pearl into my mouth. Addison's back arched off the bed as she cried out in pleasure. She tasted so sweet, and I found myself becoming addicted to her flavor with each swipe of my tongue.

"Ahh, shit!" she moaned as I pulled her piercing with my teeth.

I alternated between flicking my tongue and sucking on her pearl. I gingerly glided my finger up her slit and wanted to growl at how wet she was. Her hand grabbed my head, pushing me deeper into her sex and I had no complaints. I could stay in between her legs all day and night. Pushing her legs up and further apart, I dove my tongue into her opening. Addison hissed as she pulled at her nipple rings and thrashed underneath me.

"Se-Seojun. I-I can't." She cried out.

"Yes. You. Can. Baby." I said with each thrust of my tongue. Her legs trembled and I could tell she was about to cum. I groaned. I wanted every single drop of her delectable juice like I was dehydrated. I slipped my tongue out and grabbed her clit again before biting her. A rush of her sweet nectar flooded my mouth, making me roll my eyes in the back of my head. She tried to push my head away, but I held on to her until I got my fill. "Yeobo, that was the best thing I've ever eaten."

She huffed out a giggle as her chest rose up and down. "That was...intense."

"What do you want me to do to you now, yeobo." I hovered over her, cupping each of her breasts before flicking my tongue across each nipple.

"I want to feel you inside of me." She whispered in my ear.

I smiled down at her before lifting off of the bed. I finished unbuckling my pants before allowing them to drop to my feet. I damn near moaned with relief as I released my throbbing dick. Addison's eyes widened as she stared at my naked body. Lifting her hand, she crooked her finger, beckoning me to her.

Moving back on top of her, I rubbed my dick over her wet slit. "Are you ready, baby?"

She nodded as she pulled me down and tasted my lips. Addison moaned as she licked my lips, tasting her own juices. I held onto my shaft and slowly pushed the head inside of her. She hissed before digging her claws into my back. I pushed a little further in, allowing her walls to adjust around me.

"Are you okay, yeobo?"

Addison's eyes were clamped closed, and her mouth was slightly opened. I leaned down and kissed all over her face, but I didn't move any more until she said she was ready. Her pussy was so tight and wet that I was about two minutes from exploding. I felt her body loosen up as she peeked one eye open. Licking her lips, she moved her hips, giving me the signal that she was good.

Without hesitation, I slid in and out of her, biting down on my lip as moans began bubbling in my throat. I would forever be the type of man that moaned for my woman, and I had no shame in it. Besides, Addison felt amazing, and I couldn't hold my groans back even if I wanted to. Her walls had my dick in a tight hold and I only had a few more strokes left in me before I exploded.

"You feel so good, baby" she moaned, wrapping her legs around my waist.

I groaned. "F-fuck, Addison. You're so fucking tight." My strokes became harder, and the sounds of our wetness filled the room.

"Choke me!" She demanded.

Without missing a beat, I wrapped my hand around her throat and lightly squeezed. I wish I had a camera to remember this moment. Addison's face was beautifully contorted with a mixture of pain and pleasure that had my balls tightening. She dug her nails into my back as I pumped harder.

Addison pulled my head down, her lips grazing my ear. "Cum for me, agi."

"Oh, fuck!" I shouted, throwing my head back.

I felt her walls tightening as her screams became louder. She was right there and so was I. I leaned my head down and bit down on her nipple causing a rush of her essences to cover my dick. My eyes rolled into the back of my head as my dick pulsed. I erupted inside of her. What has this woman done to me?

Chapter 31

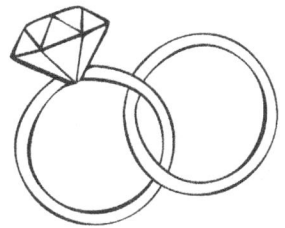

Addison

I stared down at my plate of food and smiled. Akira and I had met up for brunch while Seojun and Raheem went to got the jet ready for us to head back to Philly. Even though my best friend was talking, my mind was on my new husband. My body was sore, but everything felt so good last night that I didn't even care about the pain. This feeling I had for Seojun felt surreal and if I were being honest, it scared me. How could I fall for someone that I just met? What if I didn't want this marriage to just be temporary?

"Okay bitch, you're gonna stop cheesing over them damn eggs and tell me what the hell happened last night." Akira said, taking a sip of her mimosa.

I shook my head and bit the inside of my jaw to stop myself from grinning again. "Oh, nothing."

"Girl don't play. Don't nobody be walking around smiling like that unless they got some."

I smirked, playfully tilting my head to the side. Akira squinted her eyes for a brief moment before realization hit her. We burst into laughter as I waggled my eyebrows.

"What did you expect? It was my wedding night after all." I cooed, taking a sip of my drink.

"Well, give me the tea! How did it go? Did it hurt or did you enjoy it? Your freaky ass probably enjoyed all that pain, too." Akira rambled.

"It was everything you could imagine. He ate me out until I came so hard that I was seeing stars. Then when he put that huge dick of his inside of me, I swear he was ripping me apart. It hurt so bad yet so good. It was amazing. We fell asleep in each other's arms and he woke me up with his mouth sucking on my toes."

Akira fanned herself. "Oh, he a freak freak. Get it then, bestie!"

As we continued to laugh and joke, I saw my phone vibrating with a facetime call from Cindy.

"Hey!" Cindy sang out with Sandy behind her waving frantically. "Hold up, is that Akira with you?"

I shifted my phone, allowing K to wave at the pair. "Hey, ladies!"

"Where are yall?" Cindy asked, scrunching up her eyebrows.

"Oh, we uh, we're in Vegas."

"Vegas?" Cindy and Sandy shouted together. "What the heck are you doing back there? I thought you were in Philly to visit your grandma."

"It was a spare of the moment type of thing," Akira chimed in.

The pair stared at us and waited for an explanation. A part of me didn't want to tell them anything, but I couldn't figure out why. Cindy, Sandy, Akira, and I have been really good friends for months and we always told each other everything. Well, with the exception of my prior arranged marriage with Mr. L.

I sighed. "Long story short, I got married."

The pair stared at me in disbelief before they burst out into laughter. "Good one, Addy, but seriously, what's going on?"

Rolling my eyes, I took out the marriage certificate with me and Seojun's name on it. Cindy and Sandy's eyes grew wide. I heard the sound of someone taking a picture before the line disconnected. What the hell was that? Before I could ask, someone had grabbed my arm and yanked me out of my seat.

"Seojun?"

"How the fuck do you know Cindy and Sandy?"

My eyebrows furrowed as I turned to look at Akira. Raheem had a grip on her arm too.

"Addison, don't make me ask you again." Seojun said through gritted teeth.

"T-they are my friends I met in school. Seojun, you are hurting my arm!"

His nostrils flared as his voice lowered into a growl. "I am going to do far worse than hurt your fucking arm. You betrayed me!"

"What?'

Ignoring me, Seojun dropped my arm. "I should've known your ass was too good to be true. Here I was thinking I found someone I could see myself with for the long haul and the whole time she's been backstabbing me."

"Seojun, what the fuck are you talking about?" I shouted, throwing my hands on my hips.

"It doesn't matter," he continued, ignoring me. "This shit was only temporary. Hell, the only reason I chose you was because you have Reaper blood. If your grandfather hadn't been the former leader and my dad hadn't made a deal with him, then your ass wouldn't even be here."

"W-what?"

That's what my grandmother was trying to tell me when she was telling me about grandpa Ernest. Throughout my life, I heard bits and pieces of the Reapers, but I would have never thought my family would be involved. Even with this new knowledge, it made my heart plummet that Seojun only wanted me because of a deal. Balling my hands into fists, I lifted my chin.

"And I only married you to pay off my grandmother's debt. I guess we're both even."

Seojun's nostrils flared as he glared down at me. "Raheem, get my wife and her friend on the plane. I'll be there in a moment." He ordered with disdain.

I opened my mouth to say something, but Seojun turned on his heels and left me standing there. I didn't understand what was happening and the fact that Seojun wasn't talking was pissing me off. The moment he saw me talking to Cindy and Sandy, he flipped out, but why? How did he know them and why was speaking to them a problem? I had so many more questions, but I obviously wasn't getting any answers at the moment. Maybe when we all got on the plane, Seojun and I could talk in private so we could get down to the bottom of this issue.

After gathering our bags, Raheem got us back to the plane. I had hoped to see Seojun at some point, but the entire ride back to Philly, he was nowhere to be found. Hell, even Raheem wasn't speaking to Akira. I know I was upset, but Akira was more vocal about her anger.

"We'll be landing in fifteen minutes," Raheem said, walking past us.

"Bet! So you have fifteen minutes to tell me what the fuck is going on before I lay my hands on you." Akira spat.

Raheem looked back at her which caused her to look him up and down before she stood and got into a fighting stance. Raheem sighed with a shake of his head before going back towards the front of the plane.

"Scary hoe." Akira shouted, plopping into her seat. "This shit is stupid. How are they going to be mad, but not tell us why they mad?"

"Right! The whole situation is bullshit, but apparently, there is nothing we can do until Seojun explains what's going on."

Akira frowned as she reached over and grabbed my hands. "Love I am sorry about all of this. You gave yourself to that man and now he's acting like...this!"

I gave her a tight grin. "It's not your fault K. Seojun needs to be a man and come talk to me. That's all to it. Maybe he used to date either Cindy or Sandy? I mean, why else would he flip out like that?"

Akira shook her head as she crossed her hands over her chest. If Seojun thought he could treat me like the scum on his shoe, then he was sadly mistaken.

Chapter 32

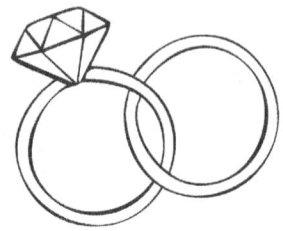

Luther

"Stupid bitch!" I shouted as Bruno's phone shattered across the floor.

"Damn bruh! You had to throw my phone?" he grumbled, walking over to inspect the damage.

"Shut your bitch ass up! If you hadn't lost Addison's ass the other night, she would still be right here! Now, she's fucking married — to Seojun, of all people!"

"The shit is wild!" X replied, running his hand down his beard.

"Fuck! This bitch has fucked up my money."

I paced back and forth in my office. I was finishing up with the contract for Mr. Omba when I was blindsided with two text messages. First, Mr. Omba sends me a picture of Addison and some man hugged up. Then Sandy sends me a picture of Addison holding up her marriage certificate. I should've known her ass was up to something. As soon as I told her that her freedom was just about up, her ass does some dumb shit like this.

My text notifications were going off, causing me to stomp to my desk and snatch up my phone.

"Fuck!"

"What's up?" Olivia asked, staring at me with confusion.

I briefly closed my eyes before opening the message; I knew this shit was coming but hoped that it didn't.

Mr. Omba: Consider our contract null and void. Also, I will no longer continue my business with you and Ms. K.

I felt my stomach begin to knot.

Me: Hold on, Mr. Omba. We have been in business together for years. Are we going to throw that away over one woman? I can get you somebody else!

My heart hammered against my chest as I waited for his response. Mr. Omba was our only client and that was the majority of our income. I mean, yeah, we had the brothel houses, and I kept a few of Seojun's massage parlors opened, but they weren't making us anywhere close to the same amount of money as me shipping people to Mr. Omba. All of the women, with the exception of Cindy and Sandy, that used to work for Seojun were in hiding under a fake name. So, the women and men I had as their replacements weren't bringing in as nearly as much revenue. Hell, I wouldn't be able to run the Cobras with that small set of income. To be honest, I didn't understand how Seojun was able to have all of that money and was able to pay his workers.

Mr. Omba: Luther, I was only giving you a courtesy text message before I spoke with Ms. K, but my decision is final.

I tried to reply back, but the text message didn't go through, indicating that he blocked me. Rage boiled throughout my body. Addison landed three days ago, and all hell had broken loose.

"What happened?" Olivia asked, rubbing my back.

I shrugged her off of me. "Fucking Addison! She went and got married and somehow her buyer found out. He just ended his contract."

"What the fuck?" Xavier spat, crossing his arms. "How the hell did he even find out? Cindy and Sandy sent the picture in our private group chat."

Olivia glared at Bruno as she pointed her finger at him. "We were all here together except for you Bruno." She looked up at me. "I don't know baby. Something seems a bit fishy."

Bruno's eye shot daggers at Olivia, but I could see the hint of terror behind them. I stared at him waiting for a response, but it never came. A dead giveaway that he was guilty. Allowing the rage to take over me, I pulled my gun out of my top drawer and shot him in the stomach. He flew back and hit the ground causing Xavier to jump up off of the couch. Bruno held onto his abdomen, dark blood oozing between his fingers as he cursed.

"You and Jerome's bitch ass had one damn job. Keep Addison's ass in line and don't let another nigga in her face. Not only did you two fail, but now her bitch ass is married. I let you slide before Bruno when Addison was sneaking out with her friend to work, but I don't do second chances. I for damn sure don't do rats in the Cobras."

Bruno coughed up blood as he laughed hysterically. "Mr. Omba knew he couldn't trust you. The moment I saw that picture and marriage certificate, I made sure he saw it. I may not have agreed with Seojun's rules, but at least he wasn't a slimy low down bitch nigga like you."

I scoffed before putting another bullet in between his eyes. Olivia shook her head as she spit on Bruno's body before lighting a blunt. I opened the call log on my phone and dialed Mama K's number.

"What do we do?" I asked when she picked up.

"I'm thinking! This Addison bitch has royally fucked us! I've been working on this damn plan for years. Ever since my brother turned me down to run the damn Jaguars, I've been working to get rid of all of them. Screw it! I'm boarding the plane and will be down there in a few hours. Get all of your men together and we'll slaughter them all."

Chapter 33

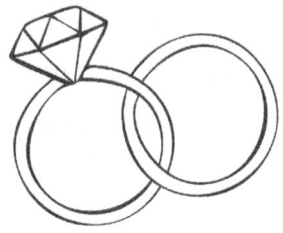

Mama K (a.k.a.) Kim

I never wanted to be Ayzo's mom until my brother officially welcomed him into the Jaguars. I thought with him having his foot in the door, he'd allow me access to the power. I tried to be in with the Jaguar's through my brother, but he didn't want me or his wife apart of that life. He used to bitch that it was too dangerous, and we'd could get hurt. I mean, for his wife, yes. She was fragile and easily manipulated. Hell, it was her biggest flaw that got her caught up as being a damn junkie.

I, on the other hand, was strong and my brother knew that. Did my strong leadership skills and ability to physically protect myself help me prove that I could be a Jaguar? Nope. I despised my brother for it, but heavily trusted Ayzo to get me in. So, imagine my disappointment and anger when he started complaining that he didn't want to be a Jaguar anymore. My son was soft, just like his damn dad and that pissed me off.

I thought my chances to become a Jaguar was ruined until I met Luther. He was a crucial key to my master plan, but he spent the first few years of his life with deadbeat parents. Thankfully, I took him under my wing when I found him. His father, T, didn't give a damn about him and his mother was dead. I was the only mother figure in his life and was going to use that to my advantage.

I made a deal with T that he could keep his son so that he could learn a bit about the streets. Luther did petty jobs here and there while I taught him the ins and outs of being a leader. I made sure he knew about his past which fueled his anger and motivated him to stick with my plan to get our revenge. Now, everything was messed up all because of that little bitch, Addison. My phone began to ring causing me to roll my eyes.

"What is it, Delilah?"

"Where's the rest of my money?"

"Bitch, don't call me with no stupid shit. I told you, once Addison was shipped out, then you'd get your money. However, it seems like your daughter has fucked that all up."

"What are you talking about?"

"Well, it seems like she married the ex leader of the Jaguars."

"What? How the fuck did she know about the Jaguars and their deal with the Reapers? I never told her shit, and my mom is too senile to remember the agreement my dad made all of those years ago."

"How the fuck should I know?"

Delilah exhaled a heavy sigh. "Look, at the end of the day, I held up my end of the bargain. I told y'all about the Reapers and where to find Addison. Just because she fucked it up for yall, doesn't mean shit to me. I still need my money."

I looked at my phone in disgust. Okay, so maybe it was her idea to go after her daughter, but right now that didn't mean shit. I didn't tell her to spill out her frustrations about her dad with me a few years ago at a bar. You see, her mother was just diagnosed with dementia and her father was already deceased. Delilah explained to me that she was under the impression that her mother was still in charge of the Reapers and she would eventually take over once her sickness became worse. Unfortunately, she later learned that wasn't the case.

She found out that her father had left the Reapers with someone else. I remembered comforting her because I could understand her frustration. I was damn near in the same boat. However, when I learned that her dad decided to pass down the group to a new powerful man up north, my interest was peaked. At the time, there was only one man who was running the north. I couldn't help but smile when she said that it was no one other than my brother, Chul-Moo, that had taken over. At that moment, the wheels in my head were in motion and my plan was being formed.

I would use Luther to officially get rid of the Jaguars which would ultimately get rid of the Reapers. However, in order to complete that task, we would need start up money. A lot of it. We were already working with Mr. Omba, so the fact that he wanted a untouched bride for himself, was the icing on the cake. So, Delilah agreed to give us her daughter's location who was still a virgin as long as she got a cut of the money. I texted Olivia to check out Addison's school and to be on the look out. I didn't exactly trust Delilah. Thankfully she was telling the truth and we found Addison. Unfortunately for her, her daughter ruined the plan.

"Delilah, get your bitch ass off of my phone. The deal is off. I'm not paying you shit and if you have a problem with that, then I'm heading to Philly now and we can solve it."

With that, I hung up the phone.

Chapter 34

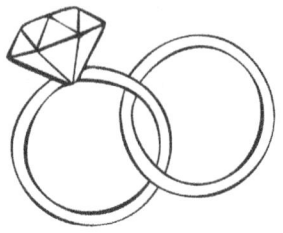

Seojun

I stared between Ayzo, Denice, and Jay and waited for their response. I had just informed them everything that has happened and why I had Addison and her friend tied up in the warehouse. To see her on the phone with Cindy and Sandy had my anger boiling all over again. I thought Addison was different. I mean, being around her had me feeling a way that I hadn't before. Even though we married out of convenience, I felt that we could make us work. I don't know if it was love or lust, but either way, I wanted her to stick around. Unfortunately, she betrayed me.

"Let me get this straight.' Denice began. "You think Addison is helping whoever set you up all those years ago?"

I nodded. "She was talking to Sandy and Cindy, who used to work for me." I stated before hopping out of my seat. "Now that I think about it, Cindy and Sandy are probably June and Tiny."

Ayzo cocked his head to the side before he nodded in agreement. "That makes so much sense! They were the only women on your payroll that you fired. They must've been the first ones to go over to the Cobras. They knew everything that happened around the Jaguars. Hell, you remember how they use to get down. They had men eating out the palm of their hands and could have easily persuaded them to jump ship."

"Shit! You are right! We can send them a message from Addison's phone to setup a trap."

Denice cleared her throat as she shifted in her chair. "Again, I ask, how is it that Addison is tied up in the warehouse? From what y'all are telling me, it doesn't sound like she even knew what was going on. Hell, this Mr. L person sounds like the you should be looking in to.. Maybe he's the one that set all this shit up."

Ayzo sat down next to Denice. "How is that, love?"

"Well, think about it. Didn't Addison say that Mr. L used to make her have mandatory doctor's visits with Dr. Johnston to make sure she is still pure."

I nodded.

"Isn't Dr. Johnston also Arnez? Coincidence?"

My mouth opened then closed. Damn, I hadn't even thought about that.

"Well, hot damn." Jay said, with arched brows.

"My baby smart!" Ayzo shouted, grabbing her face and planting kisses on her lips.

"Now we need to find out who Mr. L is. Maybe my yeobo will know more than what she is saying." I stated, cracking my knuckles.

"Seojun? Don't hurt her," Denice called after me.

I scrunched up my nose and stared at her. "She may have still betrayed me. I don't tolerate disloyalty."

"I understand that, but if she's telling the truth, the last thing you want to do is hurt her to the point that she can't forgive you."

"My baby is right cuzo. Go in there with a bit of optimism for your wife. Plus, if it wasn't for her you wouldn't have been able to hold up your end of the bargain with the Reapers."

I rubbed my chin. I am grateful that Addison agreed to marry me which helped keep the agreement with the Reapers valid. I didn't understand why we needed the Reapers before but began to understand as I got older. Merging the Jaguars and the Reapers was a smart move between the north and the south. With the Reapers and the Jaguars joining forces, we benefited off of shared power and unity making everyone's lives easier. Our connection ensured that no one could step in and try to dominate us.

However, with all of the years not keeping up with the bargain, it all seemed to crumble. I wasn't focused on keeping us strong, but instead worried about sustaining our image and keeping the cash flowing effortlessly. It was inevitable that we'd be attacked. it just hurt more when we were attacked from the inside. We were divided and eventually both groups dissolved. Meeting Addison and making her my wife, knowing she had Reaper blood, was going to rebuild the groups. Now, I'm afraid that was only going to be short lived.

If Addison truly betrayed me, then I would torture her before I ended her life. I would make her suffer for giving me false hope for restoring the Jaguars and all of the hard work my father endured to get us out of poverty. For the false hope of finding someone who understood me and potentially finding love. I mean, I didn't love her at the moment, but i could see myself falling for her the more time we spent together.

I nodded at everyone and walked through the tunnels down into the warehouse. Addison sat with her head hung down while her friend Akira cursed and yelled for someone to come out to them.

"Stop all that yelling," Raheem said, coming out of the meat locker.

"Fuck you, Heem! How dare you tie me up in this damn chair like I'm your enemy. Is that it now, Heem? You think that I am your enemy. After everything we've been through together? After I let you have me in my most vulnerable state?"

A look of guilt washed over Raheem's face before he made eye contact with me. I slightly held up my hand, motioning him to stand down.

"Until we get to the bottom of all this confusion, you two are staying in the chairs." I said, walking closer to the pair.

Addison's head lifted up and a maniacal smile spread across her face. "Seojun, when I get out of this chair, I am going to fuck you up."

"Is that right, yeobo?" I asked, hovering over her.

"Yes! Because you know I had nothing to do with you and your group being setup."

"Then who is Mr. L?" I asked, walking over to the metal table and picking up robe.

"The man who tried to sell me. Hell, he never told me what the L stood for. All I know is, he has a financial advisory business just outside of downtown. He also owns a massage parlor that doubles as a brothel house in Vegas."

I arched an eyebrow and pulled out my phone. The massage parlor sounded like the one I used to own, but I wanted to be sure.

"I am going to have Ayzo look into that. If you are lying, yeobo, then you and your friend are dead."

Addison rolled her eyes. "And when you find out I was telling you the truth, then you owe me!"

I smiled down at her as I texted Ayzo and waited for him to respond. Addison and I continued to stare at one another and I had to admit, I liked her boldness. She wasn't crying or pleading for me to not kill them. I learned to realize a lot of guilty people did that, but not her. Was she telling me the truth?

My phone began to ring, breaking my eye contact. Ayzo was calling me on FaceTime. With a confused expression, I answered the phone.

"Why didn't you just text back?" I asked.

"Fuck all that! You are not going to believe what I just found."

My heart hammered in my chest as I held my breath. I prayed that Ayzo wasn't confirming my suspicions."

"I can't believe that son of a bitch!" Denice yelled in the background.

My eyebrows scrunched together. "What is going on?"

"Mr. L is Luther Jones. Denice and I grew up with him in Chicago. He used to hang out with T and his people. When Cindy and Sandy got fired from your establishment, they must've went to Luther who was in the beginning stages of the Cobras."

I looked down at Addison who was still staring at me. "Tell me again how you got involved with Mr. L."

She rolled her eyes and dropped her head back. "I told you all of this already!"

"Amuse me."

She lifted her head and sighed. "Where do you want me to start? From the day that we met?"

I shook my head. "From the beginning."

"A few months back, I was sitting on a bench outside on campus crying because I didn't have the funds to pay for my nana's bills when this woman approached me and told me about Mr. L."

"Wait," I said, arching a brow. "What woman?"

Addison stared at me in confusion. "I don't think that matters. I mean, I'm pretty sure she worked for-"

"Yeobo, please. What woman?"

"Her name was Olivia, but I don't know her last name."

"You've got to be shitting me." Ayzo said on the other line.

"Turn the camera around so I can ask her something," Denice ordered.

I did as she asked and saw Addison's eye widening as she stared into the camera.

"Ayzo?"

"Oh, I forgot to tell you, Addison but Ayzo is my cousin." I said nonchalantly.

"We'll talk about that later," Denice said. "Addison, this Olivia, was she a Latina woman with curves for days and a fucked up attitude?"

A look of shock flashed across Ayzo's and Addison's face. Ayzo opened his mouth, but Addison had beat him to it.

"H-how did you know?"

"Olivia is my foster sister."

"Get the fuck out of here!" Ayzo shouted. "Olivia is Nicholas's ex-girlfriend that had him setup a couple of years back."

"Small fucking world," I said, rubbing my chin. "So, let me get this straight. Denice, Olivia was your foster sister when you lived back in Chicago?"

She nodded her head. "Yes. Ayzo, baby, you never met her because she had left with Luther and Xavier that night me and you hung out. About the time they all came back, you were already gone."

Ayzo shook his head. "Not quite. I mean, I had slipped out of your window, but got into it with Luther. Xavier was in the house fucking with Olivia again, but they never mentioned her name. If they had, it would have rung a bell when I moved to Philly. I had just met Nicholas and he was dating Olivia's ass up until the day-"

"Everyone turned their backs on me!" I shouted. "That was the day me and you went into hiding. I remember because you were trying to go back for Nicholas, but he was in the hospital."

All the pieces were falling into place, but the only thing I couldn't figure out was why this Luther character wanted smoke with me. I know him and my cousin had got into it over Denice, but by that time, Ayzo had long since left the Jaguars. Olivia was the common denominator, but again, what did she have to do with all of this? Her roll seemed more like the obedient girlfriend. What was I missing?

I looked down at Addison who was giving me a puzzled look. I swallowed my guilt and waved Raheem over. Throughout all of this drama, there was one thing for certain. Addison and Akira were innocent. I nodded my head at Raheem, indicating he could untie Akira. As soon as he did, she balled her fist and punched him.

"I told you we weren't involved in yall drama!" She shouted, continuing to hit him.

"Baby, wait." Raheem pled, but she wasn't listening.

"And you!" Akira shouted, pointing her finger at me. "How dare you treat my best friend like some gutta rat off the street."

She ran toward me with her fist in the air, but Raheem grabbed her before she could take a swing. He slung her over his shoulder and headed out of the warehouse, her curses still bouncing off of the walls.

"Ayzo, grab everybody and meet me outside the warehouse. We are going to end this shit tonight."

"Bet."

I disconnected the line and found my eyes colliding with fiery brown ones.

"Agi, untie me from this damn chair."

I walked over to her and kissed her forehead. "Yeobo, I am sorry. I just had to be sure."

"Untie me, now."

Doing as I was told, I untied her. I opened my mouth to apologize, but she slapped me.

"You should have believed me. Now you have to be punished."

Chapter 35

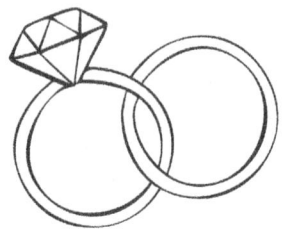

Addison

I pushed Seojun down into the chair and slapped him across the face again. I was pissed off that he didn't bother to hear me out, but instead found me guilty. It literally took three other people to show him how I wasn't involved with the bullshit Mr. L or Luther was into.

"You know, nampyeon (husband), if you expect this marriage to work, then you are going to have to learn to trust me."

A smirk spread across his face. "So, you are really learning Korean?"

"I wanted to surprise you. You have done so much for me and my family and I wanted to show my gratitude. Well, that's what I wanted to do before; but now, all I want to do is discipline you."

Seojun's dick jumped, causing me to bite down on my bottom lip. I straddled his lap and grabbed a handful of his hair before yanking it back. He hissed out a pain, but I cut it short by wrapping my hand around his throat.

"You have been a bad boy. You didn't believe your wife and tied her up! You yelled at me and said some very hurtful things."

"Baby, I'm sorr-"

"Did you mean everything that you said? Do you really only want me because my grandfather was the former leader of the Reapers?"

His eyebrows dipped. When he didn't answer right away, my hand tightened around his throat.

"N-no." he gasped.

I loosen my hold and stared down at him. "Then why did you say that bullshit to me after the wonderful night we had?"

Seojun dropped his head, pressing his forehead against mine. I briefly closed my eyes and inhaled his masculine scent.

"I was blinded by anger with the mere thought that you may have betrayed me, too."

I pushed him back and stood up. "Explain."

He sighed. "I have never been the one to show my emotions, but I have a feeling that if I don't show you my vulnerability, then I'd lose you. So, bare with me."

I tapped my foot and waited as he took in several deep breaths. I wanted to run and wrap my arms around him, but I needed to show him that he couldn't treat me anyway without consequences.

"Losing the one thing that I thought gave me purpose hit me hard. Over fifty men that I thought I could trust with my life, fucked me over and it hurt. Then, I met you. I didn't expect to fall for you so fast, but I did. You are so beautiful, smart, and just as crazy as I am. It was like you were made specifically for me. So, to even have a small possibility that you turned your back on me, too, crushed me. I was angry at the thought of losing you, Addison."

My heart raced as my hands fidgeted together. "Why didn't you just talk to me? You talked at me and accused me instead of allowing me to explain myself."

His chin dropped towards his chest. "I know and there are no excuses for me to shut you out like that. I am sorry. If you give me another chance, I promise to never hurt you like that again."

I exhaled a long breath as I paced behind his chair.

"I wouldn't blame you if you didn't forgive me. I've been a horrible man and have done some terrible things throughout my life. Screwing up the one chance of connecting with someone was inevitable. Why should someone like me deserve a woman like you, yeobo Addison?"

I threw my hand over my mouth as a sob tried to escape. Of course I was still pissed off at him, but all of this was new for the both of us. I wanted this to work and from Seojun's actions, I could tell he did, too. Still, he had to be punished.

"Stick out your tongue!" I demanded, standing in front of him.

Lust filled Seojun's eyes as he did what he was told. I leaned down and sucked on his tongue, letting a moan to escape from me. Seojun's hands roamed up my back, which I stopped, pushing him away. I stood up straight and walked over to the table.

"I didn't give you permission to touch me."

"Yeobo, I'm sorry." Seojun pouted, reaching out to me, but I slapped his hands away.

I grabbed the rope off the table and tied his hands behind his back. Repositioning myself in front of him, again, I pulled my panties down. Seojun seductively stared up at me as I pulled his head back. I leaned down and spit into his mouth before dipping my tongue inside.

"Eat up," I whispered on his lips before lifting my leg and thrusting my pussy into his face.

I threw my head back with the first swipe of Seojun's tongue. I gripped his head and held him in place as I tried to smother him. His teeth pulled at my piercing, and I exploded all over his face.

I dropped my leg and knelt down before him, loosened his pants, and pulled out his hard dick. I licked my lips and kissed the tip of his head before dragging my teeth down his shaft.

"Yeobo, why are you teasing me." He hissed.

"Do you think you deserve to cum?" I asked, dragging my tongue down his shaft. I took him into my mouth as much as I could while keeping my tongue flat like how the girls did in the videos I watched. I gagged, causing my spit to coat his dick and balls.

"Please," Seojun moaned. "I promise to trust you."

"Hmmm," I said, standing up. "I don't know if I believe you yet."

I turned around and bent over in front of him, lining my opening with the tip of his dick. I slowly sat down, allowing him to painfully fill me up before abruptly standing up. I repeated the motion a few more times, enjoying the way Seojun cursed under his breath.

"Fuck!" he groaned. "Addison, I can't take much more of this torture."

I laughed. I didn't care if he couldn't handle it because he was going to take it. I started to bounce on his dick, pretending I was twerking to one of my favorite songs. Dropping my hips, I grinded on him and it felt like his dick was punching the bottom of my stomach. I stood up and straddled his lap again, this time facing him. I continued my same movements and watched as Seojun's eyes rolled to the back of his head.

"Eyes on me!" I snapped, slapping him across the face.

He rapidly blinked before looking into my eyes, his cheek turning a deep pink. I leaned over and bit onto his lip before trailing my tongue across it.

"You hurt my feelings. How do you expect this marriage to work if you don't believe or trust me?" I asked.

"You don't want this to be temporary?"

I ran my hands through his hair and stared into his warm honey brown eyes before shaking my head. Seojun closed his eyes and exhaled a shaky breath.

"Please, yeobo, untie me."

I leaned over and freed his hands. Seojun instantly wrapped me up into his arms before kissing me slow and deep. Our tongues danced with each other and at the moment, I could tell we wanted the same thing. This wasn't going to be temporary but something we wanted for the long haul.

Before I had a chance to catch my breath, he slightly lifted me up before slamming me onto his lap, his dick burying deep inside of me. A loud scream spilled from my lips as I held on to his shoulders.

"You. Are. Mine." Seojun gritted with each thrust of his hips. "Do you understand?"

I whimpered and nodded my head, but Seojun slapped my ass and shook his head.

"Use your words, yeobo." He demanded, fucking me harder. I threw my head back as my breasts bounced in his face. Seojun leaned down and bit my nipple. "I asked you a question."

"Y-yes." I stammered, feeling my stomach quiver. "Yes, agi I understand. I'm yours!"

My legs shook as I felt my climax reach the final peak. My juices rushed down onto his dick, and Seojun cursed from pleasure. His hold tightened around my waist as he thrusted one final time, erupting inside of me. His dick pulsated within my walls as we held onto each other. I was Mrs. Seojun Yi and I wasn't going anywhere.

Chapter 36

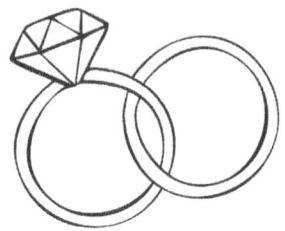

Seojun

I stared down at my trunk and nodded my head with approval. After we figured out that Luther was the culprit behind the Jaguar's fall, Jay loaded up our vehicles with everything to prepare for war. I didn't personally know the man, but he came after what was mine and he was willing to ship off my wife for a profit. He had to pay for his crimes and tonight was the night we ended all of this bullshit.

"Everyone is locked and loaded," Jay said, standing to my left.

"Whatever happens, I'll be by your side." Addison whispered in my right ear.

I looked down at her and planted my lips against hers before escorting her inside the car, motioning for Raheem to follow us. As Jay drove us through the streets of Philly, I couldn't help but feel my anxiety swarm throughout my core.

After these past two years, I was finally about to end all of this drama. I was at my lowest and felt abandon when no one was left from the Jaguars except for Ayzo, Jay, and my dad. Now, I was gaining everything back and then some.

After about forty-five minutes, we pulled up to Luther's business that Addison had told us about. It was just after midnight, yet there were cars still parked in the parking lot. I shouldn't have been surprised. This was usually the busiest time to have customers. Sex sold and the freaks came out when the street lights came on.

A black Lincoln pulled up next to us and I saw Nicholas and Ashlynn hopping out. I started shaking my head.

"Oh no you don't. Ashlynn, this is dangerous and I don't want you and the baby to get hurt."

Nicholas clapped me on the back. "I already tried that man. I thought I left her at the house, but her little sneaky ass hid in the backseat."

"Those muthafuckas kidnapped us and tried to take over my daddy's shop. I want my revenge, too. I've been taking those self-defense classes and been at the shooting range ever since then. I got this."

I looked over at Nicholas who just shook his head. "Ashlynn Shantell, the minute things get out of hand, I'm dragging your ass back to this car."

She rolled her eyes.

"You heard the man," Denice said, yelling out of the window of her challenger. "I be damned if my bestie and my niece get hurt because you want to be hard headed."

Ashlynn exhaled a breath of frustration before she agreed to stay behind all of the chaos. Ayzo hopped out of the passenger seat of Denice's car and gave me a quick hug. "How you are holding up, cuzo?"

I briefly closed my eyes and took a breath. "Ready."

Ayzo nodded. "H-hey Addison."

She looked over at him and smirked. "What's up Ayzo. We're not going to make this awkward."

I laughed and called Denice over. "Let's do quick introductions so nobody accidentally shoots the wrong person. This is Denice, Ashlynn, Nicholas, and my cousin Jay."

Addison smiled and greeted everybody. "Nice to meet you all. That's Raheem and my best friend, Akira." She nodded towards the pair who were pulling up on a motorcycle.

"Let's light these muthafucka's up!" Akira said, waggling her tongue and pointing her gun in the air.

"I like her already." Denice laughed.

A few seconds later, Bishop, my body guard pulled up on her bike next to Akira and Raheem and dipped her chin.

"I have a few people coming to surround the perimeter boss. Nobodies getting out of here without having to go through us."

"Bishop, you didn't have to –"

She gave me a pointed look. "Seojun, you have been nothing but good to the Reapers. What happened to you was unfortunate, but contract or not, we are here to support you."

I walked over and gave her a firm handshake. Jay opened his mouth to say something but quickly changed his mind. The way he stared at Bishop was very familiar. It was the same look I gave Addison. I made a mental note to talk to him about it when all this was over.

I heard more motorcycles in the distance as we strapped up. I tried one last time to convince Denice, Addison, Ashlynn, and Akira to stay behind, too, but they refused. Hell, they all damn near cursed me out because they refused to leave their man's side. I pretended to be frustrated, but deep down I was proud. These women were ready to ride for us and I know we would do the same for them.

Looking around the parking lot, I couldn't help but smile. I was betrayed in the past and lost everything. I was devastated because everything my father had worked hard for was destroyed within a blink of an eye while I was in charge. Now as I stood before the people before me, I realized that they were all there for me. Not my dad or for what the Jaguars did for them, but all because of me. I looked down and sniffed as Addison rubbed my arm. Looking over at my wife, a planted a kiss on her cheek before turning to face everyone.

"Let's end this shit!"

Chapter 37

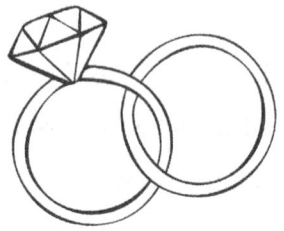

Seojun

We causally headed inside the building strapped and ready for war. I turned to the right and saw 'the playroom' with flashing red rights. A woman who was obviously strung out on whatever drug she was on, sitting in the middle of the floor. I frowned.

"Jay, Raheem, Akira, can y'all help them people out of here."

The trio nodded as they headed inside of the play room. Remembering what Z had told us a few days ago, I was pretty sure some of the individuals were here but not by free will.

Rounding the corner, we headed toward the elevators when I saw Manny talking to Cindy.

"Just the people I needed to see." I said, cocking my gun back.

Cindy screamed before trying to run, but Bishop stood at the entrance of the building with a crowbar lazily hanging over her shoulder. She tried to go the opposite direction, but the Reapers had all of the exits surrounded.

"Take us to Luther's suite so we can end this shit." Addison said, glaring at the girls.

"Why would we do that?" Manny said, rolling his shoulders. "Mr. L is our boss now."

I huffed out a chuckle. "What was the point of leaving the Jaguars, anyway? I paid you well and I know you didn't want any of the women because you had a boyfriend. So, why did you turn your back?"

Manny shrugged. "He looked better than you."

"The fuck?" Addison barked. "You betrayed the man who put food in your mouth because you thought another nigga was handsome?"

Manny rolled his eyes. "You got a problem with that, bitch?"

Before I could intervene, Addison had lifted her gun and shot him in the knee.

"Ahh! Fuck!" Manny cried out.

"First of all, watch your fucking mouth. Second of all, you sound dumb as hell. You betrayed your boss because you thought the villain looked good? I should make you eat my gun."

"Yeobo, it's okay. Let the Reapers handle him, we have bigger fish to fry." I said, planting a kiss on Addison's forehead. "Cindy, grab the key card that takes us to Luther's floor."

She stared at me and began to shake her head when Akira walked up and punched her. "Now, you two timing bitch."

Cindy flew backward as she held on to her face.

"Don't make me repeat myself," I said.

Akira took a step towards her causing Cindy to scramble to her feet and snatch up the key card from Manny's pocket.

"I like your friend," I said, nodding my head towards Akira. She arched an eyebrow at me before nodding her head back. I guess that meant she wasn't mad at me anymore for tying them up.

"Everyone's out of the playroom. We're about to start getting them home or to the hospital if they looked really sick."

Addison walked over and hugged her friend. "Be careful, K."

"I would say the same, but I know your husband will keep you safe. If not, he'll have to answer to me."

They laughed before Akira walked off.

"Fuck all of yall!" Manny spat, holding on to his leg. "I hope Luther kills you all slowly."

"Ugh, this nigga hasn't passed out yet? He's lost a lot of blood already." Denice asked, frowning down at Manny.

"Shut your hoe ass up! You ain't nothing but Luther's pussy."

Ayzo walked over and kicked Manny in the mouth, knocking him unconscious. "Shut the fuck up already."

I smirked as I grabbed Addison's hand and stepped on the elevator. Once we were all on, Cindy used the key card to scan us in to the executive suite.

"Tell me, Cindy, were you and Sandy only there to keep an eye on me?" Addison asked as we continued passing the other floors.

"And, it was you two who sold me out to Luther?" I asked, arching an eyebrow.

Cindy stared between us before tears began to form in her eyes. "It was all Sandy's idea. She was pissed that you fired us, Seojun. We were your number one girls and bringing in the most money but then you told us we were getting too old and fired us!"

"You and I both know I only said that to spare y'all feelings, but the truth of the matter was you two were not being smart. You both failed to inform me when you caught an STD and you were overcharging my clients so yall could pocket the money. I was being nice when I fired you two, but I should have just killed y'all."

The elevator doors opened, and Cindy sprinted out.

"Seojun is here-"

Before she could get another word out, I sent a bullet through the back of her head.

"The fuck?" Luther barked, jumping up from the ground.

I noticed he was rolling up a body in plastic tarp. When I got a glimpse of Jackie's face, I wanted to laugh. Luther had already done my dirty work for me and now it was only him and Sandy left to get rid of.

"Cindy!" Sandy screamed, running towards her other half. "I'll fucking kill you!"

She charged for me, but Addison had pulled her elbow back and sent her fist flying into her face. Sandy flew back, hitting her head on the ground. Addison walked up to her and placed the barrel of her gun to her forehead before pulling the trigger. Cindy and Sandy's blood coated the marble floors while Luther stood in shock.

"Luther, is it?" I asked, "It's nice to finally meet you. You remember Denice, Ayzo, and my wife, Addison?"

Hatred filled his eyes as he stared between all of us. "Denice, baby, I thought I told you to stay away from him."

"Luther, please! I belong to Ayzo. He has me, all of me and that is something I would have never given you."

"So, you opened your legs for one of the damn Yi men, too?" he laughed, shaking his head. "You know, mama K told me women went stupid over the Yi men. Naturally, I thought she was exaggerating, but now I see that she was right."

"The fuck are you talking about?" Ayzo asked.

I heard two guns cock from behind us, causing me to look over my shoulder. My eyes widened as I stared into my Aunt Kim's eyes. She had a gun at Addison's temple as she slowly walked into to the room. The other gun was on Denice as she was pulled into the room by a white man.

"Xavier? Mom?" Ayzo asked, taking a step towards her.

"Don't fucking move, Akeno." Xavier said, pushing the gun against Denice's head.

His hands flew up as he took a step back. My heart hammered in my chest as fear flashed in Addison's eyes. What the hell was going on?

"Let me tell you boys a story." Aunt Kim began. "Once upon a time, there was a girl who stood by her older brother's side when he barely had two pennies to rub together. She helped build up a small territory int the northwest. It wasn't much, but they were able to get by. Then one day, his wife decides to run away with every last penny. This caused the girl's brother to spiral into depression for not only losing his wife, but for losing all of the hard working money he saved up for. So, his sister looked for her brother's wife in hopes of getting their money back. You could imagine her surprise when she not only finds the woman a few years later drugged up, but with a son."

My mouth became dry as I stared at my aunt. "W-what are you saying? Are you seriously saying that I have a little brother?"

She nodded before looking over at Luther. "Your mother got pregnant by her dealer whose name was Terrance, but everyone called him-"

"T." Nicholas answered as he stared at a Latina woman stepping out of the side office.

"Hey, Nicolas. You look good."

"You're the bitch who shot my man?" Ashlynn spat, attempting to go towards Olivia, before Nicholas held her back.

Olivia smirked as she winked at them. "That's cute."

"Anyways," My aunt Kim continued. "Your mother gave birth to Luther two years after she abandoned you. The last time I saw her, she was doped out crying because she wanted to come back home with her family. Your dad offered to bring her back if she stopped using, but she never did. Her drugs were more important and she overdosed. When I told your dad about Luther, he didn't want to hear it."

"Lies!" I spat. "My father is all about family and you know that!"

"Call him and ask! Luther was not his blood, and he didn't care what happened to him. If it wasn't for me, your brother would've died on those streets!"

I shook my head. "Why should I believe yall?"

Luther stepped closer to me and my eyes landed on his Cobra tattoo. The date October 10th stood out to me causing me to gasp. Another date, January 9th caused my heart to drop.

"Why do you have my mother's birth date and the day she died tattooed on you?" I whispered.

Luther smirked at me. We both knew that answer. My head spun as I stared at him. How could this be? Why didn't anyone tell me?

"I was discarded like I asked to be brought into this life! I tried to become friends with you," Luther explained, looking at Ayzo. "But you stabbed me in the back by taking my woman. I tried to become a Jaguar, but you, Seojun, didn't even let me come talk to you."

My eyes scrunched up. "What are you talking about? I don't remember you coming to see me. If I had known-"

Luther burst out into laughter. "And that's another reason your men betrayed you. You made sure all of the women were taken care of but didn't give a damn about anybody else. I came to one of your massage parlors looking for you, but you were too busy. Hell, I went at least three times, but you were always too busy. So, I gave up and worked with my mother's drug dealer, T. When I found out that nigga was my father, I wanted to throw up. I was so happy the day I got to kill him."

I flinched. How could he kill his own father?

"Wait! I ran an entire group and you thought I had spare time? You should have kept trying to see me! Hell, it would've caught my attention faster if you came to my shop every single day and waited."

Luther's eyes darted over to Aunt Kim. "Mama K said if I kept bothering you, you'd ban me. Besides, she said y'all didn't want me around anyway because I was only your half-brother."

I glared at my aunt. "That is a lie! I wouldn't have cared if you were my half, full, or quarter brother. You are still my brother."

Luther's shoulder slumped as guilt filled his eyes. I took a step toward him. Even though Luther had royally fucked up, he was my blood. Maybe we'd be able to move on from the past mistakes, but right now, everything he had been told his whole life was a lie. I'm sure if my father really knew about him, he wouldn't have turned Luther away.

"Enough of this!" Aunt Kim shouted, shooting Luther in the leg.

"What the fuck?" he shouted, blood spraying on the ground.

"We had a damn plan, but here you are getting all sentimental! Did you forget that they didn't want you? Did you forget that his father didn't want you? Don't be so weak!"

"That's not true!" I shouted. "If I would've known, I would have accepted you."

Aunt Kim threw her head back and laughed. "And my brother said you were a great leader? How pathetic. See, this is why I needed to run the Jaguars. I was always stronger and smarter, but your father wouldn't even give me a chance. So, now I am taking it!"

"Wait, mama K." Luther panted.

She rolled her eyes. "X, baby, handle him."

My eyebrows furrowed. What was she talking about? Before I knew it, Xavier had pushed Denice to the floor and shot Luther in the head. Olivia screamed as Luther's brains splattered across the floor. Ayzo ran toward Denice as I stared at my brother's lifeless body.

"What the fuck, Xavier?" Ayzo shouted, helping Denice up.

Olivia wailed as she cried into Luther's chest. Xavier stepped over her and stood next to Aunt Kim. I opened my mouth to say something when he tilted her chin back and kissed her, making my stomach churn.

"Fuck him. I've been playing his obedient bitch boy for years. Now, I get to run the show with my baby. We're going to take Addison down to the Reapers since she is a descendent. They didn't want to allow her mother to be the leader because she would've fucked around and spent all of their money. Addison, on the other hand, is smart and resourceful. She would be a great leader in public while baby and I run her ass behind the scenes. We'll control her which means controlling the Reapers while we rebuild the Jaguars. We win."

My hands balled into a fist as anger washed over me. My eyes darted over to Ayzo who nodded his head. He understood that we were not leaving here without Addison. I vowed to protect my family and she was my wife. I looked over at Addison, but realized Olivia had quietly moved away from Luther and was now standing next to Aunt Kim and Xavier. With her gun pointed at Xavier, she shot him in the back of the head. I pulled my gun out and aimed it at Aunt Kim.

"I loved him," Olivia wept. "I know I've done some fucked up things for him, but he was my person." She turned and looked at Nicholas. "I wanted to shoot you because I knew that was going to please him. Garrett was working undercover as a Cobra in hopes of destroying the territory from the inside. He had a kind heart and wanted to help the younger kids get out of the gang life but that only pissed off T and Luther. That's what got him killed."

Nicholas's jaws clenched as he gripped his gun.

"Denice," Olivia continued. "Luther wanted me, but you just had to be in the picture. I thought I was able to get you off of his mind after all of these years, but he was going to always choose you. I hated you for it and I still do. He died with love for you in his heart."

With that, she dropped her gun and walked into his office before sitting on the couch and crying. I wanted to feel bad for her but I didn't. She chose to follow after a man who, deep down, never wanted her back. She thought if she did everything he wanted, he would choose her, but he didn't.

Ashlynn looked up at Nicholas and dipped her chin. He planted a kiss on her temple and followed after Olivia. She looked up at him before giving him an apologetic frown. He briefly closed his eyes as he pointed the gun at her chest, in the same position his brother was shot before he pulled the trigger.

Chapter 38

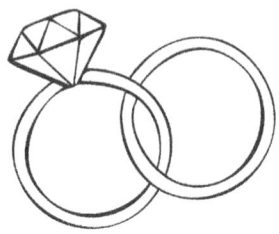

Mama K (a.k.a.) Kim

I stared between my brother, nephew, and son as I sat tied up in my brother's basement. After the Reapers and Seojun's people cleared out the building, they hauled me off to accept my fate. My eyes darted between all of them and I wish I had killed them sooner. I had nothing but hatred for them because they all ruined my life. I should've been in charge of the Jaguars. I should have been the one with all of the power, but no!

"Look, this was all her idea!" Delilah cried, tilting her head towards me. I rolled my eyes. They already knew the damn truth because I told them. If I was going down, then so was everybody else.

"Mama, please." Addison said, walking into the room, Denice and Bishop trailing behind her. "You sold me out all for some money and so that you could run the Reapers. Fyi, they never were going to accept you as their leader."

"Spare me, Addison. I was the original leader, and they would've accepted me had it not been for your ass."

"No, we wouldn't have." Bishop said, flatly.

"Please, yall have to listen to-"

I rolled my eyes. "Oh, shut the fuck up, Delilah. You are full of it."

"Aunt Kim, do you have something to say to your family?" Addison asked.

"Fuck this family! As soon as I was dismissed, I plotted my revenge. I don't give a shit about any of you!" I spat. I looked over at my son before spitting at the ground.

Denice walked pass Addison and punched me in the face. My head flew back and I could feel blood filling my mouth.

"Don't you ever disrespect him like that again!"

I slowly tilted my head up, a wide smile on my face. "Ayzo, you going to let your bitch hit your mother?"

Ayzo's eyes squinted. "I'm not your son, remember."

I laughed and shook my head.

"Now that the Jaguars and Reapers are here, Kim and Delilah, you must answer for your crimes. You both have been found guilty in conspiring against your own crew and family. For those in favor to allow them to pay back the family through hard labour say, I." Seojun said.

No one uttered a word. Rage boiled through my veins as I snarled at them. I knew it was going to come down to this, but for some reason I thought they'd spare me.

"For those who agree to death say, I."

Of course everybody agreed. I looked up at my brother and lifted my chin. "Before I die, at least tell your son the truth about his brother."

His nostrils flared as he lifted his gun. The last thing I saw was the bullet aiming to my face. I heard delilah scream and another gun shot go off before everything faded to black.

Chapter 39

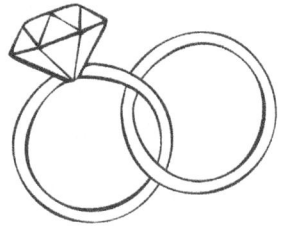

Seojun

I sat across from my dad, my hands folded on top of my desk. He refused to make eye contact with me which was a dead giveaway that he was guilty.

"Luther was really my brother?"

He sighed, running his hand down his face. "He wasn't my blood."

I knocked over everything off of my desk and glared at him. "You spent years spewing family and tradition into my ear and the whole time I had a brother out in the world that needed us."

"He. Was. Not. My. Blood! Your mother fucking abandoned us and then cheated on me with her damn drug dealer. Do you really think I wanted to look at that bastard every single day? To be reminded of the hurt that your mother put us through?"

I shook my head and paced. "You shouldn't have punished him for mom's mistakes. He didn't be asked to be born into this world."

My dad sighed. "It's nothing I can do now."

I glared at him. "It's time for you to go."

"So, you're just going to kick your father out? After everything I've done for you?"

"I just need time, dad."

Walking to the door, I opened it escorting him out. He bumped past me with a frustrated huff. I sat on the edge of my desk and dropped my head. I don't know how I was going to be able to move past my father's betrayal, but I was going to pray that I did. I loved my father, but for him to push an innocent child away because of my mother's mistakes was crazy to me. I didn't expect him to take full custody, but it would've been nice for me to get to know Luther. Had I did, things would've turned out differently.

"You okay, baby?"

I looked up to see Addison walking into the room. She stood in between my legs as I wrapped my arms around her.

Sighing, I kissed her head. "I'll be fine. How's your grandma?"

"She's comfortable. She wasn't up to talking today, but I'm used to that. I bet tomorrow she'll be better."

I nodded. "I can't wait to meet her."

Addison laughed. "Don't be surprised if she starts flirting with you."

We laughed together and fell into a comfortable silence. I rested my chin on top of her head and inhaled the vanilla scent that drove me crazy.

"Is it really all over?"

I nodded and kissed her forehead. "It's over, baby."

Epilogue

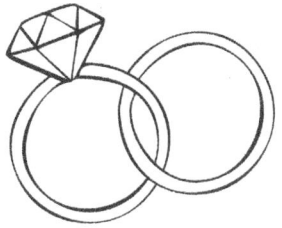

Addison 5 Years Later

"If you don't hurry up, we're going to be late!" I shouted up the stairs. Today was Renee's dance recital and we couldn't be late or Ashlynn would be calling our phones back to back. When that woman gave you a time, you had better be there at that time, but that was something I loved about her. Ashlynn and Nicholas had a beautiful baby girl and now she was six years old with her first lead role in her dance performance. The years flew by, but a lot had taken place.

After Ayzo's mom, Kim, and my mom were sentence and killed for their crimes, things started off hectic. After we rebuilt our territories, Seojun and I now ran the Jaguars and the Reapers from the Northwest down to the South. We compromised and kept two massage parlors and two escort houses open, because some of the women who worked with Seojun in the past really wanted to stay in that area. It was uncomfortable at first and I could admit my trust with Seojun was becoming shaky, but I quickly learned that it was only business. The women respected me and never did any foul shit. So, I agreed, and we kept them on payroll. Besides, Raheem and Akira checked in on them and made sure everything was running smoothly. All the other women who wanted to come out of hiding, worked at S&V Realty or at one of the many vacation resorts we had across the country.

Seojun and I mainly focused on his realty company and my therapy center. He built new homes, vacation resorts, and businesses for all of the communities with a lower annual income. He still made it his mission to help those who really needed it. I aimed to help the community especially for those who had mothers like mine and Ayzo.

After Seojun and I went down to the annual Jaguars and Reapers meeting where the contract for Seojun to marry in order to keep the Jaguars was deemed valid, things finally began to calm down. We found a comfortable routine.

Then, Seojun really stepped up and showed me his true feelings for me when my grandmother passed away last year. It hit me hard, but he was nothing but loving and compassionate while he helped me get through her passing. I'm not saying everything is peachy perfect, but I know that I have someone to lean on when grief pops up.

The same goes for my husband. It took a couple of years for him to speak to his father again. I was there through his sleepless nights and spouts of despair, and I never allowed him to push me away. It was a truly a rough time, but in the end, it only made our relationship stronger.

"What is that man doing?" Denice asked, rubbing her belly.

"Probably changing for the tenth time. You know he has to look perfect for every occasion." I chuckled with a slight shake of my head. "How's the twins?"

"Kicking my ass. I should've known better when we got married during my ovulation week and had Junior. Now look at me, celebrating our anniversary and got knocked up again."

I threw my hand over my mouth and laughed. "That's what happens when you and your husband change y'all sex life into a friendly sexual competition."

Denice laughed. "You right, but I can't help it. I like hearing him call out my name!"

"Keep playing and I'll add a third baby with the twins." Ayzo said, coming around the corner.

"Boy, hush!" Denice giggled.

"When should we tell everybody?" Seojun whispered, wrapping his arms around my waist.

I looked up at him before planting a kiss on his lips. "Later, today is Renee's day."

"Yes, yeobo." Seojun cleared his throat. "Okay, let's head out before Ashlynn starts calling."

After everything we had been through, Seojun and I remained happily married. It wasn't easy because we had to learn about one another, but the fact that we wanted us to work made it easier. Now, we had our precious blessing brewing in my stomach to expand our family. If we had to do all this over again, I wouldn't change a thing. Life was good and I couldn't wait to see what the future held for us.

The End

About the Author

I can't believe I'm writing this again because another book is officially completed. If you're new here, I'd like to take the time to introduce myself. So, my name is Jessica but as you can see, I write under the pen name J.D. Southwell. I was born and raised in DFW, TX and I've always enjoyed reading ever since I was a little girl. Unlike most kids growing up, I spent the majority of my time at my local library where I eventually found my love of Romance and Mystery books.

I wrote and published my first book, *Dating is Ghetto*: an erotic anthology novella.

After a year, I wrote and published 40hrs With A Stranger. Then, six months later, Book II, They're Not Strangers was released. After a year, the final book, Strangers No More is here! While the, Its A Vibe, series is complete, there may be a strong possibility that some of these characters will be getting a spin off series. *Wink Wink.*

Anywho, I'd like to give a special shout out to my PR Team, Pretty Girls Do Read. Thank you to Denisha and Syren who made sure I stayed on track and made marketing easy peasy! Shout out to my editor, Tylee who made sure the story was in tip top shape! Shout out to my book cover designer That One Chaotic Artist (instagram name). Shout out to my beta and ARC readers as well as my street team for supporting me. I really apperciate each and every one of you!

If you've enjoyed this story, please leave me a review and share this story with a friend. Feel free to follow me on Instagram, Threads, and Tiktok

www.jbookcollections.com
email :jd.southwell@outlook.com
Instagram:@jdsouthwells
Threads:@jdsouthwells
Tiktok:@jdsouthwell

Made in the USA
Coppell, TX
10 August 2025

52987667R00148